PUBLISHED BY RED YARROW BOOKS,
an imprint of Cerrillos Road Holdings. Santa Fe, New Mexico

Red Yarrow Books are available at special discounts for events, promotions, fundraising, or educational purposes when purchased in bulk. For more details, please contact us at *redyarrowbooks@cerrillosroad.com*

Copyright © 2025 by Bryan Wempen

Unbound Ambitions: The Candidate is a work of fiction. Names, characters, businesses, events, and dramatic incidents are the product of the author's imagination. Any resemblance to actual persons, living or dead, or events is purely coincidental and inspired by.

Cover design — Sherwin Emmanuel Minhas
Bio photo — Michella Wempen
Editor — OpenAI

Library of Congress Control Number: **2024953010**
ISBN: 979-8-9887219-4-9
eISBN: 979-8-9887219-5-6

Printed in the United States of America
Published in the City of Santa Fe, New Mexico

UNBOUND AMBITIONS: THE CANDIDATE

INTRODUCTION TO THE SERIES

In the fierce and unforgiving arena of future politics, ambition drives everything. *Unbound Ambitions: The Candidate* offers a gripping exploration of a political campaign in a world reshaped by technological advances, evolving ideologies, and a hyper-connected society. In this high-stakes environment, every decision, every gesture, and every word is part of a larger game—a game where the stakes couldn't be higher, and the price of failure is devastating.

Vic Ross, a seasoned candidate with sharp instincts and a carefully engineered public persona, is running for the highest office in the land. In an era where voters are as likely to be swayed by algorithms as by traditional media, Vic has mastered the art of navigating the treacherous waters of public opinion. But as the campaign barrels toward the finish line, the challenges become more personal and complex. It's no longer just about policy platforms or the latest poll numbers; it's about survival in a system that demands absolute sacrifice.

Unbound Ambitions: The Candidate delves into the darker side of ambition, where morality bends under the weight of ambition, and power comes at an unforgiving cost. As Vic grapples with the relentless pressures from his team, invasive media scrutiny, and the ghosts of past decisions now exposed by advanced AI-driven opposition research, he must confront the ultimate question: how far is he willing to go to win? From choreographed photo ops targeting undecided micro-demographics to debates broadcast across immersive virtual platforms, every moment tests his character and limits.

This novel explores the futuristic machinery of a political campaign and the enduring human elements that underlie it: the drive, fear, and ambition that push individuals to the edge. In this technologically augmented battlefield, Vic's journey is one of unrelenting pressure, where the pursuit of power exposes the cracks in even the most seasoned candidates.

In this race, nothing is certain, and every move counts. Welcome to *Unbound Ambitions: The Candidate*, where the fight for power in a near-future world is as brutal as it is compelling—and no one walks away unscathed.

PROLOGUE

The capital buzzed with life; its skyline dominated by glowing skyscrapers and the endless hum of drones crisscrossing the night sky. Campaign slogans danced on holographic billboards, and streets pulsed with the energy of a nation gripped by the final days of an election. From his penthouse, Vic Ross watched it all—the city that had crowned him a political force and now threatened to swallow him whole.

Behind him, the low hum of his AI dashboard filled the room, lines of code flickering across translucent screens. Sentiment analyses, voter trend projections, and real-time media monitoring systems worked tirelessly, anticipating every twist and turn of the race. The data was relentless, and tonight it was all telling the same story: Vic Ross was losing.

The light of the holograms reflected off his sharp suit and perfectly styled hair, but Vic barely noticed. His gaze was fixed on the city below, where he imagined every voter, every algorithm, and every journalist conspiring to decide his future. He had spent decades climbing to this moment, and now, standing at the edge of his ambition, the weight of it all threatened to crush him.

His phone vibrated on the countertop behind him, displaying a flood of notifications: Morales trending on every major social platform, analysts dissecting her latest rally, and projections narrowing his chances with every hour. He picked up the phone, scrolling through headlines as his jaw tightened.

"Morales Inspires in Virtual Town Hall."
"Can Ross Still Connect with a Changing Electorate?"

Vic tossed the phone back onto the counter. He didn't need the headlines to tell him what was wrong. Morales had momentum. Her campaign was sleek, adaptive, and powered by AI systems that made every speech and gesture an almost perfect match for the electorate's desires. Meanwhile, his own team felt slow, reactive—scrambling to keep up with a race that had shifted beneath their feet.

A sharp chime echoed through the suite as the door slid open. Slater entered, a tablet glowing in his hand. The campaign manager's face was as composed as ever, but the tension around his eyes gave him away. He walked past Vic to the screens, syncing his tablet with a wave of his hand.

"Sentiment's still dropping," Slater said, the glow from the screens illuminating his features. "We're losing the relatability edge. The analytics team suggests targeting undecided in key districts—working-class families and minority voters. It's going to take face time."

Vic turned, his tone sharp. "Facetime? In the middle of an election where Morales is winning with a virtual damn hologram? What do you suggest—another barbecue or a pancake breakfast?"

Slater glanced at him, unfazed. "The food truck event tomorrow. It's already in motion. You show up, smile, and shake some hands. It's not the event—it's the optics. They're looking for authenticity. The AI says it's worth at least a two-point shift in the Midwest quadrant."

Vic scoffed, pacing back to the window. "Optics. Everything's about optics these days. A taco truck photo op isn't going to save this campaign."

Slater didn't respond immediately, scrolling through data on his tablet. When he finally spoke, his voice was steady but firm. "No, but a taco truck photo op doesn't hurt. And if we lose the optics war, we lose everything."

Vic said nothing, watching his reflection in the glass. Behind the polished exterior, he felt the exhaustion creeping in. This campaign had taken everything: his time, his family, pieces of himself he wasn't sure he'd ever get back. And now, as the finish line approached, it felt like even that might not be enough.

His phone vibrated again, another stream of alerts flashing across the screen. The final debate loomed—a chance to seize control of the narrative. Or a disaster waiting to happen.

Slater's voice cut through his thoughts. "You need to win tomorrow, Vic. We're out of room for mistakes."

Vic nodded, but his thoughts were elsewhere. He had fought his way to the top of this game, clawing for every inch in a system that rewarded ruthlessness and crushed hesitation. If the taco truck were what it took, he'd do it. But he couldn't help wondering—was this campaign still about winning? Or was it about holding on to what was left of himself?

As Slater left the room, Vic stayed at the window, staring out over the city that had made him and might unmake him. Tomorrow, the circus would start again, and he would step back into the arena, armor polished and mask firmly in place.

This wasn't just another campaign. It was the future. And losing wasn't an option.

— 1 —

Vic Ross stood at the floor-to-ceiling window of his penthouse, a cigar smoldering between his fingers, and surveyed Washington, D.C. Below, the city sprawled like a blueprint of his ambition, a landscape he'd learned to manipulate, with the Capitol dome gleaming in the morning light—a beacon reminding him of what he had fought for and intended to keep. His opponents might mistake this for nostalgia, but for Vic, it was simply resolve.

Down on the streets, people scrambled to work, lives preoccupied with mundane worries—groceries, childcare, bills. Vic had long since left those concerns behind. High above them all, his world was the territory of political moves and influence, untouched by the concerns of the people he claimed to represent.

Vic took a long draw from the cigar, the rich smoke curling lazily toward the ceiling. The burn in his chest was a welcome distraction from the never-ending drumbeat of stress that fueled him. A bottle of expensive whiskey sat half-empty on a nearby table, a testament to the nights he spent chasing sleep that never came. He glanced at his reflection in the glass: a tall, imposing man, built like he used to play football and never quite lost the frame, though age and pressure had hardened him rather than softened him.

His dark hair, always on the verge of needing a trim, showed the first streaks of gray, while his jaw was perpetually set like he was bracing for impact. The suits he wore, usually dark and impeccably tailored, seemed more like armor than clothing, a uniform for a man who never stopped working. His eyes, a steely blue, carried the weight of sleepless nights and relentless ambition, and even the whiskey couldn't dull the sharpness of his gaze. Relaxation wasn't something Vic ever allowed himself; every breath was another investment in his survival, another moment to press his advantage.

With politics as his sole passion, Vic's life was streamlined, and every minute was a calculated investment. He lived in strategy sessions, fundraisers, and high-stakes calls, where each word was a subtle manipulation for support or a deal. Even his penthouse, sleek and cold, reflected that drive—abstract art lining the walls, chosen by a designer to suggest taste rather than personal interest. He rarely noticed them, truthfully. To him, they were mere symbols of the life he'd carved out, standing in for what he actually enjoyed: the control he wielded over it all.

Vic took a final sip of black coffee, wishing it was whiskey, and checked his phone. A message from Slater, his campaign manager, suggested an early Zoom to discuss the latest polling numbers. He grimaced. The polls had been slipping for weeks, and with it, the narrative of Vic as the unstoppable incumbent had begun to show cracks. He couldn't afford to lose his grip.

Another buzz: a donor demanding a brief call to discuss his upcoming check—another trade-off, another favor in the bank.

Finishing his coffee, Vic set the cup down with precision. It was the same discipline that shaped his days. This penthouse had no place for relaxation; it was an engine room, not a haven. At most, he might allow himself a rare cigar on the balcony, staring down at the city that powered his ambitions. And as for the day-to-day interactions that exhausted most people? His team handled that. When he moved from one place to the next, it was within a fortified bubble of privilege and security, courtesy of the new Candidate Service, the agency now assigned to protect major candidates like himself. The Secret Service might be the standard for sitting presidents, but The Candidate Service's agents were experts in anticipation, anticipating every potential threat with precision.

Just yesterday, their training had been on display after an unexpectedly chaotic event. Within moments, the agents moved seamlessly around Vic, ushering him to safety before a crowd could breach their perimeter. His position was secure—for now—but every misstep of his campaign was a reminder that he was still vulnerable, and people like Jen Morales were circling, looking for any opening.

Settling at his desk, Vic dialed Slater, skipping pleasantries. "What's the latest?"

"Morales's numbers are climbing," Slater replied, his tone clipped. "Her ad buys are eating into our base."

Vic gripped the edge of his desk, frustration simmering. Morales had been a New Mexico idealist, a small state official, he thought. She should have been easy to undermine, yet her idealism somehow translated into credibility with voters. It threatened everything he'd built.

"We'll hit her hard," he said, his voice dropping a degree. "Target her lack of experience, shouldn't be that difficult. Make her look unprepared. Get whatever you can on her—that's why I hired you, isn't it?" He sneered, and the edge in his tone underscored the stakes.

Slater's response was quick, but Vic detected a hint of hesitation. The strategy wasn't going as expected, and everyone knew it.

He hung up and leaned back, letting a wave of irritation wash over him. His ascent wasn't built on luck but on foresight, connections, and careful investment. His wealth was an inheritance, yes, but it was Vic's shrewdness that had turned it into something of lasting power. Politics wasn't just his career; it was his empire. His penthouse overlooked his dominion, and as far as he was concerned, he had earned every inch of it.

He poured himself a Scotch—an early concession to the weight of the day's pressures. The dark amber liquid burned as it slid down his throat, an indulgence that sharpened his focus. He wasn't about to let "Mexican Morales" take what he had spent years cultivating. She was insignificant, a name that wouldn't even last in the minds of those she tried to reach. He chuckled at the idea of calling her out that way—though it couldn't be about race; his known appreciation for Hispanic culture (and Latina women, especially) was his shield against being called a racist, which mostly he wasn't, so his name calling was an internal dialog only.

As he swirled the Scotch in his glass, his mind drifted briefly to that moment yesterday when The Candidate Service had closed ranks around him. He recalled the glint in one of their eyes—a look that wasn't just protective but calculated like he was an asset in a larger game. He wondered if the agency's allegiance extended beyond him or if he, too, was simply another fixture in the machinery of power. But such thoughts were best left to others; Vic's sights were set squarely on victory.

— 2 —

The rain drummed steadily against the windows of the campaign headquarters, a relentless rhythm that matched the pounding in Ethan

Grant's head. His office, usually a hub of activity, felt like a pressure cooker. He stared at the whiteboard on the wall, a long list of tasks scrawled across it in his increasingly illegible handwriting. Each item represented another fire to put out, another promise to fulfill, another favor to call in. But the biggest fire of all was Carly Bishop, and her demands were dangerously close to becoming an ultimatum.

His phone buzzed again. Another text from Rick Slater.

"What's the status on Bishop? We can't afford to lose her. Get it done."

Ethan squeezed his eyes shut, trying to ward off the headache that had been building all morning. He was tired of Slater's constant demands, tired of feeling like they were running in circles just to keep the campaign alive. There was a time when he had admired Slater's efficiency, his ability to stay ten steps ahead of their opponents. But now, it felt like they weren't moving toward anything real anymore. They were just trying to survive.

The door to his office swung open, and Riley Daniels, the campaign's communications director, walked in without knocking. She took one look at Ethan and raised an eyebrow.

"You look like hell," she said, dropping into the chair opposite his desk. "Let me guess, Slater's barking orders again?"

Ethan let out a bitter laugh. "You don't know the half of it. Carly Bishop's ready to blow, and Slater's acting like we're a few phone calls away from fixing everything. He doesn't get it. Every time we give Carly what she wants, she comes back for more."

Riley snorted. "That's what you get when you make deals with people like Carly. She's not in this for the vision or the policy. She's in it for the power, and she'll bleed us dry if we let her."

Ethan knew she was right. Carly Bishop didn't care about Vic Ross's ideals—whatever was left of them. She didn't care about their campaign's message. She cared about leverage. Her husband's contracts. Her influence. And if she didn't get what she wanted, she would pull her support and take half of their financial backing with her.

"I'm going to see her," Ethan said, standing up and grabbing his coat. "She needs to hear from me, not just Slater. She needs to understand that we're still in charge, not her."

Riley gave him a wary look. "Be careful. Carly's not the type to play nice if she thinks you're crossing her."

Ethan nodded, but he was already out the door, his mind racing.

He couldn't keep playing this game much longer. But if they lost Carly, the campaign would collapse, and with it, everything he and Vic had worked for.

Carly Bishop's penthouse was more traditional than Ethan had expected, yet like her—cold, calculated, and devoid of warmth. He rode the elevator up, each floor bringing him closer to a confrontation he dreaded. When the doors opened, Carly was already waiting, a glass of red wine in hand and her expression unreadable.

"Well, well, the campaign manager himself," Carly said, her tone dripping with faux warmth. "What can I do for you, Ethan? I thought you were sending Slater to handle all the dirty work."

Ethan forced a smile, though it felt hollow. "I thought it was best to handle this personally, Carly. We value your support, but I wanted to clear up any misunderstandings."

Carly's smile widened, but her eyes remained cold. "There's no misunderstanding. You made promises, Ethan. My husband's company was supposed to get those contracts, and instead, I'm hearing excuses. I'm not interested in excuses."

Ethan swallowed hard, forcing himself to stay calm. "I understand your frustration. The process has been slower than we anticipated, but we're doing everything we can to push it through."

Carly took a slow sip of her wine, her gaze fixed on his. "I don't care how you do it. Just get it done. Or I'll find someone who can— and you know exactly what that means for Vic."

As Ethan walked out of the penthouse, Carly's words echoed in his mind. She didn't give second chances. And if he couldn't deliver, the campaign would fall apart.

Back at headquarters, Slater was waiting for him, his face a mask of irritation. The campaign wasn't just about winning anymore. It was about survival. And every day, the line between the two became harder to see.

— 3 —

Jen Morales stood in front of a small crowd gathered in the Santa Fe community center, the familiar scent of brewing coffee and desert sage wafting through the air. Her hometown. Her refuge. As she looked out at the faces of old friends, neighbors, and local supporters, she felt the tug of something she hadn't had time to feel in months—comfort.

But comfort was a luxury Jen couldn't afford, not now.

"We need to restore people's faith in the system," Jen said, her voice steady despite the exhaustion that had been pulling at her bones for days. "We must remind the country that leadership isn't just about wielding power—it's about service. It's about doing what's right, even when it's hard."

The small crowd applauded, some nodding enthusiastically. But as Jen scanned the room, she caught a glimpse of doubt in a few faces, and that doubt weighed heavier on her than she liked to admit. This campaign had taken more out of her than she had expected. She had fought for every inch of ground, but the closer they got to Election Day, the more she felt the walls closing in.

Jen was strikingly beautiful in an unpretentious way. Her warm, deep brown eyes revealed both her sincerity and unspoken worries. Her skin, kissed by the New Mexico sun, carried a healthy, natural glow, but the lines of stress at the corners of her eyes hinted at the burdens she bore. Her hair, a rich chestnut brown, often fell into soft waves around her face, though it was usually pulled back into a practical ponytail on the campaign trail.

She had a vibrant smile that could light up a room, but it had become a rare sight lately, reserved for the moments when she let herself relax, usually in a fit of laughter she shared with close friends or Nathan. Jen's athletic build was a reminder of her past as a high school soccer star, and she still maintained a level of fitness that spoke to her disciplined, driven nature. Yet beneath her confident exterior lay a deeply introspective soul, someone who carried her community's hopes and her own fears in equal measure.

After the speech, Nathan Carter, her future running mate and trusted friend, approached. His calm presence was a welcome relief in the campaign's whirlwind.

"That was a good speech, Jen," Nathan said, his voice low and steady. "You're getting through to them."

Jen managed a faint smile but shook her head. "It's not enough. We've been fighting an uphill battle for months, and it feels like no matter what we do, we can't break free of Vic Ross's shadow. The media is still buzzing about Tom Albright's arrest, but Vic's numbers barely falter. His machine just keeps grinding forward, while we're struggling just to stay afloat, let alone gain any ground."

Nathan crossed his arms, his brow furrowed. "People want what Vic's selling—he's promising a better tomorrow without confronting today's hard truths. 'Make the Nation Excellent Tomorrow.' But we're the ones telling it like it is, and that's not always what people want to hear."

Jen sighed. Nathan was right. Vic Ross's campaign thrived on distorted facts, polished promises, and carefully spun narratives. He talked big about change and reform, but beneath it all was a web of dark money and backroom deals. Usually, a future VP candidate's arrest would be a campaign disaster, but Tom Albright's scandal barely slowed his momentum. Jen couldn't help but wonder if people had simply stopped caring about integrity in politics.

Across the room, she saw Grace Howard, a local volunteer and one of her most dedicated supporters, setting up a makeshift table for voter outreach. Grace had been with the campaign from the beginning, rallying support and organizing phone banks. But even Grace had been looking more and more worn out lately, her smile a little tighter, frown lines showing, and her movements a little slower.

Jen crossed the room to join her, offering a hand as they began packing up materials for the next event.

"Thanks for everything you're doing, Grace," Jen said, her voice soft.

Grace looked up, brushing a stray hair from her face. "It's nothing, Jen. You know I believe in you—we all do. You're our future."

But Jen could hear the doubt creeping into Grace's words. People were tired. The relentless grind of the campaign was wearing on everyone, and Jen couldn't shake the gnawing fear that no matter how hard they fought, it might not be enough. Without hesitation, Jen stepped closer and wrapped Grace in a brief, reassuring hug, hoping to convey the strength they both needed.

Later that evening, Jen and Nathan sat in the back of a modest SUV, making their way to the next event. The New Mexico high desert stretched out endlessly on either side, bathed in the golden hues of the setting sun. Jen watched the landscape pass by, her thoughts drifting back to her family—her parents, who had instilled in her a deep sense of justice and service, and her younger brother, who still believed she could change the world.

"You're quiet," Nathan said, glancing at her from the passenger seat. "What's going on in that head of yours?"

Jen smiled wearily. "Just thinking about how hard this has been. I knew running for this office would be a fight, but I didn't expect it to feel like constantly swimming upstream while getting whacked over the head with a truck like a game of whack-a-mole."

Nathan nodded. "It's the way the game is played, unfortunately. The people who play it dirty have been doing this for a long time. We're the outsiders, the ones trying to change the rules. And that makes us dangerous to people like Vic."

Jen turned her gaze back to the window, watching the landscape blur past. "I just wonder if it's worth it sometimes. We talk about integrity, about restoring faith in the system, but it feels like the system is so broken. Can it even be fixed?"

Nathan's voice softened. "Jen, if you don't believe it can, no one will. That's why you're running. That's why people are behind you."

Jen nodded, but the doubt still lingered, a familiar weight in her chest. She remembered her first campaign, when she ran for Secretary of State. It had been a hard-fought victory, the kind that seemed impossible until she made it happen. Winning that race was about more than just a title—it was about proving that she could make a difference, that she could help keep New Mexico at the forefront of election security and reliability.

She'd thrown herself into the role, determined to preserve the state's reputation as the leader in fair and secure elections. Under her watch, New Mexico fortified its voting systems, expanded voter education, and fought back against the rising tide of misinformation. She'd worked late into the night, seven days a week, reading reports, consulting with cybersecurity experts, and visiting communities to ensure that every vote counted and every voice was heard. It wasn't glamorous work, but she took pride in knowing that, for a time, she helped restore a bit of faith in the democratic process.

Jen could still remember the letters she received—thank-you notes from citizens who appreciated her efforts and messages from rural voters who felt seen for the first time. Those small victories had meant everything to her. They were proof that change, however incremental, was possible. But now, as she looked ahead to the challenge of this campaign, the stakes felt so much higher, the opposition so much fiercer.

As the car slowed to a stop in front of a town hall in a small rural community, Jen took a deep breath and straightened her shoulders, forcing the weariness aside. This was what she had signed up for—the long days, the endless battles, the moments of doubt. But she reminded herself of that first victory, the difference it had made. If she could do it then, maybe she could do it again.

She turned back to Nathan, a small but determined smile tugging at her lips. "You're right. We have to keep pushing, no matter how tough it gets. We've done it before—we can do it again. This campaign is bigger than any of us, especially my moments of insecurity."

Nathan gave her a reassuring nod, and together, they stepped out of the car, ready to face whatever lay ahead.

The town hall was packed—more people than Jen had expected in this quiet corner of New Mexico. Farmers, teachers, and small business owners all gathered to hear what she had to say. As Jen stepped onto the small stage, the murmurs quieted, and all eyes turned to her.

She scanned the room, taking a deep breath. This was why she was running: these people, these communities. They were the heart of the country, and they deserved leadership that cared about more than just winning elections.

"We're at a crossroads," Jen began, her voice strong and clear. "This election isn't just about policies. It's about who we are as a nation. It's about the kind of world we want to leave for our children. For too long, we've allowed politics to become a game played by the rich and powerful. But it doesn't have to be that way."

The crowd listened intently, a few nodding in agreement. But Jen could see the skepticism in some faces—people who had heard promises before and been let down. She understood that feeling—she had felt it herself.

"I'm not going to stand here and tell you that it'll be easy. Change never is. But I believe that together, we can rebuild this system. We can create a country where everyone's voice matters, not just the ones with money and power. We can fight for justice, for fairness, for integrity."

As the applause broke out, Jen felt a spark of hope. It was small, but it was there. Maybe, just maybe, they could do this.

Across the country, in a sleek conference room in Washington, D.C., Vic Ross sat at the head of a long table, surrounded by his top advisors. The tone of the conversation was starkly different from the one at Jen's town hall.

Rick Slater stood at the opposite end of the table, a stack of papers in front of him. "Morales is gaining traction," Slater said, his voice cold and clinical. "She's still way behind in the polls, but her base is getting louder, and we're seeing some movement."

Vic's jaw clenched. He had hoped Jen would burn out by now, that the weight of her ideals and lack of funding would crush her under the pressure. But she was still standing. And that was a problem.

"What's our next move? Goddamnit!" Vic snapped, his voice hard and edged with frustration.

Slater smiled, that familiar **predatory gleam** in his eyes. "We hit her where it hurts. She's running on integrity, on this whole 'faith in the system' narrative. We will show people that she's just like everyone else—just another politician making promises she can't keep."

Vic nodded slowly. It wasn't the first time they'd taken down an opponent like this, and it wouldn't be the last. The goal wasn't just to win—it was to destroy, to ensure no one could stand in their way. You didn't just cut off the head; you burned, drowned, and buried the opponent—at any cost.

— 4 —

The serene expanse of Lake Superior shimmered in the early morning light, a view captured in a photograph that adorned the walls of Vic Ross's Washington, D.C., office. For Vic, the image was more than just decoration—it was a carefully chosen artifact, a nod to the state that had propelled him into the national spotlight. Minnesota, the "Land of 10,000 Lakes," had been his stepping stone to power, though Vic's roots in the state were far shallower than he allowed most people to believe.

When Vic moved to Minnesota five years before his gubernatorial campaign, it was less about putting down roots and more about seizing opportunity. A lucrative business deal had taken him to Minneapolis, where he found himself enamored not with the state, but with its untapped political potential. He saw a divided electorate—a landscape ripe for a candidate who could craft a compelling centrist narrative.

By the time he declared his candidacy, Vic had fashioned himself as a champion of Minnesota values, touting a narrative of rugged determination and Midwestern pragmatism. He spoke earnestly about his deep admiration for the people of Minnesota, weaving stories of their resilience and grit into every speech. The reality, however, was far more calculated. Vic viewed the state less as a home and more as an opportunity—a platform to launch his ambitions. Behind closed doors, his disdain for the very people he claimed to represent occasionally slipped through. More than once, he referred to his constituents as "fucking idiots," a sentiment overheard by aides who learned to either ignore his outbursts or spin them into jokes. His early campaign commercials featured him chopping wood at his newly purchased cabin—a rustic symbol of his supposed deep connection to the state. In truth, the cabin was as close to Minnesota's wilderness as Vic preferred to get.

Vic's ascent to the governorship was not part of a lifelong plan but the result of political serendipity. Many opponents referred to him as the "Accidental Governor," a label that he initially bristled at but later learned to wear as a badge of resilience. A scandal-plagued incumbent had left Minnesota's political landscape in disarray, and Vic, a relative outsider with a sharp wit and a talent for spinning a compelling narrative, stepped into the void. He branded himself as a pragmatic centrist—a businessman who understood the struggles of working Minnesotans but wasn't afraid to challenge entrenched political interests. His message resonated in a state divided by urban progressivism and rural conservatism, tapping into the frustrations and aspirations of voters who felt overlooked by the status quo.

When the final votes were tallied, Vic's narrow victory shocked both his critics and his supporters. "Ross won? The corporate guy?" pundits exclaimed, their disbelief palpable. But Vic saw it differently: he had been underestimated and planned to use it to his advantage.

Vic's governorship was marked by both achievements and controversy. Early in his first term, an investigation revealed that one of his largest campaign donors had secured a lucrative state contract. Vic claimed ignorance, shifted blame to a subordinate, and launched an independent audit that distanced him from the fallout. It wasn't the last time his name would be tied to scandal. Accusations of favoritism, questionable campaign donations, and an extramarital affair that circulated in whispers all threatened to derail his political career.

Yet, time and again, Vic emerged unscathed. His ability to deflect, pivot, and control the narrative became his signature. He leaned on his media savvy and a network of loyal consultants to bury controversies under a flood of good press. For every headline about his missteps, there were two touting Minnesota's job growth under his leadership or the success of his green energy initiatives. He perfected the art of steering attention away from his flaws and toward his achievements.

After two terms in office, Vic left Minnesota behind with surprising swiftness. His public farewell was framed as bittersweet, full of tributes to the state he had claimed to love. "Minnesota will always be my heart," he declared at his farewell press conference, standing in front of a North Star flag, his voice heavy with manufactured emotion. Privately, Vic was already packed for D.C., eager to leave the "hillbilly" state behind and dive into the sophistication and power of the nation's capital.

In truth, Vic had never intended to stay. A year after stepping down, he sold his Minneapolis home and officially relocated to Washington, keeping only the cabin as a symbolic gesture. It served as a convenient backdrop for media profiles and campaign ads, reinforcing the myth of his enduring connection to Minnesota. But in reality, Vic rarely set foot there, preferring the polished corridors of D.C. to the rustic charms of the Northwoods.

As he positioned himself for the presidency, Vic made one thing clear: he did not want to be referred to as "Governor Ross." His communications team emphasized data showing that no governor in the past 32 years had successfully ascended to the presidency. "Former Governor" was a title that, while accurate, he deemed politically limiting. Instead, he insisted on being called "Presidential Candidate Vic Ross," branding himself as forward-focused and national in scope, not tethered to his state-level past.

In D.C., Vic established Ross Strategies, a political consulting firm that capitalized on his experience and connections. The firm catered to high-profile clients seeking to influence legislation, win elections, or navigate public relations crises. With contracts from energy companies, tech firms, and lobbying groups, Vic's wealth skyrocketed. The same strategic acumen that had allowed him to sidestep scandals as governor now made him indispensable in the capital's power circles.

Vic Ross maintained a sizeable PR and branding budget to aid his uncrackable image management. Though he rarely returned to Minnesota, Vic ensured that the state remained part of his public identity. His speeches often referenced his time as governor, painting a romanticized picture of his service. Campaign ads for his consulting firm featured aerial shots of the Boundary Waters and clips of him shaking hands at state fairs. "Minnesota made me who I am," he often proclaimed, his tone thick with sincerity. But those who knew him well recognized it as yet another carefully crafted line, designed to keep the myth of his Midwestern roots alive while he continued to climb the political ladder in Washington, D.C.

To his critics in Minnesota, Vic's departure symbolized everything they disliked about him—a man who had used the state as a launchpad and discarded it when it was no longer useful. To his supporters, he was the pragmatic leader who had brought jobs and innovation to the state, even if his love for Minnesota was more concept than reality.

Vic's tenure as governor had been one of contradictions: scandals deftly avoided, accomplishments touted louder than their complexities, and a connection to the state that was more performance than substance. But in the end, Vic Ross had achieved what he set out to do. Minnesota had served its purpose, and he had moved on—leaving the North Star State behind as he reached for bigger and brighter horizons.

— 5 —

The bar was dimly lit, and the smell of stale beer and whiskey couldn't be missed. Ethan Grant took a long swig of his gin rocks, feeling the burn as it slid down his throat. He had been here for an hour already, his jacket draped over the back of the stool, his tie loosened. He hadn't planned on drinking tonight, but after he met with Carly Bishop, it felt inevitable.

Ethan slammed the glass back down on the counter, the sound barely cutting through the low murmur of conversations around him. His phone vibrated on the bar, another message from Rick Slater, no doubt. He didn't need to check it to know what it said: ***Get it done***.

"Fuck him," Ethan muttered under his breath, running a hand through his already messy hair. He motioned to the bartender for another round. It had been months since he had allowed himself to get this drunk, but right now, it seemed like the only option. If he was going to drown, he might as well drown in decent gin.

As the bartender slid the next drink across the bar, Riley Daniels appeared beside him, sliding into the stool without a word. She had that look on her face—the one that said she knew exactly what was going on, and that she wasn't going to let Ethan off the hook.

"You look like shit," Riley said, her voice cutting through the haze of alcohol in Ethan's mind.

"I feel like shit," Ethan replied, taking another long drink. "What the hell are you doing here?"

"Looking for you," Riley said, nodding to the bartender for her own drink. "And not surprised I found you in the bottom of a bottle."

Ethan smirked, though it didn't reach his eyes. "Not at the bottom yet, and seems like the only place that makes sense anymore."

Riley raised an eyebrow, taking a sip of her whiskey. "Care to elaborate? Or are we just going to sit here and pretend you haven't been spiraling for the past month?"

Ethan sighed, rubbing a hand over his face. "I talked to Carly today. She's threatening to pull out if we don't deliver on the contracts."

"And?"

"And Slater expects me to just...fix it. Like it's that fucking easy." Ethan took another drink, the liquid numbing the rising anger in his chest. "I can't keep doing this, Riley. We're so deep in shit, I don't even know what the hell we're fighting for anymore."

Riley tilted her head, studying him. "You didn't honestly think running a campaign like this would be clean, did you?"

"No, but I didn't expect it to be...this," Ethan said, gesturing vaguely with his drink. "I mean, Christ, we started this thing talking about integrity, about reform, and now? Now we're just trying to keep people like Carly Bishop happy, so they don't bury us."

Riley shrugged. "Welcome to politics, sweetheart. Everyone's dirty. The only difference is how well you hide it."

Ethan barked out a bitter laugh. "I don't think I'm hiding it very well."

"Not with that attitude," Riley said, smirking. She leaned in, her tone softening. "Look, I get it. This isn't what you signed up for. But if you walk away now if you quit? Slater will steamroll over you, and everything you've worked for will go up in smoke."

Ethan stared into his glass, watching his thoughts swirl like melting ice. "And if I stay? What's left of me when this is all over? I'm selling shit—and I'm starting to smell like it, too."

Riley didn't answer, but the look in her eyes told him everything he needed to know. There were no good answers here. Just choices. And none of them came without a heavy price.

Back at the campaign headquarters, Vic Ross was pacing the floor of his office, a glass of old smokey Scotch in hand. The burn felt good—sharp and clean, a distraction from the mounting frustration that had been gnawing at him for weeks. Every day brought another crisis, another problem to fix. And Tom Albright's arrest had left a stain that just wouldn't come out, no matter how hard they scrubbed.

Slater sat calmly at Vic's desk, flipping through pages of polling data like it was just another day at the office. Nothing rattled him, and that infuriated Vic. He needed Slater to care more and feel the pressure. But instead, the man was as cool as ever, sipping his drink and pretending everything wasn't about to go up in flames.

"Do you ever fucking worry?" Vic snapped, swirling his drink as he glared at his advisor.

Slater looked up, raising an eyebrow. "Worrying doesn't change anything."

"Jesus, Rick. We're slipping here. Morales is pulling in tons of grassroots support, and she's got celebrities who never endorse actually working the phones for her. Fuck me! The swing states are getting tighter. We're hanging on by a thread, right, and you're sitting there like its business as usual."

Slater leaned back in his chair, his expression unreadable. "It *is* business as usual, Vic. This is what happens with every campaign. There's always a moment when things feel like they're getting less stable. But that's when we double down."

Vic shot back the rest of his Scotch, slamming the glass down on his desk. "And what the hell does that look like? Hitting her harder? Going after her family? Her fucking pets?" He leaned forward, eyes blazing. "Motherfucker, give me some specifics. I'm not in the mood to guess how you plan to save my campaign for President."

Slater's lips curled into a faint smile. "If that's what it takes."

Vic stared at him, a sinking feeling settling in his gut. He had always known that Slater was willing to cross lines, but the further they went, the blurrier those lines became. And now, they were standing on the edge of something he wasn't sure he wanted to see through.

"I'm serious, Rick," Vic said, his voice low. "How far are we willing to go?"

"As far as we need to," Slater replied, standing up and pouring himself another drink. He turned to face Vic, his eyes cold. "You want to win? Then you better be ready to get your hands dirty."

Vic poured himself another drink, the tension in his chest

tightening. He knew what Slater was saying and that if he let this campaign fall apart now, everything he had built—everything he had fought for—would be for nothing. But the deeper they went, the more he felt he was losing himself this time; that scared the hell out of him.

"Jen Morales isn't the problem," Slater said, his voice cutting through Vic's thoughts. "The problem is that you're letting this get personal. You're hesitating. And hesitation, in this game, gets you killed."

Vic shot him a glare. "I'm not hesitating."

"Aren't you?" Slater's smile was thin, calculated. "You want to win, but you're still trying to convince yourself you've already got it in the bag, trying to keep things sorta clean. Let me tell you something, Vic—there's no clean path to the power you're after. You either play the game with headbutts and fists or get crushed by it."

Vic stared at the drink in his hand, the amber liquid swirling in the glass. He knew Slater was right, but that didn't make it any easier to swallow, and he sure as hell wouldn't admit it.

"We'll hit her harder," Vic said finally, his voice low. "But if we do this, we do it my way. I'm not burning everything down just to sit on the ashes."

Slater gave a slow nod, a flicker of approval in his eyes. "As long as you understand that in the end, it's not about how you get there. It's about winning."

Vic downed the rest of his drink in a single gulp, the burn barely registering. "Yeah. We understand each other."

Across town, Jen Morales sat alone in her hotel room, nursing a cold coffee. She had stopped drinking it hours ago, opting instead to take slow pulls from a cigarette as she stared at the wall, the weight of the campaign pressing down on her.

The day's events played in a loop in her mind—the faces of the people she'd spoken to, the questions she hadn't been able to answer, the promises she wasn't sure she could keep. Whenever she thought she had made progress, the shadow of Vic Ross loomed larger, his campaign machinery churning out polished lies faster than she could combat them with the truth.

"Fucking bastard," she muttered, taking another drink. She had tried to play it clean, to run a campaign that was about more than just power. But power was all that seemed to matter anymore.

Her phone buzzed on the nightstand, and she picked it up to see a message from Nathan. *You okay?*

Jen stared at the message for a long moment before replying. *Yeah. Just...tired.*

Nathan responded almost immediately. Me too. We're still in this, though—don't forget that. PS. A bottle of wine or drinking won't ever help.

Jen put the phone down without replying. They were still in it. But for how long? She wasn't sure how much more she could take. Yet, despite herself, she cracked a small smile. How in the hell did he know she was thinking about wine? Weird.

She took another long pull, her lungs burned, and leaned back against the headboard, closing her eyes. She had to keep fighting. She had to. But as weariness dulled the edges of her thoughts, a question crept in—what the hell was she fighting for anymore? The thought lingered as her grip awareness lessened, and eventually, her eyes drifted shut.

— 6 —

Vic Ross leaned back in the plush seat of his campaign bus, trying—and failing—to find a comfortable position. The vehicle lumbered along a narrow Iowa highway, its rumbling engine and the distant hiss of the air brakes grating on his nerves. The golden light of early evening washed over cornfields, stretching endlessly in both directions, but Vic could only think about how much he hated this bus. It felt painfully analog and amateur, with its faux wood paneling and outdated upholstery. No amount of polished campaign branding or high-tech gadgets scattered around the cabin could hide that.

Compared to the sleek, black SUVs that usually whisked him from place to place or his private plane outfitted with luxurious leather seats and in-flight service, the bus was a relic. It reminded him of student field trips and local roadshows—not the powerful image he preferred to project. Yet, the campaign messaging team had insisted: "You need to be seen on the ground in the Midwest," they'd said. "We have to show you're connected to the heartland."

Vic had tried to argue. The plane was faster and more efficient. It got him to more events in less time. But even Ethan Grant, his deputy campaign manager supported the idea. The optics mattered. The bus had become a rolling stage, a symbol of his dedication to grassroots outreach—whether or not he liked it.

He smoothed his expression as the bus turned into the gravel lot of a community center, bracing himself to deliver the next carefully crafted speech. If the voters noticed the lines of irritation around his mouth, they might see the cracks beneath his polished surface. So he plastered on his campaign smile, determined to perform the role once again.

Day One: Iowa

Vic stepped onto the makeshift stage set up in front of the center, facing a crowd that had gathered despite the biting wind. Farmers, families, and the occasional curious onlooker stood with their arms crossed, some nodding in polite greeting as he approached the microphone. Vic glanced at Ethan, who gave him an encouraging thumbs-up.

"Thank you all for coming out," Vic began, his voice practiced yet warm. "I know what's important to Iowans: family, faith, and the dignity of hard work. And I promise, if you trust me with your vote, I'll put policies in place that protect the heartland."

A murmur of agreement rippled through the crowd, though Vic could still sense the intense skepticism. He pivoted, launching into a story about his grandfather, a farmer who had faced tough times. It was a story his PR team had fine-tuned, one that usually resonated well. But here, the reactions felt subdued, wary. As he wrapped up, he saw an older man in a weathered cap eyeing him with doubt, arms crossed.

Day Two: Wyoming

The bus groaned its way across the Wyoming plains, and Vic found himself staring out the window at the rugged landscape. He longed for the quiet interior of his private plane, where he could sip Scotch in peace while hurtling above the clouds, far removed from the dust and miles of emptiness. But here he was, stuck in this lumbering, glorified school bus because the voters demanded proximity, humility, and visibility.

When the bus finally pulled into the small town hall, Vic stepped out, brushing imaginary dust from his suit. The place had a worn-down charm, with cowboys and ranchers gathered, many of them holding battered hats in hand as a sign of respect.

Vic's speech here was more personal, tailored to the rugged individualism of the region. "I understand that Washington doesn't always hear your voices," he said. "But I promise, I'm here to change that." He referenced land rights and fair cattle trade, buzzwords that typically won applause.

An older rancher stepped forward during the Q&A session, his face lined from years of hard work. "We've heard promises before," he said. "What makes you different, Sir?"

First, it's Vic, not Sir. Vic's campaign smile slipped, but he caught himself. "What makes me different is I've been listening. I'm not just here to give empty promises; I'm here to take your concerns straight to the Capitol, Courts, and anywhere else I need to support you."

The rancher nodded slowly, his expression unreadable, and Vic knew he hadn't entirely won him over. Back on the bus, Vic sat across from Riley Daniels, his communications director. "We need to make sure they feel it, Riley," he said. "The authenticity. Otherwise, we're losing them."

Riley raised an eyebrow. "Might help if you actually believe it," she shot back, but there was no malice, only tired honesty. Vic frowned but said nothing.

Day Three: Nebraska

The Nebraska stop was in a high school gymnasium, the stands packed with voters ranging from young college students to older veterans. As the bus pulled up, Vic tried not to show how much he detested the way it creaked and sighed to a stop. He could almost hear the whispers of his wealthy donors back in D.C., who would never understand the optics game he was forced to play.

Vic leaned into the microphone, his voice projecting strength and confidence. "Nebraska knows the meaning of resilience," he declared, recounting stories of communities rebuilding from floods and crises. The crowd listened, some nodding, others with folded arms.

A young man in a college sweatshirt stood to ask a question. "You say you care about our future," he said. "But what about climate change? Droughts and floods have hit us. What are you doing about that?"

Vic paused. His prepared answer touched on green initiatives balanced with job preservation, but he felt the pushback in the young man's tense shoulders. Afterward, Vic rubbed his temples as the bus pulled away from the school.

Ethan sat next to him, looking at polling numbers on his tablet. "We need momentum, it's like we're in neutral," Ethan said grimly.

Vic knew it, felt it in his bones. But in this relentless grind of promises and doubts, he wasn't sure if he was gaining ground or just treading water.

— 7 —

The room smelled of burnt coffee and cheap disinfectant, a scent Jen Morales had come to associate with safety. In the circle of folding chairs, no one asked her about campaign strategies, press releases, or the latest polling numbers. Here, she wasn't a gubernatorial candidate. She was just Jen—a woman with her own struggles, trying to keep herself together.

For two years, the members of her Alcoholics Anonymous group had protected her anonymity like it was their own. Even in Santa Fe, her hometown, where the line between private and public lives often blurred, they had been her shield. When the press had started digging into her background, speculating on personal details, the group closed ranks. Jen always knew she was safe here.

But now, sitting in her usual spot near the back, she felt a creeping sense of detachment. The familiar ritual of sharing and listening, once a lifeline, felt distant—like a version of herself she was leaving behind.

The meeting ended with the "we version" of the **Serenity Prayer**, the group reciting the words in unison, their voices steady and deliberate. As the others began to chat and refill their coffee cups, Jen stayed seated, staring at the empty cup in her hands.

"Hey, Jen," a soft voice called, breaking her thoughts. It was Nora, one of the regulars. Her expression was kind, but there was a trace of concern in her eyes. "You doing okay, important lady?"

Jen hesitated. She'd heard the question a lot lately, but this time, the answer felt heavier. "I'm fine," she said, her smile not quite reaching her eyes.

"Campaign keeping you busy?" Nora asked her tone light but knowing.

"Yeah," Jen replied. "It's... a lot."

Nora nodded, her concern softening into understanding. "Just don't forget to take care of yourself, okay? You've come so far. We're all here if you need us."

Jen nodded quickly, her throat tightening. She muttered a goodbye and slipped out into the cool night air before Nora could say anything else.

The streets of Santa Fe were quiet as Jen walked to her car. The city lights cast long shadows across the adobe walls, their familiar shapes a reminder of home. This town had always protected her, its people rallying around one of their own when the campaign trail grew too intense. Lately, though, Santa Fe has felt distant, like it belonged to someone else.

Sliding into the driver's seat, Jen stared at the wheel for a long time. The words from the meeting played in her mind: ***Take care of yourself. You've come so far.***

Had she? The campaign was grueling, with a relentless barrage of debates, interviews, and donor events. Every moment felt like a test of her resolve, her ability to hold it all together. But no one saw the cracks forming beneath the surface.

Her phone buzzed in the cupholder, the screen lighting up with a message from Nathan: "Donor dinner tomorrow. Be ready for questions on water policy."

Jen exhaled and leaned back, her thoughts clouded. The pressure of balancing everything—her campaign, sobriety, and identity—was becoming unbearable.

When Jen arrived home, the house was dark, and its silence was comforting and oppressive. She moved through the kitchen, turning on a single light over the counter, and opened the cabinet where she kept her coffee mugs. Her hand hovered briefly before shifting to the bottle of red wine tucked behind them.

It had been a gift from a supporter, untouched since the day it arrived. For two years, it had been her silent challenge, her proof that she could hold her ground. But tonight, as the weight of the campaign pressed down on her, it felt like something else entirely.

Jen poured herself half a glass, the deep red liquid swirling under the light. She stared at it for what felt like forever, guilt and longing warring inside her.

"Just a little," she whispered to herself. "Just enough to take the edge off."

The first sip was hesitant, a rush of warmth filling her chest as the wine hit her tongue. Relief followed—not just from the stress but also from the suffocating sense of always being watched and judged. Here, in her kitchen, she was alone.

The guilt came next, sharper than she expected. She glanced at the clock as if tracking how long she'd allowed herself this moment. But another part of her pushed back: *I deserve this. I can handle this.*

The next morning, Jen stared at her reflection in the bathroom mirror, searching for regret, maybe, or a sign that she'd made a mistake. But her face looked the same: tired, determined, and unwilling to back down.

She needed to be sharp and focused. The meetings had helped for a while, but they tied her to a version of herself she wanted to outgrow. She wasn't just Jen from Santa Fe anymore; she was a candidate, a leader. And if a single glass of wine helped her cope, wasn't that better than falling apart completely?

At least, that's what she told herself.

Her phone buzzed again, a reminder of the packed schedule ahead. Jen swiped the screen, ignoring the AA group text blinking at the top. She hadn't responded in days, and she didn't plan to.

"I've got this under control," she murmured to herself, the words more fragile than she intended.

That evening, at a private campaign dinner, Jen nursed another half-glass of wine as donors quizzed her on policy and praised her poise. She took measured sips, was careful never to finish, and always maintained control.

Nathan caught her as the night wound down, his expression approving. "You seemed more relaxed tonight," he said. "That's exactly the energy we need."

Jen smiled, but the weight of his words lingered. The energy he wanted wasn't coming from speeches or strategy—it came from the quiet rebellion she'd allowed herself the night before.

Later, as she sat in the car, she scrolled through her phone. The group text from AA was still there, filled with well-meaning check-ins. She hesitated, her thumb hovering over the screen, then swiped the notification away.

The meetings had been her safety net, her protection. But the campaign demanded something else entirely.

"I've got this," she whispered again, but the doubt in her voice echoed in the car's silence.

— 8 —

The pounding bass of the music reverberated through the floor as Ethan Grant stared down at his empty glass, the dim light of the club casting long shadows across his face. He'd lost count of how many drinks he'd had—too many, probably—but tonight, he didn't care. The gin had dulled the constant buzzing in his head, the relentless noise of the campaign, of Slater's demands, of Carly Bishop's threats. All of it, gone, at least for now.

The club was loud and packed, bodies moving in sync with the music, a mess of heat and sweat that Ethan didn't feel like joining. He leaned against the bar, signaling the bartender for another round, his tie hanging loose around his neck, his shirt untucked. He was past the point of giving a damn about appearances.

As he waited for his drink, his phone buzzed in his pocket. He knew who it was before he even looked. Riley Daniels had been texting him all night, checking in, telling him to stop drinking and get his ass home. But he wasn't ready to leave yet. Not when the weight of everything still pressed down on him so hard.

He glanced at the screen: **Where the fuck are you?**

Ethan smirked and typed a quick reply. *Out. Don't wait up.*

A few seconds later, the phone buzzed again. *You're a fucking idiot.*

Ethan didn't respond. Instead, he downed his next drink and motioned for another. The bartender gave him a raised eyebrow but said nothing as he poured the gin. Ethan wasn't interested in small talk tonight.

He leaned back against the bar, letting the music pulse through him, trying to lose himself in the noise. But even as the alcohol worked its way through his system, the nagging thoughts wouldn't leave. Slater's voice echoed in his mind: **Fix it, or you're done**—Carly Bishop's threats. Vic's face tightened with pressure. And that unshakable feeling that the more he did for this campaign, the less of himself he had left.

Then he felt someone slide into the seat beside him. Ethan didn't bother looking up at first—he wasn't in the mood for company. But when a familiar voice broke through the music, he couldn't help but glance sideways.

"I figured I'd find you in a place like this."

Riley. Of course, it was her. She never could leave well enough alone.

Ethan sighed, pushing his drink away slightly. "What the hell are you doing here?"

Riley shrugged, her eyes sharp as they locked onto his. "Saving you from yourself, as usual."

Ethan let out a bitter laugh. "Seems like a waste of time, don't you think?"

Riley leaned in, her voice low. "I think you're making a bigger mess than you realize, and if you don't pull your shit together, it's all gonna fall apart. You're not the only one in this, Ethan."

Her words hit harder than the gin. He knew she was right. But he wasn't ready to admit it yet.

"Why do you fucking care so much?" Ethan asked, his voice softer now, the edge gone. "Why are you always cleaning up after me?"

Riley didn't answer right away. Instead, she reached over and grabbed his glass, downing the rest of his drink in one go. She set the glass back down with a thud, her eyes never leaving his.

"Because someone has to."

A few minutes later, they stumbled out of the club, Riley guiding them both as the cool night air hit like a slap to the face. The streets were quiet now, most of the late-night crowd long gone. Riley flagged down a cab, and they slid into the back seat, the mingled smell of sweat and alcohol heavy between them.

Ethan leaned his head back against the seat, his eyes half-closed. He could still feel the gin swirling in his veins, dulling the sharp edges of his thoughts. But he couldn't shake the feeling of Riley sitting beside him, her body close enough to feel the heat radiating off her.

"You really are a goddamn mess, you know that?" Riley muttered, her voice a blend of annoyance and amusement.

Ethan turned his head to look at her, a lazy grin spreading across his face. "And you're still here. So what does that make you?"

Riley rolled her eyes, but there was a flicker of something in her expression—something that wasn't just exasperation.

They didn't talk much on the ride back to Ethan's place, the silence between them stretching out, heavy and charged. By the time the cab pulled up outside his building, Ethan wasn't sure if he was thinking clearly or if the alcohol was doing the talking. Either way, he found himself holding the door open for her, half-expecting her to turn and leave.

But Riley didn't.

They made their way upstairs, the tension thickening with every step. When they reached his apartment, Ethan wasn't thinking about anything except the heat radiating between them. He fumbled with the key, his hands shaky from too much gin and too little sleep, but Riley didn't move to help. She just stood there, watching him with that same unreadable expression.

When the door finally swung open, they stumbled inside, and everything seemed to blur together—the soft click of the door closing, the feel of Riley's hand on his chest, the way she didn't push him away.

And then they were kissing—hard, urgent like neither of them could afford to stop. The room spun around them as they stumbled toward the couch, clothes half ripped, half discarded. There was nothing gentle about it. Nothing soft. It was raw, desperate, fueled by months of frustration, anger, and the unspoken tension that had been building between them since the campaign started to fall apart.

Ethan's hands were all over her, his breath hot and heavy in her ear as she pulled him closer, her nails digging into his back. It wasn't clean. It wasn't pretty. But it was what they both needed, and neither of them was about to stop.

By the time they collapsed onto the couch, tangled in each other, their breathing ragged, the gin had finally caught up with Ethan. His head was spinning, but it wasn't just from the alcohol anymore.

Riley lay next to him, her chest rising and falling with deep, even breaths. She didn't say anything. Neither did he. They just lay there, the weight of what had just happened hanging in the air between them, thick and suffocating.

Ethan closed his eyes, trying to block out the thoughts that were already clawing their way to the surface. What the hell had they just done? And what the hell was he going to do now?

But there were no answers tonight. Just the pounding in his head, the burn of the gin still lingering on his lips, and the feel of Riley beside him—solid, warm, and just as fucked up as he was.

Across the city, in the quiet of his penthouse, Vic Ross poured himself another Scotch, the liquid gleaming amber in the low light. The city spread out before him, glittering in the darkness, but Vic's mind wasn't on the view.

His thoughts were on Jen Morales.

He'd underestimated her. She was still hanging on, still pulling in support from places he hadn't expected. He'd figured she didn't have the balls to play at this level. But she wasn't breaking. And that meant she had to be dealt with.

Vic took a slow sip of his drink, letting the heat settle in his chest. Slater had already laid out their next moves—ways to undermine her, to chip away at her reputation. But Vic was tired. He was tired of playing defense and waiting for the right moment to strike.

Maybe it was time to hit her harder. Maybe it was time to end this, once and for all.

Vic downed the rest of his drink and set the glass down with a decisive thud. His mind was made up. They'd go after her tomorrow, and they wouldn't stop until she was finished. It was time to unleash the social media counter-assets, to spread whatever false information it took to bring her down.

"Fuck her," he muttered, taking a deep breath as he steadied himself and headed toward the bedroom.

— 9 —

Ethan Grant woke to a pounding headache and the bitter taste of regret. His eyes cracked open just enough to take in the mess of clothes scattered across the floor, the half-empty bottle on the coffee table, and the faint morning light creeping through the blinds. His body felt heavy, as if every bone was weighed down by the drinking the night before, and the choices he didn't want to think about.

Riley lay beside him on the couch, her hair tousled, still asleep, her back turned to him. For a moment, he considered reaching out, maybe saying something—an apology, a joke, anything to break the suffocating silence between them. But what was there to say? They'd crossed a line they couldn't uncross, and now, they had to deal with the fallout.

Ethan closed his eyes again, willing the pounding in his skull to ease up. His phone was vibrating somewhere on the floor, but he ignored it. He knew what it was—Slater, calling to bark more orders, to remind him that the world didn't stop just because Ethan's life was falling apart.

Eventually, Riley stirred, sitting up slowly and rubbing her eyes. She didn't say anything as she stood and gathered her clothes, slipping into her jeans and pulling on her shirt in silence. The awkwardness between them was almost unbearable.

"Riley—" Ethan started, his voice hoarse, but she cut him off with a wave of her hand.

"Don't," she said, her tone flat, avoiding his gaze. "Last night was a mistake. We were both drunk. Let's just...forget about it."

Ethan nodded, though he knew it wouldn't be that easy. Nothing ever was.

"See you at the office," Riley said, her voice sharp and professional, before grabbing her bag and heading for the door without another glance. The sound of it closing behind her felt like the final nail in the coffin of whatever control Ethan had left. His life was officially a dumpster fire.

He sat up, his head throbbing, and reached for the bottle on the coffee table. He poured himself another drink—hair of the dog, right? Just enough to get through the next hour, then maybe he could face the day. But as the bourbon burned its way down his throat, mixing with the gin already churning in his stomach, Ethan couldn't shake the feeling that he was sliding deeper into something he couldn't escape. He was definitely going to puke—a fitting metaphor for the mess of his recent choices.

Jen Morales paced her hotel room, the tension practically radiating off her. She hadn't slept much—how could she? And drinking again didn't help.

The latest polls showed Vic Ross closing in on her in key swing states, and to make matters worse, the press was suddenly picking apart every little detail of her campaign, questioning her fundraising tactics, her strategy, and even her commitment to the causes she'd championed for years like election security, human rights, and hope.

It was bullshit, all of it. But bullshit or not, it was sticking.

Nathan sat on the edge of the bed, scrolling through his phone. His face was a mask of calm, but Jen knew him well enough to see the worry in his eyes.

"This is Slater's work," Nathan said, his voice low but clear. "He's good at this kind of thing. Smear campaigns, quiet leaks to the press, planting seeds of doubt on social media. We knew it was coming."

Jen clenched her fists, her mind racing. "Yeah, but I didn't think they'd hit us this hard. Not like this." She paused, staring out at the sprawling desert beyond the city. "They're making me look like I'm no different from Vic—just another politician out for herself. I hate those motherfuckers!"

Nathan stood and crossed the room, his hand resting on her shoulder. "You're not, Jen. Anyone who knows you, knows that."

She turned to face him, her jaw set. "But not enough people know me yet, outside New Mexico, Nathan. And those who don't? They're going to believe the noise. They'll think I'm just like the rest."

Nathan sighed, his hand dropping to his side. "So what do we do? Fight back how?"

Jen shook her head. "We can't go down that road. I'm not playing Slater's game. If we start mudslinging, and misinformation campaigns we're no better than they are."

Nathan nodded, but his expression was grim. "I get that, Jen. But we have to be smart. We need to find some of their own tactics to use against them—countermeasures. They're coming at you with everything they've got, and if we don't push back, we'll lose what little ground we've gained."

Jen exhaled slowly, the weight of the decision pressing down on her. She had promised herself she wouldn't play dirty or compromise her principles. But now, with the campaign hanging by a thread, she wasn't sure how much longer she could hold that line.

"I need some time to think," she muttered, brushing past Nathan and grabbing her jacket. "I'm going for a walk."

Back at Vic Ross's headquarters, the mood was decidedly different. Vic was standing at the head of the conference table, his hands braced on the wood as he stared down at the stack of reports in front of him. Polling numbers. Swing state projections. Fundraising goals. It was all bullshit to him now. The game had changed.

Rick Slater sat opposite him, as cool and composed as ever, with a smirk tugging at his mouth's corners. "Quiet today, Vic."

Vic straightened up, running a hand through his hair. "Just thinking."

"Thinking about how close we are to finishing her off?" Slater's smirk widened. "Because we're almost there. We've got the press on her, and her numbers are slipping. If we keep pushing, we can force her to make a mistake. She's desperate. She'll crack."

Vic took a breath, his mind swirling with a mix of satisfaction and unease. Slater was right—they were close. They'd hit Jen's campaign hard, and the press was eating it up. All they needed was one more push and scandal to break her.

But something about it wasn't sitting right with Vic. He'd told himself from the beginning that he wanted to win on his own terms. But now? Now it felt like he was winning on Slater's terms.

"I'm not sure about this," Vic said quietly, his eyes fixed on the reports in front of him.

Slater's smirk disappeared, his gaze sharpening. "Not sure about what?"

"All of this," Vic muttered, waving a hand over the stack of reports. "We're going after her hard, Rick. Harder than I ever thought we'd need to."

Slater leaned back in his chair, crossing his arms. "What's the problem, Vic? You wanted to win, didn't you? This is how we win."

"Yeah, but at what cost?" Vic muttered more to himself than to Slater, a brief crisis of conscience moment.

Slater's eyes narrowed. "The cost is irrelevant. Do you want to be president? This is how you get there. You don't like the process? Tough shit. That's how the game is played. You hired me to win."

Vic didn't respond immediately, the words sinking in like stones on his chest. He knew Slater was right. This was how the game was played. But as he stared down at the reports, all he could think about was the people who would get crushed along the way—people like Jen, who had once believed in something better.

"Heavy is the crown, Vic," Slater said, his tone steady, almost smug.

Vic sighed and reached for the bottle of Scotch on the table, pouring himself a glass. He took a long drink, the burn of the alcohol doing little to ease the tension in his gut. Slater was watching him carefully, waiting.

"You want to win, Vic," Slater said softly, his voice almost a whisper. "And I'm going to get you there. But you have to decide now—how far are you willing to go?"

Vic stared into his glass, the amber liquid swirling slowly. He had already crossed so many lines. What was one more? Scotch hadn't let him down yet—everyone and everything else did daily. But people like Slater, he thought, were the most unpredictable of all.

He turned his gaze to Slater, the room seeming to shrink around him. "Are you going to let me down?" he asked, his voice tinged with desperate vulnerability.

Slater's smile was cold, his eyes gleaming with calculated confidence. "Not a chance," he said smoothly. "You won't regret this."

But Vic wasn't convinced.

Jen found herself walking aimlessly through the streets, the quiet hum of the city lulling her into a trance. The sun had set when she returned to her hotel, and the sky was deep indigo streaked with orange and pink. She hadn't made any decisions, hadn't figured out how to deal with the shitstorm Vic and Slater were raining down on her.

The hotel bar was quiet, with only a few scattered patrons nursing their drinks. Jen slipped inside, her footsteps slow and heavy, her mind a swirl of exhaustion and frustration. She needed to clear her head, needed a moment to breathe before everything came crashing down again.

She ordered a glass of wine, sipping it slowly as she sat at the bar, staring at the swirling red liquid. It didn't take long for the familiar feeling of hopelessness to settle in. How the hell was she supposed to beat Vic when he was willing to burn everything down just to win?

The sound of footsteps drew closer, and Jen glanced sideways as Nathan slid into the seat beside her. He offered a small, weary smile, a glass of whiskey resting in his hand.

"Knew I'd find you here," he said softly, taking a sip. "Rough day, huh?"

It was only a matter of time before Nathan brought up her drinking again.

Jen sighed, swirling the wine in her glass and watching the dark liquid shimmer in the light.

"Yeah, well, we're all feeling it," Nathan said, his voice low. "You don't have to carry it all yourself, Jen."

She gave him a half-smile, though it didn't reach her eyes. "Feels like I do sometimes."

Nathan shook his head, his gaze soft. "You're not alone in this."

For a moment, they sat in comfortable silence, the weight of the campaign hanging between them, unspoken but heavy. Jen felt a flicker of gratitude, maybe, or just relief that Nathan was here, that someone was still standing with her, even when everything else was falling apart.

She set her nearly empty wine glass on the bar, her movements slow and deliberate. Her heart raced, the steady beat louder than she wanted to admit. "Maybe I don't want to be alone tonight," she said, her voice barely above a whisper.

Nathan's gaze flicked to the glass, then back to her, his expression soft but tinged with concern. "Jen," he said gently, "have you considered calling someone from AA? Just to check in?"

Her cheeks flushed as she turned away, his words landing heavier than she expected. "I'm fine," she murmured. "I'm being careful."

He leaned in, his voice calm but firm. "I know you are. But being careful doesn't mean doing it alone. It's okay to reach out."

She sighed, the tension easing as she nodded slowly. "You're right. I'll think about it."

Nathan offered a faint smile and set his glass down. "Good. And hey, let's put the emotional juggling act on hold tonight, okay?"

A quiet laugh bubbled up, and she nodded, a genuine smile breaking through. "Deal."

— 10 —

The next morning, Ethan Grant woke up to an alarm he didn't remember setting. The shrill sound stabbed through his skull like a jackhammer, and he groaned, slapping his hand across the nightstand until his fingers finally silenced the noise. His eyes cracked open, and the sight that greeted him was far from promising—his apartment was a disaster zone. Empty glasses littered the coffee table, a pizza box half-open on the floor, and a couple of rumpled papers that probably held something important he should have looked at weeks ago.

He sat up slowly, rubbing the sleep from his eyes. His head was throbbing, his mouth felt like sandpaper, and the last remnants of last night's bourbon clung to his breath like a bad decision. Then he remembered the worst part of all—Riley.

A groan escaped his lips. Not because of what happened between them but because he knew she wouldn't let him live it down. She'd probably show up at the office with that knowing smirk on her face, ready to bust his balls at every opportunity.

Dragging himself off the couch, he stumbled into the kitchen, reaching for a cup of coffee. But as he poured, the memory of last night brought a small smile to his face. Despite the mess, despite the regrets, Riley had been there. She always was. And honestly, maybe that's what he needed—someone to remind him that, despite all the pressure, there was still a little bit of his old self buried under the campaign grime.

Just as he took his first sip of coffee, his phone rang. He fumbled to answer it, the hot coffee sloshing onto his hand as he saw Riley's name on the screen.

"Morning, sunshine," her voice chirped through the phone, way too cheerful for what he knew she was about to drop on him.

Ethan groaned. "I swear to God, if you're calling to remind me of last night, I'm hanging up."

Riley laughed, and Ethan couldn't help but grin. "You mean the part where you drunk-splained campaign strategy to me while barely able to string three words together? Yeah, that's a moment I'm holding onto forever."

"I thought we agreed to forget about it," Ethan muttered, but the smile in his voice gave him away.

"Nope. Besides, it's rare to see you like that. I mean, stumbling around, all worked up over the campaign...it was kinda adorable."

"Adorable?" Ethan snorted. "Well, that's definitely not what I was going for."

"Hey, just letting you know—next time you decide to drink like a frat boy, let me know so I can clear my schedule. I don't do babysitting for free."

Ethan shook his head, leaning against the kitchen counter. Despite everything, Riley always had a way of cutting through the bullshit. "You know, there's a part of me that wishes you were as professional as you pretend to be. Then maybe I wouldn't have to live with the constant embarrassment."

"Oh, you love it," Riley shot back. "Besides, somebody has to keep you in check. Anyway, I'll see you at the office. Don't be late. Slater is in one of his delightful moods."

"Great," Ethan sighed. "That's just what I need. Another day getting ripped to shreds by a sociopath."

"Buck up, cowboy. You're good at taking punches. Just make sure you don't roll into the office smelling like gin and regret."

Ethan chuckled as the call ended. Something was comforting in the way Riley could laugh at everything, even when it was falling apart. It was what kept him sane, at least for the moment. He took another sip of his coffee, letting the small wave of humor wash over him. But reality was already creeping back in—the meetings, the pressure, the deals. There would be no hiding from it today.

Later, Jen Morales found herself in a situation she hadn't expected—stuck at a local diner in the middle of nowhere, waiting for her car to be repaired. The diner was a throwback to the 1950s, with checkered floors, vinyl booths, and a waitress named *Betty* who was probably born the same year as the establishment itself. Jen wasn't sure if this detour was a curse or a blessing, but it was starting to feel like a weird kind of escape.

She had been on her way to meet with campaign volunteers when the car started making a noise that sounded like a dying whale. After pulling over and calling for help, she wound up in this tiny roadside diner, where the smell of greasy bacon and coffee overwhelmed her senses.

Nathan slid into the booth across from her, shaking his head and grinning like an idiot.

"Car trouble, huh? You sure this isn't just a ploy to avoid another strategy meeting?"

Jen rolled her eyes, sipping her coffee. "Yes, Nathan. I secretly sabotaged my car just to hang out in a greasy diner with you. But saying it out loud, seems more like a great idea!"

"Well, mission accomplished. You've dragged me into it, too," he said, picking up a menu and scanning the list. "Hey, look on the bright side—at least we get to eat something that isn't delivered from a plastic container for once. When's the last time you had a proper diner breakfast?"

Jen smirked, setting her cup down. "I don't know. Sometime before, my life became an endless blur of campaign events and political landmines."

"Then we'll count this as a win," Nathan said with a grin. "You deserve a break anyway. I mean, I've seen you give the same stump speech a dozen times this week. You're practically on autopilot at this point."

Jen let out a small laugh. "That bad, huh?"

Nathan shrugged. "Hey, it's a great speech. But every time you say 'this country deserves better,' your eyes glaze over a little more. Thought you might fall asleep during the last one."

Jen couldn't help but smile. Nathan's humor was always dry but somehow hit the right notes. He had been with her from the beginning, the steady hand guiding her through every storm the campaign had thrown their way.

Just then, Betty reappeared with a plate of pancakes big enough to feed an army, setting them in front of Nathan with a smirk. "Don't say I never gave you anything."

"Thanks, Betty," Nathan said, flashing her a grin before turning to Jen. "Come on, we've got a few minutes before the world crashes down on us again. Pancakes?"

Jen shook her head, but she couldn't deny the tiny flicker of lightness in her chest. "Fine. But I'm stealing some of yours."

The moment felt almost surreal—a brief pause in the chaos, a chance to just be human for a second. It wasn't much, but it was enough to remind Jen that there were still small pleasures in life, even if they came in the form of pancakes in a dusty diner off the highway.

"Hey, at least we've got a good story now," Nathan said between bites, his grin widening. "The day the candidate's car broke down on the way to save the country.' Has a nice ring to it."

Jen laughed, feeling some of the tension slide off her shoulders, even if only for a moment. "Yeah, that's exactly how I want to be remembered."

Back at Vic Ross's campaign headquarters, there was no diner breakfast. There was only tension, meetings, and the sound of phones ringing off the hook. Vic stood in front of a whiteboard covered in hastily scribbled numbers and state projections, listening as Slater rattled off strategy points that sounded like pure venom.

Vic took a deep breath, his hand reaching for his third cup of coffee of the morning. "Jesus, Rick. Do you ever think about just…easing up for five seconds? Maybe going outside, touching some grass?"

Slater gave him a look that was somewhere between confusion and condescension. "I'm sorry, what?"

"I mean, have you ever just…stopped being such a relentless bastard for a minute?"

Slater didn't miss a beat. "Nope. Not my style."

Vic shook his head, rubbing his temples. "Sometimes I think you might actually be a robot."

"If I am, at least I'm an efficient one," Slater deadpanned, crossing his arms. "We don't have time to lighten up, Vic. Jen's campaign might be struggling, but she's not out yet. We've got to finish this."

Vic sighed, leaning back against the wall. "I know. I just…I don't know. Maybe I'm losing my edge."

Slater raised an eyebrow. "Losing your edge? You sound like you're ready to retire."

"Maybe I am," Vic muttered under his breath, though he knew

damn well he wasn't going anywhere. Not until this thing was over.

Slater's phone buzzed, and he glanced down at the message before looking back at Vic. "Well, you can think about retirement later. Right now, we've got work to do."

Vic let out a low chuckle. "Yeah, yeah. Don't get too excited. It's not like I will start holding yoga classes in the office."

"Good. You'd look ridiculous in spandex."

Vic smiled despite himself. For all of Slater's sharp edges, there was something about his brutal honesty that Vic couldn't help but respect. He might be a relentless bastard, but at least he didn't pretend to be anything else.

— 11 —

Vic Ross stood at the center of his war room, analyzing the projected map on the wall like a general surveying the battlefield. Phones rang, aides dashed in and out with status updates, and strategists clustered over laptops in intense discussion. Around the room's perimeter, The Candidate Service agents stood like sentinels, their presence underscoring just how high-stakes this campaign had become. Jen Morales was still in the race, still a threat. But Vic wasn't looking to simply defeat her; he wanted to end her political career for good. It was time to get the amateurs out of the way.

"Where are we on the Morales scandal?" Vic's voice cut through the commotion, instantly drawing the attention of his senior strategist, Rick Slater, who leaned against the far wall with his arms crossed, a lazy smile on his face.

"We've planted enough seeds. The press is starting to bite," Slater replied, his tone brimming with satisfaction.

Vic narrowed his eyes. "Not enough. I want it bigger. She's got too much goodwill. We need something that sticks."

Slater straightened, the lazy smile becoming a calculating grin. "You want a bomb? We'll give them a bomb. I've got a few more... explosive details ready to leak. Just depends on how deep you want to dig."

Vic weighed the choice, feeling the oppressive pressure of the decision. He knew precisely what Slater was offering: a nuclear scandal that would forever taint Morales's reputation, maybe even destroy her personal life. But for Vic, the stakes had risen beyond victory. It was annihilation or nothing.

Vic's gaze flickered briefly to one of The Candidate Service agents, a woman named Parker, who monitored the room with her sharp eyes, always vigilant. Vic had grown accustomed to the Service agents' silent presence, a reminder that he wasn't just any candidate—he was a target. Any serious misstep would attract more than political enemies; it could bring real danger. He looked back at Slater, calculating the fallout. "How far can we go without it blowing back on us?" he asked quietly.

Slater's grin sharpened, his eyes gleaming with that predatory edge Vic knew too well. "We're already wading through the mud, Vic. Might as well wallow in it. She's built her image spotless—let's shred it."

"Scandals sell. People eat them up. They'll believe everyone's hiding skeletons before they'll buy a clean slate. Voters relate to flaws faster than virtues. Sad truth—if I cared." Slater's shrug was as indifferent as his tone, the weight of morality no match for the game of power.

Nearby, Agent Ramsey's earpiece crackled, and she tilted her head, listening intently before muttering something Vic couldn't hear. She shot him a quick glance, a subtle reminder of the thin line he walked between candidate and protected asset. But Vic knew his choice. The campaign had reached a point where retreat was impossible. He would either emerge triumphant, or he would fall—utterly.

"Do it," Vic ordered his voice firm. "Whatever you've got, use it. I don't care how ugly it gets."

Slater's smile turned cold like a shark catching the scent of blood. "Consider it done."

At her own headquarters, Jen Morales tried to stay focused despite the oppressive tension filling the air. Her team was exhausted, having spent the last several hours scrambling to handle the relentless wave of negative press and increasingly invasive questions from the media. She scanned the latest headline accusing her of fraudulent campaign financing, her frustration growing as her campaign manager, Nathan, paced beside her.

"What the hell is going on?" Jen muttered, tossing the tablet onto the table. "This is spiraling out of control."

Nathan's face was tight with frustration. "It's Slater. He's dredging up every piece of dirt he can find, spinning half-truths and huge lies into headlines. The press is loving it."

Jen pressed her fingers to her temples, feeling the stirring of a stress headache. She had prepared for a tough race, but this? This felt like a constant ambush. Every time she tried to get her message out, another scandal erupted, keeping her team in constant defensive mode.

And now, it was getting personal.

"They're claiming I used funds from my old nonprofit to fund my campaign," she said, voice edged with anger. "It's complete bullshit. I worked hard to raise that money legally. How can they get away with this?"

Nathan leaned in, hands clasped. "They don't need it to be true, Jen. They just need to plant doubt. That's how this works. If they throw enough accusations, something sticks."

Jen clenched her fists, fighting the urge to let her anger overtake her judgment. "I won't play this game. We fight with integrity. That's the only way I want to win."

Nathan sighed, studying her closely. "I know that's what you want. But if we don't hit back soon, they're going to bury us."

Jen stood up and began pacing, frustration coiled tightly in her chest. This wasn't the race she had envisioned when she'd entered the political ring. She wanted to restore faith in a broken system, to make real change. But it was becoming harder to hold onto those ideals when every headline twisted her intentions and every news segment piled on the smears.

"Let them sling their mud," Jen said, her voice growing steadier. "We'll stay focused on the issues, the policies, and improving people's lives. We'll remind everyone what we're fighting for."

Nathan hesitated. "You're sure? Because we're past the point of playing nice."

Jen looked him squarely in the eyes. "We fight with integrity, Nathan. That's how we have to win."

He nodded, though worry lingered in his gaze. "All right. But brace yourself. This isn't going to let up. It'll get a lot worse."

As Jen sat back down, she felt the weight of the campaign pressing in on her like never before. "I can handle it. We've come too far to back down now." But even as she spoke, a cold knot of doubt tightened in her stomach, as she said the Serenity Prayer to herself.

Later that evening, Vic and Slater settled into a secluded booth at a high-end bar, away from the prying eyes of the press. A television above the bar played a news segment about Jen's alleged misuse of nonprofit funds, and Vic's mind buzzed with the thought of his rival's slow downfall. His Scotch swirled in his glass, the ice clinking softly.

"So," Slater said, reclining with a smug grin, "ready to watch Morales burn?"

Vic didn't answer immediately, his eyes fixed on the television as the anchors dissected the latest scandal. Ramsey, his ever-present Candidate Service agent, sat at a table nearby, her gaze watchful. Her attention, so professionally fixed on any sign of threat, momentarily unsettled him. Was this level of destruction truly necessary to secure victory?

"This is what you wanted, right?" Slater asked a dark thrill in his voice. "Doesn't matter how. We're about to take her out of the race, Vic. She'll never recover from this."

Vic took a long drink, barely tasting the burn of the alcohol. He had convinced himself he needed this—needed to secure his place, no matter the cost. But as Slater gloated, Vic wondered if this truly was the path he'd wanted.

"Yeah," he said quietly, setting his glass down. "This is what I wanted."

Slater raised his glass in a mock toast. "To Morales's career. May it be as swift and brutal as she deserves."

As they clinked glasses, Vic felt a flicker of doubt in him. He had gone too far to turn back now, but a part of him wondered if he'd crossed a line he could never uncross.

Back in her hotel room, Jen felt the toll of the day's events sink in as she sat on the edge of her bed, replaying every attack, every twisted rumor in her mind. Her phone buzzed, and she saw a message from one of her top volunteers, Grace: ***Hang in there, Jen. We believe in you.***

Jen's chest tightened. This campaign wasn't just for her; it was for everyone who believed politics could mean more than name calling, backroom deals, and smear campaigns. She closed her eyes and let out a long, steady breath. She had to hold on, even if it felt like the world was against her.

But as the night wore on, and her resolve seemed to settle deeper into fatigue, Jen couldn't shake a creeping fear. Slater's ruthless tactics were testing her beyond anything she had imagined. Was integrity enough, or did she need to get dirty to survive?

She felt the answer weigh heavily, a question lingering as she drifted to sleep: *Could she hold to her principles, or was winning worth everything?*

— 12 —

Rosa Delgado didn't enter rooms quietly; she made sure of it. The door to Vic Ross's war room swung open, and the chatter that had filled the space died immediately. Rosa's sharp heels clicked against the tile as she strode in, her dark hair pulled back in a sleek ponytail, her tailored black suit hugging her frame-like armor. She wasn't tall, but her presence made her seem like a giant.

Vic had never seen her in person before, but he recognized her immediately from the briefings. Rosa Delgado, political operative, fixer, and professional cleaner for some of the dirtiest campaigns in the country. A Mexican-American powerhouse with roots in both corporate law and the political underworld, Rosa was the kind of person you called when things got ugly—and when you didn't want to leave any fingerprints.

"I take it you're Vic," Rosa said, her voice smooth and controlled as her eyes scanned the room, taking in every detail.

Vic stood up from his chair, feeling a strange mix of curiosity and apprehension. "And you must be Delgado. I was told you were effective."

Rosa smiled, though it didn't reach her eyes. "Effective is one word for it. You don't call me if you want to win clean. I'm here to make sure Morales doesn't see the inside of a ballot box."

She said it so casually as if they were discussing the weather. But there was an edge to her words that told Vic she wasn't messing around.

Slater leaned back in his chair, his smirk widening as Rosa approached the table. "I told you she was good," he said to Vic, his voice laced with approval. "Rosa's going to make sure Morales doesn't just lose. She's going to disappear."

Rosa crossed her arms, staring Vic down. "Here's how this works. Tell me your limits, if you have any, and I'll work around them. If you don't have any, I'll handle things my way. But once we start, there's no stopping. Morales is about to become a ghost."

Vic's stomach twisted, the familiar unease creeping in again. He had agreed to hit Jen hard, to do whatever it took to win.

Slater cut in before Vic could respond. "We don't have limits."

Rosa raised an eyebrow, clearly unimpressed. "You sure about that?"

Vic glanced at Slater, feeling the weight of the decision pressing down on him. He wanted to win. He needed to win. But the idea of completely destroying Jen Morales—of wiping her out so thoroughly that she could never recover—felt like a step too far.

But what choice did he have now? He had already crossed so many lines. One more wouldn't matter.

"No limits," Vic said quietly, forcing the words out. "Do whatever you have to."

Rosa nodded, her smile returning. "Good. Then let's get started."

Jen Morales sat alone in her hotel room, staring at the headlines on her tablet, each one more brutal than the last.

—Morales Campaign Under Investigation for Misuse of Funds.
—Morales' Ties to Radical Activist Groups Exposed.
—Morales Drunk Again.

It was all bullshit. Every single piece of it, even the drunk again. But the more they repeated it, the more it stuck. And now, she could feel the support slipping away, her chances of winning getting smaller by the hour.

Her phone buzzed on the nightstand. She didn't want to answer it, but when she saw the name Rosa Delgado flash across the screen, her heart skipped a beat.

Rosa Delgado. The woman she had once called a friend. The woman who had helped her during her early days in local politics, back when Jen had been a city councilor in Santa Fe, fighting against corporate interests and entrenched corruption. Rosa had been her ally then—sharp, fierce, uncompromising. But somewhere along the way, they had taken different paths.

Jen had chosen integrity. Rosa had chosen power.

Jen answered the call. "Rosa."

"Long time no talk," Rosa's calm and collected voice said through the phone.

"What do you want?" Jen asked, her throat tight.

There was a pause on the other end of the line. "I think you know what I want. I'm here to bury you, Jen."

Jen gripped the phone tightly, her knuckles whitening as the words hit her like a punch to the gut. "Why? Why are you doing this, Rosa?"

"You could've joined me," Rosa's voice came through, low and steady, laced with quiet reproach. "We could've fought together, side by side, against the real threats. But no—you chose the hard way. You chose to make enemies instead of allies."

Jen's voice wavered with anger, her grip tightening on the phone. "I chose to fight for something bigger than myself, Rosa. Something worth believing in." Her voice broke slightly, but she pressed on. "You? You sold out. And that… that is the real disappointment."

The silence on the line was deafening, every second stretching painfully long.

Rosa laughed, cold and devoid of humor. "Sold out? No, Jen. I just realized how the game is really played. And if you don't learn it fast, you'll get crushed. This isn't about idealism anymore. This is about power."

Jen gripped the phone even tighter. "You can throw whatever you want at me, but I'm ready to fight."

"You won't have a choice," Rosa replied, her voice soft but heavy. "By the time I'm done, no one will remember your name for anything good."

Later that night, Jen's phone buzzed again. This time, it wasn't another attack or demand. It was a message from Andrea, one of her AA sponsors in Santa Fe.

Haven't seen you in a month, Jen. Is everything okay? We're worried about you.

Another message came through almost immediately.

The group misses you. Let me know if you want to talk. No judgment, just support.

Jen stared at the screen, her chest tightening as her eyes brimmed with tears. The group had been her rock, her safety net when everything felt impossible. But now? How could she face those meetings when she was barely holding it together—her campaign, her sanity—it all felt like it was crumbling around her.

She swiped the messages away, her guilt gnawing at her as she turned off her phone.

"I'm fine," she whispered to herself. "I've got this."

But as she sat alone in the silence, her reflection in the darkened window staring back at her, she wondered how long she could keep lying to herself.

— 13 —

She leaned back in her chair, legs crossed, a glass of tequila on the rocks in one hand and her phone in the other. She'd given up wine—it felt too girly and always left her bloated. The war room buzzed around her with the usual campaign chaos: phones ringing, emails pinging, and frantic conversations. But Rosa remained calm, unbothered. She had survived worse. Politics was dirty, and no one knew that better than she did. Hell, she'd helped make it that way.

Vic Ross stood across the room, staring at the latest poll numbers on the screen. He wasn't calm. He was far from it. His hands were clenched, tension rolling off him in waves. Despite all the dirt they were throwing at Jen Morales, she wasn't out of the race yet. Not completely.

Slater walked over to Rosa's table, raising an eyebrow. "So what's the next move?"

Rosa took a slow sip of her drink, savoring the tequila burn as it slid down her throat. "We hit her where it hurts most. You want her out? We'll drag her through the mud so deep she'll choke on it."

Slater grinned, clearly enjoying this. "How?"

Rosa placed her glass down, her eyes dark and cold. "I've got some skeletons. Morales thinks she's untouchable and that her little activist days are ancient history. She doesn't know shit. I've got a file on her that'll make people think she's been cozying up to all the wrong kinds of friends. That's the thing about the past—it always bites you in the ass."

Vic crossed his arms, clearly uncomfortable. "What exactly are we talking about?"

Rosa's smile widened. "Back home, this is how we'd say it: *En la guerra y en el amor, todo se vale.* Everything's fair in war and love. Morales made enemies during her rise. We're going to make sure everyone knows about them."

Slater laughed, raising his glass. "I like it. She won't know what hit her."

Vic, however, was less enthused. His fingers twitched as he reached for his own drink—another glass of whiskey. He took a long pull from it, hoping to drown out the sinking feeling in his gut. "What are these 'skeletons?'"

Rosa leaned forward, her voice dropping as she flipped through her phone. "Radicals. Leftist groups she supported in her early days. Activists, maybe a few who've got a shady history with violence. All public records if you know where to look. We'll make it look like she's been in bed with extremists this whole time. Trust me, she won't survive it."

Vic's jaw tightened. "And none of this will blow back on us?"

Rosa waved her hand dismissively. "You worry too much. I'm not sloppy. You brought me in to do this, and I don't fail."

Vic drained the rest of his whiskey, the burn doing little to settle the unease gnawing at him. This wasn't just politics anymore. This was a full-on assassination, and Rosa was the one holding the knife. He had come this far—no turning back now.

He poured himself another drink.

Across town, Jen Morales sat in her campaign office, surrounded by chaos. The noise of her team—frantic conversations, phones ringing off the hook, the faint buzz of the television news showing yet another hit piece on her—was unbearable. Her head was pounding, and her throat was tight with anxiety. She hadn't slept in days, and hadn't eaten in what felt like forever. She really wanted a drink. But she couldn't stop. Not now.

Nathan leaned against the doorframe, arms crossed. "It's getting worse. You saw the latest?"

Jen nodded, her voice hoarse. "Yeah. They're hitting us from every angle. I can't even keep up with the lies anymore."

"They're trying to connect you to those activist groups from years ago," Nathan said, walking into the room and lowering his voice. "You know the ones I'm talking about. It's bad, Jen."

"I know," she muttered, her hands trembling as she picked up her phone and scrolled through the avalanche of messages. "They're making me look like some kind of...radical."

Nathan sighed. "This is Rosa Delgado. It's got her fingerprints all over it. I've heard how she operates. She knows how to tear people apart."

Jen raised an eyebrow, her lips twitching with a half-hearted smile. "You've been practicing your Spanish." Her stomach growled softly, reminding her she hadn't eaten all day. She made a mental note to grab something—anything—before her next call.

Nathan shrugged. "Figured I'd learn a few new words. Seemed fitting."

But the humor faded quickly as the weight of their reality sank back in. Jen had always known this campaign was going to be a fight, but she hadn't expected to be suffocating under this much shit. They weren't just attacking her platform—they were attacking her character, her past, everything.

"How do we fight back?" Jen asked, her voice barely audible over the pounding in her chest.

Nathan didn't answer immediately. Instead, he reached into his bag, pulling out a bottle of whiskey, and set it on the table between them.

"First, we drink," he said, pouring two glasses without waiting for her reply.

"You sure, Nathan?" Jen hesitated, eyeing the glass as he slid it toward her.

Her hands hovered over it, the craving clawing at her resolve. Fuck it, she thought, picking it up. She downed the whiskey in one sharp motion, the burn in her throat a brief but welcome distraction from the crushing weight of her anxiety.

Nathan poured her another. "Look, Jen, the only way we fight this is by keeping it real. No bullshit. No mudslinging. We hit them with the truth, over and over again."

"You've seemed to get your drinking under control. AA taught you moderation, and that's great," Nathan said with sincerity, his tone gentle but encouraging.

Ignoring the comment, Jen shook her head. "The truth doesn't matter anymore. People believe what they want to believe."

Nathan leaned in, his voice low but firm. "You still have people who believe in you. They need you to stand your ground."

Jen met his gaze, her eyes heavy with exhaustion. "And if we lose?"

Nathan smiled grimly, knocking back his own drink. "Then we lose fighting."

Nathan paused, then leaned forward, a spark of a new idea in his eyes. "We start leaking to the media. Open-ended questions, not direct accusations—about the VP. He's easier to get to than Vic."

Across the country, Rosa leaned back in her chair, a self-satisfied smile playing on her lips as she watched the latest hit piece unfold on television. The news anchors were in a frenzy, dissecting the leaked emails, photos, and rumors that tied Jen Morales to fringe activist groups with questionable reputations. The story was gaining traction, exactly as Rosa had planned.

Rosa wasn't afraid of taking risks. That's why she was the best. That's why campaigns that had hit rock bottom called her when they needed someone to drag their enemies through hell.

Slater walked over, glancing at the screen with satisfaction. "It's working. Morales is getting buried. You think she'll try to fight back?"

Rosa laughed, a dark sound that sent a chill down Vic's spine as he stood nearby, nursing his whiskey. "She'll try. But it won't matter. The damage is done."

Vic looked at Rosa, still uneasy. "What if she finds a way to flip this?"

Rosa's smile was sharp, her eyes gleaming. Vic. Don't even dream about it. This campaign's dead. It's only a matter of time before she folds."

Vic nodded, but the whiskey in his hand didn't soothe him the way it used to. He felt like he was drowning, and no matter how hard he tried to stay above water, the deeper he sank. The campaign was spiraling, and even though it looked like they were winning, Vic wasn't sure he recognized himself anymore.

Rosa watched him carefully, her smile fading slightly. I get it. You're feeling the heat. But trust me, this is how the game is played. There's no clean way to win. Not anymore."

Vic stared into his glass, the words swirling in his mind. No clean way to win. He had known that when he hired Rosa. He just hadn't expected it to feel this...dirty.

Slater clapped him on the back, his voice low. "Relax. We're almost there. Just hold the line."

But Vic wasn't sure how much longer he could keep the weight of it all from crushing him. The lies, the destruction, the endless cycles of manipulation—each one tightened around him like a noose, and he could feel himself slipping, making dangerous mistakes. Even Rosa, with all her charm and ruthless allure, had become just another reminder of how this game had devoured him, piece by piece.

Jen woke in the middle of the night, a cold sweat covering her skin. Her head was spinning, a combination of too much whiskey and not enough sleep. The room felt like it was closing in, the weight of the campaign pressing down on her chest. She wanted another drink to calm her but had nothing in the room.

Her phone buzzed, and she reached for it, blinking against the harsh light. A new headline greeted her.

More Morales Emails Leaked—New Details Surface.

She stared at it, her heart sinking. How much more could they throw at her? How much longer could she hold on?

She pressed her palms to her face, feeling the overwhelming urge to scream. But what good would it do? This was a fight she wasn't sure she could win. Not anymore.

Her phone buzzed again—a message from Nathan. *You're strong. We'll figure this out.*

Jen let out a shaky breath, her hands trembling as she typed a response. *I'm trying. But I don't know if it's enough.*

As the message sent and the room settled into silence, Jen knew one thing for certain: this was the darkest moment of her campaign, and the only way out was straight through. She repeated it to herself, over and over, anchoring herself to the words.

— 14 —

Vic sat slumped on the couch in his office, the dim light casting shadows across the bottles scattered around the room. His hand clutched yet another glass of whiskey, but the drink no longer comforted him. It only dulled the constant churn in his stomach—the same feeling he got every time he thought about what his campaign had become. The room reeked of whiskey and frustration.

"Fuck," Vic muttered under his breath, downing the last of the glass before haphazardly tossing it onto the coffee table. The glass clinked against another bottle, tipping over and spilling its contents across the stack of papers Vic was supposed to review.

It didn't matter. None of it fucking mattered anymore.

The door opened, and Rick Slater strode in, his usual sharpness in full effect. But Vic didn't even bother sitting up. He didn't care.

"What the hell's going on in here?" Slater asked, his voice full of irritation as he eyed the mess around Vic. "You look like shit."

Vic let out a humorless laugh. "Thanks, Rick. You really know how to lighten the mood."

Slater strode over, grabbed the nearest bottle of whiskey, and poured himself a drink. "We're not done, Vic," he said, his voice steady. "Rosa's work is moving the needle. We're gaining ground."

Vic didn't respond. He stared at the wall, feeling the pressure building inside his chest like a steel vice. He had sold every part of himself to this campaign. Every fucking part. His values. His conscience. His goddamn soul. And for what?

He ended up in this room, drowning in booze, while his campaign bled out.

"Rosa's handling Morales," Slater continued, clearly not picking up on Vic's mood. "We've got the press in our pocket. Her numbers are crashing. She's just about done."

Vic ran a hand through his hair, letting out a frustrated groan. "Yeah? And what the fuck are we going to be when this is all over? Huh? What the fuck do we have left?"

Slater raised an eyebrow, taking a sip of his drink. "We'll have the presidency."

"The presidency," Vic spat the words, standing up unsteadily, his voice rising. "And what will that mean, Rick? After all this—after we've destroyed everything and everyone? Who the fuck are we when we win?"

Slater's expression hardened. "We're the winners, Vic. That's all that matters."

"This isn't what I wanted," Vic muttered, his voice low and raw.

Vic stared at him, his chest heaving. He wanted to punch something. Wanted to rip the fucking walls down around him and set fire to the whole mess they'd created. But he couldn't. He was trapped. Caught in the web they'd spun, and now, there was no way out.

Slater sighed, setting his drink down and walking over to Vic, his eyes cold and calculating. "You wanted to win. And this is how we win. Stop thinking about what it's costing you. You don't get to feel sorry for yourself now. Not when we're this close."

Vic clenched his fists, his entire body trembling with barely contained rage. Slater, however, was right—this was precisely what he had signed up for. Ultimate power came at a price, and Vic had known that from the start. The Supreme Court had all but cemented this truth in *U.S. v. Commonwealth of New Columbia*, 598 U.S. 443 (2026). Even Vic harbored doubts about absolute immunity despite the personal advantages it brought him; it simply granted too much unchecked authority. But he wasn't the game's architect, just another player determined to exploit its rules to his favor. Vic's razor-sharp memory never failed him, and he recalled every detail of that landmark case, savoring how each precedent had paved his way to the top.

He grabbed the bottle and poured another drink, not stopping as the amber liquid splashed over the rim and pooled on the table. He didn't care. "Fine," he muttered, his voice heavy with defeat. "Fuck it. Means to an end."

"Now you're getting it," Slater said, his voice filled with approval. "No one remembers how the game was played. They just remember who won."

Jen Morales couldn't make herself sleep. She sat in the corner of her darkened hotel room, staring at the TV as the latest smear against her played in an endless loop. The stream, the channel—it made no difference. Every anchor spoke about her as though she were already finished, her career over, her reputation beyond repair.

And the worst part? They might be right.

Her phone buzzed beside her. She didn't even look at it. The messages were endless. Reporters asking for a comment. Supporters telling her to hang on. Campaign staff asking for guidance on what to do next and AA ladies who care about her.

But Jen had nothing left to give.

She was breaking, slowly but surely. Rosa Delgado had done her job. She had torn Jen apart, piece by piece, with surgical precision. And now, there was almost nothing left.

Nathan knocked softly on the door before entering. He looked at her, sitting there in the dark, and his heart sank.

"Jen..." His voice was soft, full of concern.

"I don't know how much longer I can do this, Nathan," Jen whispered, her voice trembling with exhaustion. "I'm losing. Everything I worked for...it's all slipping away."

Nathan crossed the room and sat beside her, his presence warm but heavy with the same stress. "We can still turn this around."

Jen shook her head, her eyes brimming with unshed tears. "How? How can we turn this around when they've buried me alive?"

Nathan sighed, running a hand through his hair. He hated seeing her like this—on the edge of broken, so vulnerable. She had always been strong, a fighter, but now...now she looked like she was drowning.

"I don't know," Nathan admitted quietly. "But we've come too far to give up now. You've come too far."

Jen's hands were shaking as she pressed them to her face, trying to hold back the tears threatening to spill over, which wasn't typical. "I'm not strong enough. They're going to destroy me. What if they win?" she whispered, her voice breaking.

Rosa Delgado sat in a smoky bar downtown, and her heels kicked up on the booth seat across from her. A cigarette dangled from her lips as she casually scanned her phone, watching the fallout from her latest move. The Morales campaign was in shambles, and she couldn't help but feel a sick sense of satisfaction. This was her art. This was what she did best—dismantling people who thought they were untouchable.

She took a long drag of her cigarette, blowing the smoke out in a slow, lazy stream before turning to the man sitting beside her. A campaign aide, young, eager, and clearly in over his head.

"So," she said, her voice low and smooth, "*Si no te das prisa, no comes.*" She smirked, watching the aide's confused expression. "It means if you don't hustle, you don't eat. Morales didn't hustle hard enough. Now she's starving."

The aide chuckled nervously, unsure what to make of Rosa's dark sense of humor. But she didn't care. He wasn't important. What mattered was that she was on the verge of winning. She had broken Jen Morales, and now all that was left was to watch the final pieces of her career crumble to dust.

Rosa took another drag from her cigarette before snuffing it out in the ashtray. "*Vamos a joderla hasta el final.* We're going to fuck her up until the end. You understand?"

The aide nodded, though his nervousness was palpable. Rosa chuckled softly to herself. She liked it when people were scared. It made things more fun.

"Finish the job," she said, waving him off. "I want every last piece of dirt out there by tomorrow."

Vic stumbled through his apartment, drunk and disoriented. The whiskey bottle in his hand was almost empty, but he wasn't done. Not by a long shot. He could barely stand, his vision swimming as he staggered toward the window, leaning heavily against the wall.

He was drowning. He could feel it—this relentless pull, this darkness creeping up inside him, consuming everything. He had tried to bury it under alcohol, tried to hide from the guilt and the regret, but it was too late.

The campaign was winning. They were destroying Jen Morales. But Vic couldn't shake the feeling that he was destroying himself right along with her.

He took another swig of whiskey, letting it burn all the way down. But no amount of alcohol could drown the voice in his head that kept telling him he had lost something—something important. Something he couldn't ever get back.

Vic dropped the bottle, watching as it shattered on the floor, shards of glass scattering across the room.

"Fuck..." he muttered, his voice cracking.

And for the first time in a long time, Vic Ross felt the crushing weight of failure. Not the failure of losing the campaign—he was still on track to win. But the failure of losing himself, of becoming the kind of man he had always promised he wouldn't be.

But there was no turning back now.

— 15 —

Morales hadn't expected to find salvation sitting in a dimly lit coffee shop, wearing a hoodie and tapping away at a laptop like nothing in the world was wrong. She'd thought about quitting a dozen times in the past week—hell, even in the past hour—but then Diego Castillo showed up.

Nathan had been the one to make the introduction, bringing Diego into her campaign like some last-minute Hail Mary. They didn't have many options left. Jen had been backed into a corner by Rosa Delgado's scorched-earth tactics and was on the verge of being wiped out.

But Diego was different. He didn't operate like anyone else on her team. He wasn't loud. He didn't offer empty reassurances. He didn't even flinch when Nathan explained how bad things had gotten. Instead, he'd sat quietly, taking it all in before simply saying: ***"I can fix this."***

And now, as Jen sat across from him, watching him work, she didn't believe he really could.

Diego barely looked up from his laptop as he spoke, his fingers flying over the keyboard. "Rosa's good—and vicious. I've seen her work before with other campaigns. She's a master at using the media to spin whatever narrative she wants. But there are ways to cut her off at the knees—using her own ego and arrogance against her."

Jen frowned, leaning forward. "How? She's got every outlet eating out of her hand right now."

Diego paused, tapping a few more keys before looking up, his dark eyes calm and focused. "They're using smear tactics. Disinformation. If you want to counter that, you have to expose the mechanisms behind it. Show the world *how* they're manipulating the narrative, not just that they're doing it. The public doesn't trust the media but will trust the truth when framed right."

"Diego's done this before," Nathan said, nodding toward him. "He knows how to fight dirty but not too dirty. He knows how to *think* like Rosa."

Diego's lips curled into a faint smile. "In my hood, we'd call this — dirty war. And in a dirty war, the most important thing is not just hitting back. It's making them show their hand first."

Jen sat back, still skeptical but desperate enough to listen. "And you think we can do that? You think we can turn this around?"

Diego met her gaze, his expression unreadable. "I don't think. I know. But it's going to get ugly."

Jen let out a shaky breath, the tension coiling tighter in her chest. "Ugly I can handle. I've been living in ugly for weeks now."

Diego tapped a few more keys, bringing up a series of screens that flashed with data. "Here's how we do it. We start by tracking the sources of the disinformation. Every piece of fake news, every smear, every social media post they're planting—there's a trail. They don't think anyone's looking, but I am. I will trace it back to their networks, find the connections, and then we expose it. Not just to the public, but to the people running the media outlets. Some of them will back off once they see they're being played. Others? We'll handle them differently."

Jen leaned in, intrigued despite herself. "And what happens when they try to bury us again?"

Diego smiled faintly. "They won't be able to. Not when we've exposed the game. You see, Rosa thinks she's untouchable because no one's figured out her patterns and game yet. But I know them. And once I start pulling at the threads, her entire operation will start to unravel."

Nathan crossed his arms, watching Diego closely. "And if Rosa catches wind of what we're doing?"

Diego's eyes darkened slightly, but he didn't flinch. "Then we make sure she doesn't."

Jen listened to the flood of suggestions, the tactics, and strategies they proposed to turn the tide pressing so hard against her. She took a moment, closed her eyes, and murmured a silent prayer for strength. Then, she looked up, meeting each of their eyes with a steady resolve.

"All right," she said firmly. "Let's push back just as hard."

She leaned forward, her voice low but filled with purpose. "Are Vic and his team paying off the news outlets? Is he running a pay-to-play game with his politics? And what about Slater? Is he pushing this hard just to cover his own tracks—a pardon, maybe, for the list of felonies he's already neck-deep in?"

They nodded, her determination sparking a renewed energy in the room. This time, they would fight back, matching Vic's team blow for blow.

Back at Ross headquarters, Rosa Delgado was leaning over a table covered in campaign documents, her mind whirling through strategies. Her team was finalizing the next round of smears, preparing to drop another wave of attacks on Morales before the weekend.

She didn't even blink when Slater walked in, looking pleased with himself.

"You see the latest?" he asked, dropping a printout on the table. "Morales is fuck-done. Numbers are plummeting, and the media's eating it up."

Rosa barely glanced at the papers. Her voice was calm, but underneath it was the sharp edge of a hunter waiting for the kill. "We need to keep the pressure on. One more hit, and she'll fold."

Slater poured himself a drink, watching Rosa carefully. "You sound almost disappointed. I thought you'd enjoy this more."

Rosa gave him a tight smile, shrugging. "*En mi país, decimos que nunca celebras antes de matar al toro.* Never celebrate before you've killed the bull. Morales isn't dead yet."

Slater raised an eyebrow. "You really think she's still a threat?"

Rosa chuckled, a low, dangerous sound. "I know how this works. The moment you think you've won, that's when they hit you where it hurts."

"Relax. She's done," Slater said, downing his whiskey. "We've got the media in a chokehold, and her campaign is out of money. What's she going to do? Send out a press release?"

But Rosa didn't relax. Her instincts were screaming that something wasn't right. Morales should have been finished by now. The way they had buried her...there shouldn't have been anything left.

"*Voy a revisar unas cosas.*" Rosa muttered, more to herself than to Slater.

She pulled out her laptop, her fingers moving quickly as she accessed her network of contacts and tools. Something wasn't adding up. She scanned through the recent activity on the disinformation channels, the fake social media accounts, the articles they had planted. It was all going according to plan—but there was something...off. Then she saw it. Subtle. Almost invisible. Someone had been following her trail.

Rosa's pulse quickened. "*Hijueputa.*"

Slater frowned. "What is it?"

Rosa didn't answer right away. She scanned the network logs again, her mind racing. Someone had been tracking their operations—quietly, methodically. It was sophisticated. It's way above Morales's team.

She slammed her laptop shut, her expression dark. "I need to go check something out."

Diego Castillo leaned back in his chair, the faint glow of his laptop illuminating his face with a triumphant smirk. He had done it. He'd traced Rosa's digital trail back to its source, pinpointing the network of fake accounts, AI video hubs, and bot farms responsible for flooding the internet with disinformation. A series of IP addresses on his screen linked the operation directly to Vic's campaign. It was all the proof they needed to show that dirty money was fueling the digital attacks.

"I'm good, but honestly, they got sloppy and overconfident." Diego shook his head.

With a steady hand, Diego saved the evidence, his mind already racing through the next steps. Finally, they had something concrete to turn the tide.

Jen sat across from him, her nerves frayed but her eyes sharp with determination. "You have it? Just like that?" She shook her head, half in disbelief. "I thought Rosa was the best."

Diego leaned forward, a faint grin tugging at his lips. "She is. But everyone leaves a trail if you know where to look. And like even the best, she got a little too comfortable."

Jen let out a breath she didn't know she'd been holding, a new spark of hope lighting in her chest.

Diego nodded, his face calm. "I have it. And I'm sending it to every major media outlet as we speak."

Nathan, standing behind them, let out a low whistle. "You think this will work?"

Diego didn't flinch. "It will work. I've exposed them. The media won't be able to ignore this, not when they see they've been played."

Jen swallowed hard, her heart pounding in her chest. She had been on the verge of giving up, but now...now there was a sliver of hope. A chance to fight back.

"Thank you," she whispered, her voice trembling slightly.

Diego gave her a slight nod. "We're not done yet. But this is the first step."

Rosa was already on the phone, barking orders to her team. "Shut it down. I don't care how. Just shut it the fuck down."

Her voice was sharp, her face tense. Whoever was coming after her knew what they were doing, and Rosa wasn't used to being on the defensive. But she wasn't about to let her entire operation crumble because of some tech nerd.

"Get our news brokers on the phone, right fucking now! I'll take them in order from CMM down by audience size," Rosa screamed.

Slater watched her pace the room, his expression unreadable. "Think Morales is fighting back?"

Rosa glared at him. She's desperate. Desperate people are more dangerous."

Slater's expression shifted, his usual confidence replaced with a rare seriousness. "So, what do we do?" he asked, his tone low, almost wary.

Rosa stopped pacing, her gaze sharp and icy. "We move the pieces. Create false doors, exits, and windows—anything to throw off whoever sniffed out the digital trail. Then we find them, and we bury them." She clenched her jaw, her voice dropping to a steely whisper. "And Morales? She's going to regret ever thinking she could win."

— 16 —

He was trying to ignore the gnawing headache that had been with him for days. The whiskey wasn't working anymore, but it didn't stop him from pouring another glass. He watched the amber liquid staring back at him in the glass, hoping it would silence the nagging voice in his head telling him what a piece of shit he'd become.

"Vic!" Slater's voice cut through the fog as he barged into the office, a grin spread across his face. "You're going to love this."

Vic glanced up, his eyes bloodshot. "What now, Rick?"

Slater plopped a folder down on the desk in front of Vic, his excitement barely contained. "One of our influencers, you know, Marisa Blake—the social media star with millions of followers—suggested something... unconventional. She's pushing this angle with her followers about a medium—some psychic or whatever—who's supposedly had visions about your victory."

Vic frowned, rubbing his temple. "A medium? Are you fucking kidding me?"

"Hold on," Slater said, raising a hand. "This isn't as stupid as it sounds. Marisa's followers eat this shit up, and they are our voters. The idea is we leak a story that this medium—some lady named Selena Cross—has been consulting with the campaign, predicting a massive victory. Marisa thinks it'll go viral. People will eat it up as a fun, offbeat angle, which'll humanize you a little."

Vic shook his head, reaching for his drink. "Jesus Christ. We're really at the point where we're pushing psychics now?"

It seems you've provided a snippet of dialogue in which a character discusses a strategy for capturing younger voters' attention.

Vic took a long swig of his drink, considering it. It was ridiculous, but at this point, nothing was too ridiculous. He was willing to try anything to keep Morales in the mud.

"Fine," he muttered. "If it'll help, go for it. I'm up to my neck in this gimmicky crap."

Slater smirked, already pulling out his phone to relay the news. "Knew you'd come around."

Surprise, surprise—Selena Cross wasn't just a medium. She was a masterful scam artist, a fraud who'd built an empire by swindling the desperate. Her charm was disarming, her readings eerily convincing, and her reputation carefully curated to keep the illusion intact. But behind the mystique was a woman who meticulously covered her tracks. She changed her name twice, ensured her sessions were cash-only, and kept a web of little companies to funnel her earnings. If anyone got too close to exposing her, she had a repertoire of diversion tactics: anonymous threats, phony lawsuits, or an abrupt disappearance until the heat cooled. Selena had perfected the art of keeping people invested in her lies—and keeping herself just out of reach.

And now she was connected to the Vic Ross campaign.

Rosa Delgado sat in front of her laptop, staring at the glowing screen with mounting disbelief and fury as she watched Marisa Blake's latest viral video. Marisa, with her carefully curated image and millions of followers, was gushing about how Selena Cross had "seen" Vic's win, how the psychic had been consulting with the campaign, offering guidance and predictions.

"What the *fuck* is this?" Rosa muttered to herself, her fingers digging into the arms of her chair.

Marisa's video was blowing up, with hashtags like #VicRossVictory and #SelenaSees trending across social media. It was all bullshit, of course, but Rosa knew how the game worked—people didn't care about the truth. They cared about the spectacle.

As Rosa dug deeper into Selena Cross's background, she realized the situation was far worse than she'd anticipated. Selena wasn't just a harmless con artist; she had a track record of fraud cases spanning multiple states—a series of elaborate scams that had left a trail of lawsuits from furious clients, many of them older and vulnerable, cheated out of thousands of dollars.

Fuck.

Rosa clenched her jaw, her eyes blazing as she started dialing. Slater picked up on the second ring, his voice as smug as ever.

"Rosa, what's up?"

"What the hell is going on with this Selena Cross bullshit?" Rosa snapped, her voice low but furious. "Do you have any idea what you've just done?"

Slater laughed, clearly not taking her seriously. "Relax. Marisa's all over it. The whole psychic thing is trending. People are loving it."

Rosa's eyes narrowed. "You're a fucking idiot, Rick. That 'psychic' has a record of fraud longer than your fucking arm. She's been sued for scamming people out of their life savings. And now you've tied her to this campaign!"

There was a pause on the other end of the line. Rosa could practically hear Slater's brain catching up to the disaster.

"You've got to be kidding me," Slater muttered, his smugness evaporating.

"No, I'm not kidding," Rosa growled. "You just gave Morales the biggest gift of her fucking life. She's going to drag us through the mud with this. They'll use it to paint us as frauds, as liars, and they'll have evidence to back it up."

Slater was silent, and Rosa's rage only built. "You need to shut this down. Now. Kill the story, scrub the connections, and get Marisa to take down the fucking video before it goes any further."

"Right. I'll handle it," Slater muttered, his voice tight.

Rosa slammed the phone down, her chest heaving with anger. She couldn't believe the stupidity of it all. One misstep like this could destroy weeks of careful planning. The medium story was supposed to be a distraction, something to lighten the campaign's image. But now it was about to backfire spectacularly. That *pendejo,* she thought bitterly, her frustration flaring.

She needed a drink. Badly.

Diego Castillo stared at his screen, his lips curving into a slow, satisfied smile.

He had been watching the social media feeds, tracking Vic Ross's digital footprint when he stumbled across the goldmine: the medium, Selena Cross. It was almost too good to be true. There was a documented fraudster tied to the Ross campaign through one of his major influencers. And now, with Marisa Blake's video going viral, they had just handed Diego everything he needed to strike back.

"*Perfecto.*" Diego leaned back in his chair, his fingers steepled as he pulled up the fraud cases against Selena. Multiple lawsuits, charges of false advertising, and even a local news investigation that had exposed her as a con artist against senior citizens. It was all public record, and it was about to be the Vic Ross campaign's biggest nightmare.

Jen Morales was sitting across from him, her face pale from exhaustion but her eyes glinting with something that looked almost like hope.

"What is it?" Jen asked, leaning forward.

Diego turned the screen toward her, showing her the evidence. "Selena Cross. The psychic they're using to drum up buzz about Ross. She's a fraud. And we're about to expose it."

Jen blinked, the weight of the information sinking in. "You're serious?"

Diego nodded. "Very. We have her entire history—court documents, news stories, everything. Ross's campaign is linked to her now through Marisa Blake. We will push this out to every media outlet, reporter, and blog. By the time we're done, no one will be talking about Morales's 'radical ties.' They'll be talking about Ross and his fraudster psychic."

Jen's heart raced. It was a lifeline. The first real lifeline they'd had in weeks. "You think it'll work?"

Diego smiled faintly. "It'll work. We're playing their game now. And we're about to beat them at it."

Rosa Delgado paced the war room like a caged animal, her phone glued to her ear as she tried, desperately, to control the damage. The video was still up. Marisa hadn't taken it down yet, and now more outlets were picking it up—laughing at the absurdity of a presidential candidate consulting a psychic.

And the worst part?

The fraud stories were already starting to break.

Slater stormed into the room, his face flushed with anger. "She won't fucking listen. Marisa thinks this is just some 'haters' trying to ruin her image. She won't take the video down."

Rosa slammed her fist onto the table, making everyone in the room jump. "*Puta madre*. I knew it. I fucking knew it. This is what happens when you let amateurs run the show."

Slater threw his hands up. "We were just trying to get some good PR! How the hell was I supposed to know the medium was a con artist?"

Rosa's face twisted into a scowl. "You should've fucking vetted her! A little history lesson for you: do you remember years back when Congress allowed the President-elect to bypass the FBI background checks for all those cabinet appointments because they 'believed in a handshake and a smile'? That turned into an epic dumpster fire and cost that party the next two elections. **Proper vetting, Slater!** How many times do we have to learn the same goddamn lesson?" She shouted into the ceiling, "fuck me, self-inflicted problems are the worst of all problems!"

Just then, an aide rushed into the room, her face pale. "Rosa, you need to see this."

Rosa turned to the monitor in the corner. A breaking news report flashed across it, showing images of Selena Cross and headlines about her fraudulent past plastered across the screen.

—*Ross Campaign Linked to Psychic Fraudster Selena Cross.*

Rosa's chest tightened with rage. "*Que mierda?* This is a fucking disaster."

Slater's face went pale as he watched the news. "Fuck. We're screwed."

Rosa grabbed her phone, her mind racing. "Not yet. We need to get ahead of this. Do damage control, asap."

Slater shook his head, his voice hollow. "It's too late. They're going to crucify us."

Back at Jen Morales's campaign headquarters, the mood had shifted. For the first time in weeks, there was hope. Diego's work had paid off. The story about Selena Cross was exploding across the media, and the Ross campaign was on the defensive.

Jen sat beside Diego, watching the news reports roll in, her heart pounding in her chest. It wasn't over. Not yet.

"Thank you," Jen whispered, her voice thick with emotion.

Diego didn't look up from his screen, but there was a flicker of satisfaction in his eyes. "We're not done yet. But we've hit them where it hurts."

Diego had tracked down five senior citizens willing to go on camera about the scam that had cost them each over $100,000 to Selena Cross's fraud. Some were now dealing with serious health issues after struggling to afford their prescriptions, which they'd sacrificed for months due to the financial hit. Selena had relentlessly pursued them, even sending messages to family members to pressure them further. This footage was campaign gold.

— 17 —

No stranger to chaos, Rosa had lived through more political scandals and crises than most people could imagine, and she had always come out on top. But today, as she stood in Vic Ross's headquarters, watching the fallout from the Selena Cross scandal unfold, she felt something unfamiliar creeping into her chest—panic.

Her laptop screen glowed in the dimly lit room, displaying article after article about the fraudulent medium, each headline worse than the last.

    —Psychic Scammer Center of Vic Ross Campaign Controversy.
    —Selena Cross Exposed: Ross Campaign's Latest Blunder.
    —Fraudulent Medium Tied to Political Power Play.
    —Seances Suggesting Policies.

Rosa slammed her fist onto the desk, her mind racing. The story had spread faster than she'd anticipated, and now the Ross campaign was in full crisis mode, scrambling to contain the fallout.

"This is a disaster," Slater muttered from across the room, pacing back and forth like a caged animal. "Journalists are calling every five seconds, demanding statements. What the hell are we supposed to tell them?"

Before Rosa could respond, Vic stormed in, his face flushed with rage. "Unbelievable! A psychic scammer?" he roared, his voice thick with fury. "Do you have any idea how catastrophic this is? People are calling me a con artist by association!" He slammed his hand against the wall, breathing heavily. "We're finished if we don't handle this perfectly. Who the hell let this happen?"

Rosa shot him a glare, her jaw clenched. "We deny everything. Distance ourselves from Marisa Blake. Issue a statement saying she's a third-party supporter with no direct connection to the campaign."

Vic threw his hands up in frustration. "Great. So now we're the ones backpedaling? This looks weak! Pathetic!" He shot a scathing look at Slater. "And where's our spin? Or am I supposed to be doing that too?"

Slater, momentarily thrown by Vic's outburst, quickly regained his composure, pulling out his phone. "Damage control. Got it."

But Rosa wasn't done. She knew the playbook and intended to use every trick to turn the tide.

"We deny, then flood the airwaves with 'Fake news, fake news, fake news,'" she declared, her voice rising with intensity. "It worked like a charm back in 2014, and here we are—almost two decades later—it still does."

That's where the whole 'fake news' framework got off the ground." Rosa's eyes narrowed. "We need to pivot. Shift the narrative. I want a new talking point out there by this afternoon—something to divert the media. Morales is vulnerable. She's still dealing with her past ties to those radical activist groups. Let's leak something fresh on that."

Slater's eyes brightened as he looked up. "We still have those old photos of her at the protests, right? The ones with the anarchists?"

"Exactly," Rosa replied, her voice cold and decisive. "Start circulating those. Make Morales the headline again."

Vic glared at them both, still simmering but slightly calmer. "Fine. Just fix it. I don't want to hear another word about this psychic fraud. Got it?"

Rosa and Slater exchanged a quick look, then nodded. They knew they had to move fast—and make sure Vic didn't lose his cool again.

Rosa nodded. "We've been holding onto them. Time to release them. Spread the photos and make it look like she was deeply involved with dangerous fringe groups. People won't remember the details; they'll just see the headlines."

"Old school," Slater said with a grin. "Got it. I'll feed them to a few 'reliable' centrist blogs. Let them take it from there."

Rosa smirked. "By the time we're done, no one will talk about that psychic fraud. They'll be talking about Morales being a threat to national security."

But even as she spoke, some of Rosa couldn't shake the unease creeping up her spine. This wasn't like the other fights. The landscape was changing, and there was someone on the other side who knew how to navigate it in ways she didn't.

—Diego Castillo.

Rosa had heard his name before—whispers in political circles about the young tech-savvy strategist who didn't play by the old rules. She knew he was the one pulling the strings behind the scenes for Morales, and that made him dangerous. Rosa was used to dirty games, but Diego played an entirely different one. And that worried her.

But worry wouldn't stop her. Rosa Delgado never lost.

Meanwhile, at Jen Morales's campaign headquarters, the mood had energized dramatically. Where there had once been exhaustion and despair, there was now a pulse of hope, a sense of determination. The Selena Cross scandal had given them a lifeline, and Diego capitalized on every second of it.

Jen stood beside him, watching as he worked, his fingers flying over the keyboard, his mind a fortress of calm and focus.

"They're scrambling," Diego said, glancing at the multiple screens in front of him, tracking social media, news outlets, and digital chatter. "Rosa's trying to pivot the narrative. I can see the leaks starting already."

Jen frowned, leaning in. "What are they leaking?"

Diego brought up a new screen, showing a series of photos that had just started circulating on fringe political blogs. Old photos of Jen at various protests—photos Rosa had clearly been sitting on for the right moment. They showed Jen standing among a crowd of young activists, some of whom were holding signs that could be construed as radical.

"Classic smear tactic," Diego muttered, his eyes narrowing.

"They're trying to make you look like a dangerous leftist. Typical old-school move."

Jen's heart sank as she saw the images. She remembered those protests. She had been there to fight for workers' rights and economic justice. But now, the narrative was being twisted into something ugly.

"How do we fight this?" Jen asked, her voice tight with frustration. "They're going to use this to bury me again."

Diego didn't look fazed. In fact, there was a flicker of amusement in his eyes. "They're using old tricks. But the game's changed. We don't have to play by their rules."

He leaned forward, typing furiously as he spoke. "We're going to hit them back where it hurts—online. They think leaking these photos will create doubt about your character, but they forget that the internet has a long memory."

Jen frowned, confused. "What do you mean?"

Diego smiled, a quiet, knowing smile. "Rosa thinks she's being clever with this smear, but I'm about to pull up receipts. Vic Ross has ties to corporate corruption, dirty money, and people in his past who make those anarchists look like a church choir. I've already flagged some old photos and documents that show his involvement in shady dealings years ago. We'll leak those and tie them to his current donors."

Nathan, who had been listening in, whistled low. "You're talking about going nuclear."

"Exactly," Diego said calmly. "We're not playing defense anymore. We're fighting fire with fire. But we're going to do it smarter. They're using old-school methods—backdoor leaks, smear campaigns. But we will leverage digital media, influencers, and viral marketing. Once this hits the public, Ross will be the one defending himself."

Jen watched Diego in awe and terror. She had never met anyone like him—so quiet, so unassuming, and yet so devastatingly effective. It was like watching a master chess player move pieces that no one else could see.

"What do you need from me?" Jen asked, a spark of hope igniting in her chest. They were out of options, and this felt like their last chance.

Diego glanced at her. "You just need to be ready. We will push this story out, but you have to stand strong. They'll come at you harder than ever once they realize what we're doing."

Jen nodded, her pulse quickening. She had spent weeks feeling like she was drowning in the muck of Vic Ross's campaign, but now—

finally—she was ready to fight back.

"Let's do it," she said, her voice steady.

By mid-afternoon, the media war was in full swing.

Rosa Delgado's team had successfully leaked the photos of Jen at the protests, and several far-right blogs were already running headlines about her supposed ties to radical leftist groups. The narrative was catching fire, with pundits on cable news echoing the talking points. ***Fake news reports in all the major Vic Ross-friendly news sources*** amplified the story, ensuring it reached an even wider audience and fueled the controversy.

But just as quickly as the story began to gain traction, Diego's counterstrike landed.

A series of posts, twists, and pitches from high-profile political influencers—each with massive followings—began to trend rapidly. They showcased old photos of Vic Ross shaking hands with dubious business moguls, posing alongside radical Saudi figures, mingling with controversial donors linked to environmental disasters, and attending exclusive fundraisers that reeked of foreign corruption.

One tweet in particular went viral within minutes: *"While Ross points fingers at Morales for her past, let's not forget his ties to billionaires who got rich by screwing over workers, families, and the planet. #RossForTheRich"*

Rosa's phone buzzed relentlessly as the new narrative spread like wildfire. Her carefully planned attack on Morales was being drowned out by a wave of backlash against Ross. The internet, always hungry for scandal, was now focused on Ross's connections to corporate greed and political corruption.

Rosa was already typing furiously on her laptop, trying to trace the source of the counterattack. She knew it had to be Diego—his work was always precise and surgical in execution. Just as she pieced together another clue, Slater stormed into the war room, his face flushed with frustration.

"What the fuck is happening?" he shouted. "We had this in the bag!"

But she couldn't hold back any longer. She whipped around, her voice sharp and furious. "Shut the fuck up, Slater. You're the one who found the gasoline, the fire, and the whole damn matchstick factory, then handed it all to Morales on a silver platter. If I didn't know any better, I'd think Jen was paying your salary."

Slater opened his mouth to argue, but Rosa wasn't having it. She was screaming now, her frustration boiling over. "We are in this mess because of your genius ideas. So unless you have a miracle up your sleeve, get out of my way and let me clean this up!"

"They're hitting us online," Rosa muttered, her mind racing. "Influencers, blogs, viral posts—Diego's pulling out every trick in the book. The kid is good. Jesus, he's good…"

Slater threw his hands up. "We need to hit them back. Harder."

Rosa shook her head, gritting her teeth. "*Esto es una guerra nueva.* This is a new kind of war, Rick. They're not fighting fair or predictable. They're using digital media in ways we didn't account for. The old tricks aren't enough anymore."

Slater looked at her, his face pale. "So what do we do?"

Rosa's eyes narrowed as she stared at the screen. "We adapt. Fast and flexible. But first, we need to contain this."

She pulled up her phone, dialing furiously. "Get our social media team on this. Flood the hashtags, and drown out the negative stories with our own narratives. We have to get ahead of this before it spreads any further."

But even as she barked orders, Rosa knew that they were on the defensive. For the first time in the campaign, Vic Ross's team wasn't setting the narrative. They were chasing it.

She packed up and headed to the bar, where it was quiet, and she could think faster.

At Jen's headquarters, the mood was electric. The counter-narrative was working. Diego's strategy had hit hard, and the Ross campaign struggled to regain control of the message.

Jen watched as the news shifted in real time. Headlines that had attacked her just hours earlier were now fixated on Ross's ties to corrupt donors and dirty money. The tide was turning.

Nathan clapped Diego on the back, grinning. "Man, I don't know how you do it, but you just gave us a miracle."

Diego didn't look up from his screen, his face calm but focused. "It's not a miracle. It's knowing how to use the tools at your disposal. They underestimated us. That was their first mistake."

Jen felt adrenaline surge through her veins. For the first time in weeks, she felt like they had a real chance. *Can it be this easy?* she wondered, the thought lingering as the thrill coursed through her. They were fighting back, and they were winning.

— 18 —

Ross stood in the center of his campaign war room, tension radiating off him in waves. His face was flushed, his hands clenched into fists, and his patience—what little he had left—was hanging by a thread. The Selena Cross debacle had thrown his campaign into a tailspin, and the Diego Castillo counterstrike had turned a viral disaster into a full-blown media nightmare. Now, as more and more of his team scrambled to contain the damage, Vic was running out of time.

Rosa Delgado sat across from him, her eyes narrowing and jaw tight. She wasn't used to being on the defensive. She wasn't used to losing. But as the media continued to hammer them with stories about Ross's dirty connections, she knew they were in dangerous territory.

"We're done playing defense," Vic growled, his voice a low, dangerous snarl as he paced like a caged predator. "I'm fucking done reacting. We're hitting Morales—harder than she's ever been hit. Get personal, dig up rumors, hell, make shit up if you have to. I don't care how dirty this gets. Burn it all down if that's what it takes."

He paused, his eyes blazing. "I didn't come this far to get sidelined by an amateur."

Slater, seated nearby, glanced at Rosa uneasily. "We've already thrown everything at her, Vic. What more do you want?"

Vic's eyes burned with rage as he slammed his fist onto the table. "I want her destroyed," he seethed. "I want you to slit her career's throat and leave her in the fucking dirt."

Rosa's gaze flickered as she watched Vic unravel. The pressure was breaking him, and while that was dangerous, it also gave her the green light to unleash the full arsenal she'd been holding back. Subtlety had no place here anymore. This was war. His outburst didn't faze her; it confirmed what she'd been waiting for.

"All right," Rosa said, her voice sharp and unwavering. "If we're going all in, we'll hit her with shock-and-awe tactics. Flood the media with dirt, throw out so many accusations that Morales can't keep up— can't get up once she's down. We create a narrative of chaos: paint her campaign as corrupt, reckless, and unstable. It makes people question her character, and her competence. And we tie it all back to her. Let's fabricate some invoices, and make it look like her campaign funded that medium and the social media mess. We make it look like this chaos started with her."

Vic's eyes darkened with satisfaction. "Now that's more like it. Light it up."

Slater chimed in, his usual smirk returning. "We've still got some ruthless tricks we haven't played yet. We can stage some incidents at her rallies, and make it look like her supporters are getting violent. Stir up fear."

Rosa nodded. "We'll leak reports to the press about internal strife in her campaign, say she's losing control of her team, that her closest advisers are jumping ship. Create doubt in the public's mind that she can handle the pressure."

"And we'll dig deeper into her personal life," Slater added, his voice cold and calculated. "Find something—anything—affairs, drugs, skeletons in the closet. We smear her character, true or not."

Vic downed the rest of his whiskey, feeling the fire in his gut flare. "Good. I want her name to be poison by the end of the week. Do you all fucking hear me?"

Jen Morales had seen this playbook before, she had been living it. She could feel the F5 tornado coming—a storm of attacks designed to overwhelm her, drown her in scandal, and make her look unfit to lead. But something had changed. She wasn't that drowning candidate anymore. They'd weathered the storm thanks to Diego's tactical precision and even struck back. And now, Jen was taking back control—not just of her campaign, but of her destiny.

Her eyes flicked toward the man sitting across from her. His white hair was combed neatly, and his expression was calm but serious. Former New Mexico Governor Bill Prescott had once been one of the most respected political figures of his time. Old-school, tough as nails, and the kind of man who didn't suffer fools gladly. Prescott had known Vic Ross for years—back when Ross was just a slimy operator, making backroom deals to claw his way into power. Prescott had witnessed firsthand what Vic was capable of, and that's exactly why he'd stepped up to help Jen's campaign.

"I'm going to make sure Vic Ross never sees the inside of the White House," Prescott said, his deep, gravelly voice slicing through the tension in the room. "That son of a bitch has burned too many bridges, and it's time he learns there are still a few of us left in this business who won't let him win. He played a part in elevating that party to power twelve years ago—a power that's already proven dangerous to democracy and global stability. This isn't an exaggeration. We've seen the damage, and Ross in the presidency would set us back years trying to contain and mitigate the reach of that opportunistic force."

Jen smiled, grateful for the unexpected support. She hadn't anticipated someone like Prescott—an establishment heavyweight—to back her grassroots campaign. But his disdain for Ross ran deep, and his influence in political circles still carried weight.

"Thank you for joining us," Jen said. "We need your experience, perspective, and grit."

Prescott gave her a sharp nod. "You've got a good team here. Diego's a goddamn genius with tech. But Vic's going to come after you hardest now. He's got no boundaries, and you can bet he's about to flood the airwaves with every dirty trick in the book. The only way to fight back is to make sure you're ten steps ahead of him."

Diego, who had been quietly listening, leaned forward. "I've been tracking their digital activity. It looks like they're about to unleash a coordinated smear campaign. They plan to overwhelm us with false stories, plant fake incidents at our events, and create chaos online. If we don't move fast, it's going to snowball."

Prescott smirked. "Of course they are. That's Vic's style. The louder the noise, the more often he shouts a lie, the harder it is for people to hear the actual truth."

Jen frowned. "So how do we stop it?"

"We don't just stop it," Prescott said, his eyes gleaming with determination. "We hit back above, beside, and around him. Old school meets new school. Diego can handle the tech, but we will bring the fight directly to Vic. He thinks he can overwhelm you. Fine. We'll overwhelm him. We flood the media with positive stories about your campaign—your history, vision, and wins. We counter every lie with the truth, fast and hard. And we start building relationships with media outlets he doesn't control."

"The strategy weakens everything around him until the whole campaign—or Ross himself—collapses," Prescott said with resolve.

Diego nodded, his fingers already tapping away at his laptop. "I've got contacts in independent media—journalists who've been waiting for a chance to expose Vic. They've been on the sidelines, but now they're ready to run stories about his corrupt donors and backdoor deals. If we move fast, we can control the narrative before his team can strike."

Jen's pulse quickened. "Do it. Get the truth out there."

"And while we're at it," Prescott added, his voice low and deliberate, "I'm going to lean on some old friends in Washington. They've got dirt on Vic from back in the day. It's time to air it out, and that old pack of wolves owes me."

Diego stood at the front of the dimly lit room, a faint glow from his laptop screen illuminating his focused expression. Around the table, Jen, Bill, Nathan, and a few other key players watched him closely, sensing the urgency of what was about to unfold. Diego had a plan—something big enough to turn the tide in their favor.

"I'd like to introduce two new additions to our team," Diego began, gesturing to the two individuals seated beside him. "This is Mara," he said, nodding toward a sharp-eyed woman with a quiet intensity, "a top-tier AI specialist with a focus on real-time data monitoring and nextgen agentic AI. And this is Leo," he continued, nodding to a man with an easy confidence, "an expert in counter-communications and psychological operations."

Jen raised an eyebrow. "**Counter-communications?**"

Diego nodded, a hint of a smile flickering at the corners of his mouth. "If we're going to stay ahead of Ross and his people, we need to control the story before they even realize there's a problem. I've developed a protocol—an eight-minute response system—to intercept, evaluate, and neutralize any threat or smear campaign that comes our way."

He clicked a button on his laptop, and the name Project Thunderfuck—or Thunderdome, depending on who you asked— flashed across the wall at the end of the room.

"The idea is simple," Diego continued, leaning forward. "Any negative mention of our campaign, any potential threat, and Thunderdome picks it up instantly. Mara's AI agents are constantly monitoring and getting smarter by the minute, processing data from every digital path you can imagine—social media, streaming apps, news sites, blogs, forums, even converting audio and video into digital text."

Mara nodded in confirmation. "The AI does an initial scan to set the baseline, analyzing sentiment, source credibility, and impact potential. Using a scoring algorithm, it classifies each mention as Minor, Moderate, or Severe. This happens in milliseconds, so we know exactly what we're dealing with immediately."

"And the eight-minute part?" Bill asked, leaning forward.

"Exactly," Diego said. "By minute one, we know the severity, and if it's Moderate or Severe, it goes straight to Leo and me for a human review, using a custom build program to help us with speed and integrate into Mara's model."

Leo spoke up, his tone smooth and precise. "We don't just react. We choose the angle and decide whether to issue a direct rebuttal, redirect the narrative, or sometimes, let silence work for us. Our goal is to outmaneuver Ross's team. Make them react to us, not the other way around."

Diego continued, "From there, we're in execution mode. We have a library of pre-approved responses that can be customized and adapted depending on the issue. Within five minutes, we're already posting across our channels, drowning out any negativity with a focused, relentless response."

Nathan whistled, clearly impressed. "And if the original response isn't enough?"

"We've planned for that, too," Mara said calmly. "The AI keeps tracking reactions. If the first approach doesn't do the trick, we escalate—reinforce the message or pivot to a different narrative, all while the influencers and allies are backing us up online."

Jen glanced around the table, eyes narrowing with approval. "This is incredible, Diego. Ross's campaign won't know what hit them."

Diego nodded, his eyes dark with determination. "Exactly. Every time they try to throw dirt at us, we'll make sure they're the ones left scrambling." He paused, his gaze steady. "Give me three hours," he added. "I'll present an additional plan of attack then."

Jen straightened in her seat, feeling a renewed sense of power and purpose. *Project Thunderfuck* was ready. They were about to take the offensive, and for the first time, she felt that Ross's campaign wouldn't just be stopped—it would be overwhelmed.

Vic Ross wasn't used to feeling cornered, but the pressure was closing quickly. Rosa had deployed her shock-and-awe campaign, and while it was starting to have an effect, there was something Vic hadn't expected—the backlash. Every time they hit Morales with a dirty story, her team hit back harder, countering the lies with facts, flooding the media with her accomplishments and support from high-profile allies.

They were countering the punches before they were even thrown, leaving Ross's team scrambling and utterly ineffective. It was infuriating, like watching a boxing match on a glitchy livestream, stuck at 76% buffering while the action raged on without you.

And now, Vic felt the sting of the old-school establishment turning against him. He had always thrived in the shadows, making deals with the sleaziest operators in the business to avoid getting caught. But Governor Bill Prescott? That was a whole new level of threat. The man was a relic of the political world Vic thought he had escaped—one that still played by rules, one that valued integrity and loyalty. And Prescott had made it clear he wouldn't let Vic win.

"We're losing the fucking plot," Slater muttered, his face pale as he scrolled through the latest reports. "The smear campaign isn't sticking as we predicted and hoped."

Rosa's eyes flashed with anger. "That's because Morales is being smarter and faster. They're using digital media and advanced AI to counter every attack before it gains momentum. And now that Prescott's involved, we've got a bigger problem."

Vic's eyes narrowed. "We need AI and cyber expertise, now. Hit them harder. Make it untraceable—whatever it takes, just make it happen."

Rosa looked at him carefully, her lips pressed into a thin line. "Be careful, Vic. There's a line we don't cross. If we strike the way you're talking about, we risk more than the campaign. This could mean prison time if it blows up in our faces."

Vic's jaw clenched, his temper barely contained. "To hell with the line. I'm not losing. We win, I pardon—simple as that. It's just one step in the staircase."

Slater cleared his throat, uncharacteristically nervous. "There's one more play we could make," he hesitated. "But it's risky."

"Do it," Vic snapped. "Whatever it takes. But don't tell me the details—I still need a little space."

Diego Castillo watched as the Ross campaign's shock-and-awe tactics unfolded in real-time. They were throwing everything at Jen— claims of internal strife, fake scandals, and even staged violence at one of her rallies. But for every punch they threw, Diego was there to block it, countering each attack with rapid responses that kept Jen's image clean and her supporters energized.

"Vic's getting desperate," Diego said, glancing at Prescott and Jen. "They're pushing harder than I expected. They've even staged some incidents at our events, trying to make it look like your supporters are out of control."

Prescott grinned, his expression full of grim satisfaction. "Good. Let them get sloppy. Desperation makes people make mistakes. And

Vic's about to make a big one."

As if on cue, Diego's screen flashed with a new alert. "They're going after personal records now. They're digging into your private life, Jen. Trying to find something they can exploit."

Jen's heart pounded, but she took a deep breath, her resolve hardening. "Let them dig. I've got nothing to hide."

"That's exactly what they're hoping for," Diego muttered. "They'll twist the smallest detail into something scandalous. But don't worry—I'll make sure it doesn't stick."

Prescott leaned back in his chair, his eyes narrowing. "The deeper they dig, the more vulnerable they get. Vic's about to cross a line he can't come back from."

Within hours, the counterattack had begun. Independent journalists were publishing stories about Vic's deep ties to corrupt corporate interests, his shady backroom deals, and his attempts to manipulate the media. Prescott's contacts in Washington were already leaking stories about Vic's past scandals—stories that had been buried for years.

— 19 —

Staring at the screen, Vic Ross felt the steady rhythm of his pulse finally returning as the news reports rolled in. Headlines blared across every major outlet:

—Massive Cyberattack Cripples Morales Campaign.

Every update brought him a new wave of schadenfreude. Her emails were inaccessible, communications stalled, and rumors about compromised voter data were starting to swirl. For the first time in days, Vic felt like he was back in control.

"We don't even have to lift a finger," Slater grinned, his eyes alight as he scrolled through the breaking news on his phone. "The Russians or Iranians did our dirty work for us."

Vic's lips twisted into a satisfied smile. Russia, of course. Nothing was confirmed yet, but everyone knew about the Russian government's extensive history of deploying state-sponsored cyberattacks to interfere in foreign elections. And now, it looked like Jen Morales was their latest target.

"They're saying it's a coordinated attack," Slater continued, relishing each word. "Hit her fundraising, internal networks, voter data—everything. She's going dark."

Vic leaned back in his chair, the tension finally loosening in his shoulders. "Good. Let her drown. She's dead in the water now."

Across the room, Rosa Delgado didn't share his satisfaction. She sat quietly at her laptop, eyes flicking back and forth over her screen as she pulled up the latest intelligence briefings on the attack. Her brow furrowed, and she muttered under her breath.

"This is going to blow back on us," she said, her voice laced with concern.

Slater shot her a dismissive glance. "Why? We didn't order the attack."

Rosa's eyes narrowed. "Doesn't matter. This is Russian interference in a U.S. campaign. People are going to ask questions, and they'll be looking at us too. If anyone even suspects this ties back to Vic, we're screwed. Half the country might like Russia, but it can still be framed negatively and drag us down, true or not."

Vic waved her off, unconcerned. "No one's tracing anything. Let them think whatever they want. As long as Morales is down, we're winning, and we actually didn't fucking do it."

Jen Morales stood amidst the chaos at her campaign's command center, staring at the screens as her team frantically tried to handle the fallout. The cyberattack had hit with brutal precision, cutting through their infrastructure like a blade.

"Everything's down," Nathan said, rushing to her side, his face pale. "Fundraising, voter databases, internal emails—everything. We're dead in the water."

"How bad is it?" Jen asked, her voice tight and panicked.

Diego Castillo, her head of IT, hands flying over his keyboard as multiple screens displayed audit and diagnostic logs of their compromised systems. His face was set, grim but not panicked.

"This is a state-sponsored attack," Diego said, glancing at Jen with grim determination. "Russian, by the look of it. They've exploited every weak point we had. I'm working to contain them into isolated sectors so we can shut it down. I'll get us running off data backups in the meantime."

Jen's heart raced. "What do we do?"

Diego's fingers moved faster, running rapid commands to isolate the infected systems. "We need someone who specializes in attacks like this. I can hold the line, but this is bigger than anything I can handle alone. We'll talk later about how it happened."

Jen nodded, her mind spinning. "Who do we call?"

"Sam Lee. Best in the business. He used to work with government agencies that don't even have names. Now he secures Fortune 500 companies and critical infrastructure. If anyone can shut this down and get us back online, it's him."

Jen took a steady breath, feeling her resolve harden. "Get him on the phone. Bring him in."

Diego didn't waste a second, dialing Lee's private 24/7 number. "He'll secure this better than anyone in the game. And we'll make sure they don't get another shot at us. He's stupidly expensive, but when the alphabet agencies need a brainstorm, he's the one they call."

Three hours later, Sam Lee sat in his quiet San Francisco office, listening intently as Diego outlined the details of the attack. Sam had previously dealt with Russian state-backed cyberwarfare, but this level of intrusion targeting a political campaign was rare for a few unsettling reasons. He recognized it immediately: Advanced Persistent Threats (APTs), crafted to siphon data, dismantle systems and erase traces with surgical precision. But one detail made him pause—everything had been launched from a brand-new mobile device that Diego hadn't even known existed.

"I'm heading to the private flight service in ten. I'll be there in ninety minutes," Sam said, already tapping into his network. "But we need a full team on this. This breach is advanced—nothing but **Premier League talent. No MLS minds** on this."

Before hanging up, Sam had already called in favors with his trusted contacts, including *BlueOpsX36*, a top cybersecurity firm with branches in Santa Fe and Washington, D.C. He reached out to BlueOpsX36's CEO, an old lifelong friend.

"We're on it—whatever you need," the CEO replied, his voice intense. "I'll have a team on-site within the hour. We'll deploy some AI tech—military-grade, still in the R&D phase, but it works faster than anything I've seen out there. We understand the urgency."

Once his flight was in the air, Sam made his next call—to the Board Chairman of a major cloud security provider. In less than 50 minutes, Jen's campaign data would be fully migrated to a military-grade cloud environment, secure against any additional state-sponsored threat.

When Sam Lee's plane touched down just eight minutes from Morales headquarters, the BlueOpsX36 team was already working remotely and on-site. They'd set up new AI-driven monitoring and threat detection systems and network analysis hardware to contain exposure to their proprietary code. As Sam stepped into the bustling command center, his quiet confidence lifted the morale of everyone present, a steadying presence amid the high-stakes operation.

"Thank you for coming," Jen said, shaking his hand firmly. *I know this isn't going to be cheap,* she thought, *but it's money that has to be spent.*

Sam nodded. "Let's get to work. BlueOpsX36 monitors the complete estate—everything coming in and out of your networks. We've redeployed advanced threat detection across every device—laptops, mobile phones, cloud servers. No one's getting in without us knowing. And if they try, we'll let them walk right in… then guillotine those motherfuckers."

Diego, still focused, didn't look up as he spoke. "They've breached our voter data too. We need to make sure they can't use it against us. It's time for some countermeasures on that data." He paused, muttering under his breath, "God, I need to take a piss."

Sam's face darkened. "I've contacted a data forensics firm to crawl through an audit quickly. They'll trace exactly what was taken. Once we're secure, all data and every communication will be monitored. If they return, we'll catch them before they can cause any damage."

"This still doesn't make complete sense," Sam mused aloud. "Nothing on the dark web, and none of our contacts in foreign intelligence circles have heard a thing about the Russians swinging their dick over this."

Around the room, the BlueOpsX36 team worked like clockwork, seamlessly coordinating with Sam's private-sector contacts. They rolled out poly-factor authentication (PFA) across all user accounts and enforced advanced encryption protocols to lock down every facet of the campaign's operations. Real-time threat intelligence streamed in from BlueOpsX36's Network and Security Operations Centers (NOC/SOC), giving the team a critical advantage in monitoring every potential entry point. "Only eleven companies in the world can see and do what we've deployed in 90 minutes," someone remarked, a note of pride cutting through the tension.

In his office, Vic Ross watched the news with growing horror as reports rolled in: Jen Morales's campaign had survived the attack and emerged stronger. The media was ablaze with stories of how Jen's team had brought in several top-tier cybersecurity experts to rebuild their defenses in a matter of hours, turning a disaster into a narrative of resilience.

"What the hell?" Vic growled, his face turning pale. *We can't catch a fucking break*, he thought, *I swear.*

Slater slammed his fist on the table, seething. "They're back online. Lee's team locked down everything."

Rosa scrolled through the latest updates, her expression dark. "They rebuilt their digital systems from scratch. With the tech they've deployed, there's no way in. They've got tech, and even state actors would struggle against it."

Vic's hands trembled angrily as he flung his phone across the room. "This was supposed to destroy her campaign! Fucking incapable Russians."

Rosa glanced at him, her face impassive. "She's not just surviving, Vic. She's using this to make herself stronger."

— 20 —

Jen Morales sat amidst her team at her newly fortified campaign headquarters, her fingers still from typing, her face a mixture of exhaustion and fierce determination. The attack had been brutal, but with Sam, Diego, and the BlueOpsX36 team, they'd quickly restored and rebuilt stronger than ever. Jen's phone buzzed with a new message from an old supporter: ***"You survived. We believe in you. Keep fighting."***

She smiled, the flicker of hope in her heart flaring into something stronger. The game had changed, and for the first time, she felt they might have a fighting chance.

— 21 —

The campaign season had become a whirlwind of new regulations and strategic maneuvering. Still, one rule change had altered a fundamental aspect of every presidential race: the timing of the vice-presidential announcement. Under the revised election laws, campaigns were now mandated to officially announce their vice-presidential candidates no sooner than 40 days before the election.

Jen Morales sat in a quiet corner of her campaign headquarters, reviewing the updated playbook with Nathan Carter, her running mate and most trusted ally. The clock was ticking, and the tension in the room was palpable. Nathan leaned forward, a thoughtful look on his face.

"Forty days," he said, breaking the silence. "It feels like we're racing the clock."

Jen nodded. "It was designed to keep us on edge, to make sure no one gets too comfortable."

The new rule had been implemented after years of debate about the influence and impact of vice-presidential picks. In previous elections, candidates often used their VP selections to bolster their campaigns early, leveraging the media frenzy and consolidating voter blocs well in advance. However, critics argued that this allowed campaigns to focus more on theatrics than substance, turning the VP choice into a spectacle rather than a considered decision.

In response, election reformers had pushed for the change. By delaying the official announcement until the final stretch, they hoped to keep voters focused on the presidential candidates' platforms and policies. The thesis behind the why is it ensured that the selection wasn't made just to pander to a specific demographic or generate short-term momentum.

Nathan rubbed his chin, thinking it through. "It puts more pressure on us to make the perfect choice," he said. "But at least it makes the electorate take the presidency itself more seriously."

Jen sighed, feeling the weight of the decision. "It's a double-edged sword. We get to keep our opponents guessing, but it also limits our ability to build momentum early with your name out there. No one will remember how it was in eight or twelve years."

Nathan offered a reassuring smile. "Well, we've been making history from the start. Why stop now?"

Jen appreciated his optimism. She knew that when they finally announced his candidacy, it had to be powerful and meticulously planned. Every day they waited was a gamble, but it also meant the final sprint to election day would be electrified with fresh energy.

"This forty-day rule is a goddamn nightmare," Vic muttered, pinching the bridge of his nose. "We're used to having months to integrate our VP into the campaign narrative to solidify our base. Now we have to drop a bombshell and hope it detonates the way we need it to."

Ethan leaned forward, his expression unreadable. "The key is making sure our choice shifts the momentum. It's a final push, not a slow build. We need someone who can capture attention instantly and change the conversation in our favor. Do we maybe go with Slater?"

Vic scowled. "Easier said than done. We've been keeping our options open, but we can't afford a misstep. The wrong pick, and we blow our last shot at turning the tide."

Ethan knew Vic had a point. The new rule made the vice-presidential selection more of a gamble, and they were playing a high-stakes game. In the past, a long rollout had allowed campaigns to test messaging, gauge public reactions, and fine-tune their strategies. Now, it was all about timing and impact, a sudden and strategic strike.

"And let's not forget," Ethan added, "Jen Morales's camp will do the same thing. We're not just trying to land our pick—we're trying to outmaneuver hers. We have to anticipate how her announcement will play with the public and plan accordingly."

Vic sighed, leaning back in his chair. "Jen's running on the reformer narrative," he mused. "Her pick is probably, Carter, squeaky clean, someone who reinforces her whole message of integrity. We need a contrast—someone who'll make people forget her 'clean politics' shtick and remember why sticking with us is the safer bet. Unless her guy's screwed up in ways we don't know about yet."

Ethan's mind was still running through all options, weighing pros and cons. The challenge was finding someone who could match Jen's momentum without feeling like a blatant political calculation. It was a delicate balance, one that could make or break their campaign in those crucial final days. Slater has been kept out of this because he was an option, an odd situation.

Both campaigns were fully aware of the new landscape: the delayed vice-presidential announcement would add an element of suspense to the race, but it would also make the final push to election day more unpredictable. Each side had its own strategy, its own strengths and vulnerabilities. As the countdown to the 40-day mark continued, the pressure to get it right was almost unbearable.

Back in her headquarters, Jen tried to channel the anxiety into determination. Her team would make the most of every second, and when the time came, she and Nathan would be ready to make their case to the American people.

Across town, Vic Ross prepared for his own announcement, knowing that this election was a battle not just of policies and promises, but of strategy, timing, and the perfect execution of a plan that had been years in the making.

— 22 —

With 40 days left until the election, the pressure was suffocating. Every move mattered. Every dollar raised could be the difference between victory and defeat. Both campaigns had maxed out their financial raises, relying now on in-kind contributions to scrape by. In the heart of Jen Morales's campaign headquarters, the hum of activity was relentless, a constant churn of phone calls and strategy sessions. But just beneath the surface lurked a heavy tension. Despite their recent win against the cyberattack, money was tight. Too tight to breathe.

Jen sat in a strategy meeting, surrounded by her closest advisers— Diego Castillo, Sam Lee, Bill Prescott, and Nathan. The glow from their laptops and phones reflected the data in real time: fundraising goals, media buys, ad placements, and the endless parade of emails begging for donations.

"Where are we with cash flow?" Jen asked, her voice steady but laced with concern.

Nathan pulled up the latest numbers, his expression grim. "We're about $3 million short of where we need to be by next week. Our grassroots donors are tapped out, barely able to contribute anything under the in-kind rules. They're giving what they can, but we're hitting dead ends. We need to catch a bit of lightning."

Jen leaned back in her chair, her mind racing. From the start, they had refused to take corporate gray-area PAC money, especially under the new rules. It had given them the moral high ground, sure, but now it was becoming painfully clear how hard it was to compete with the relentless spending power of Vic Ross's campaign.

"We're not going to hit those numbers if we stay the course," Nathan continued, glancing at Jen. "I'm not saying we sell out, but we need to consider other funding sources."

Jen raised an eyebrow, knowing exactly what he meant. "You're talking about gray-area PACs."

Nathan hesitated, but he nodded. "The legal ones. The ones we know won't be a liability."

Jen's jaw tightened. She knew Nathan meant well, but this was a line she wasn't willing to cross. "No."

Nathan sighed. "Jen, I get it. But Vic's campaign will outspend us 3-to-1 in these last few weeks. He's already got the backing of some powerful dark money groups, and they're flooding the airwaves with attack ads. Without PACs, we'll never get to the cap. We can't just ignore the fact that we need money to keep pace."

Jen's eyes hardened. "I'm not taking money from any PACs that can't stand up to scrutiny. And I'm especially not taking dark money. I don't care if it puts us behind financially. We're not playing that game."

Diego, sitting quietly at his laptop, looked up. "We can still make this work. We've got strong grassroots support, and we can leverage digital campaigns to get small donors to brainstorm and incentivize in-kind work. The cyberattack gave us a boost in visibility, and we need to ride that momentum."

Nathan frowned, glancing at the numbers again. "Digital is good, but it won't be enough to close the gap. The ads Vic's campaign is running—those are PAC-funded. He's got millions coming in from shadowy new versions of former super PACs and dark money groups that side-step disclosing their donors."

Jen crossed her arms, her voice firm. "That's exactly why we can't go down that road. Vic might be willing to take money from these people, but we're not. Our supporters believe in us because we're running a clean campaign. We will win this the right way, or not at all."

Vic Ross, on the other hand, had no such moral reservations.

In a private room at his campaign headquarters, Vic sat across from Rosa Delgado and Slater, his fingers drumming on the table as they discussed the numbers. Despite the optics of their campaign, they were burning through cash faster than they could raise it. Ads, consultants, legal fees—it was all piling up. And now, with the election only 40 days away, they were in a financial bind.

"How are we on the money?" Vic asked, his voice sharp.

Slater didn't look up from his phone. "We're short, but we've got a few backdoor deals in the works. Some gray money groups are ready for another cash infusion."

Rosa's eyes flickered with something close to disdain. "How much?"

"$10 million, give or take," Slater replied. "It's coming from some PACs that don't disclose their donors. We can funnel it through an old super PAC—completely untraceable. All above board, technically. Sort of. Probably won't hold up next cycle."

Rosa crossed her arms. "Vic, you realize this will be a problem if it ever comes out. People are already suspicious about where we're getting our money from. If the press digs into this..."

Vic waved her off. "We need the money. Morales is catching up, and she's getting free publicity thanks to that damn cyberattack. We don't have time to be picky about where the cash comes from."

Rosa's lips thinned into a hard line. "If you take this money, you're selling your soul to the devils behind it. They don't illegally fund campaigns out of charity. They'll expect favors, and it won't be possible. And when they come to collect, it won't be pretty."

Vic leaned back, a smug grin on his face. "I've dealt with demons before. This isn't new to me."

Slater grinned. "We'll use the money to drown Morales in attack ads. Hit her on everything from her ties to leftist groups to her inexperience. If we blitz her in these final weeks, she won't recover."

Rosa watched Vic carefully, her mind calculating. She had never opposed getting dirty, but even she understood the long-term risks of dark or gray money, and prison-level dirty. Still, Vic wasn't going to change his mind.

"Fuck me, I don't want to do prison time for your lack of budgeting," Rosa snapped. "I know nothing, and I'm not attending these meetings. Period." She exited the room swiftly.

Back at Jen's campaign headquarters, the team was in overdrive. Sam Lee had fortified their digital infrastructure after the cyberattack, locking down every vulnerability. Now that they were secure, the focus had shifted to one thing: closing the fundraising gap—a problem that felt increasingly insurmountable.

Diego was head down analyzing their data streams, monitoring every piece of information flowing through their networks. He had implemented systems that tracked donations in real time, analyzing donor behavior and predicting where the next wave of contributions would come from.

"We've seen a surge in small-dollar donations to specific nonprofits from small donors, who can consult with marketing companies, all totally legal and a gray area, since the attack," Diego said, glancing at Jen. "But we need to keep the momentum going. I'm running predictive models that show which segments of our donor base are most likely to give again. We'll target those people with tailored text messages and HeyYouApp campaigns."

Nathan rubbed his temples, still thinking about the money they needed. "How much can we realistically raise this way?"

Diego tapped the screen, showing a series of graphs and numbers. "If we hit every potential donor in our database with the right message, we could bring in another $2 million. It won't be easy, but it's possible."

Jen nodded. "Let's do it. Every dollar helps. We still need more than $2 million, and it takes a couple of days to get through the nonprofits, so the sooner we start, the better."

"And we need to ramp up the pressure on Vic," Diego added, his eyes narrowing. "I've been tracking the super PACs trying to funnel money into his campaign through shady, possibly illegal channels. I just can't prove it yet. There are a lot of shadowy groups backing him—some with ties to foreign interests."

Jen's brow furrowed. "Foreign interests?"

Diego nodded. "It's subtle, but there's a pattern. Some of these PACs are getting money from overseas, likely laundered through intermediaries. We can't prove it yet, but we can get close."

Nathan leaned forward, interested. "So what are you suggesting?"

Diego smiled faintly. "We start pushing the narrative that Vic's campaign is being funded by dark money and foreign interests. We get journalists and independent media outlets to ask questions and dig into these shadowy channels and PACs. Even without a smoking gun, the suspicion alone will hurt him."

Jen's mind raced. It was a risky move but one that could pay off. If they could frame Vic as a candidate controlled by dark, unaccountable money, it could turn public opinion against him in these crucial final days.

"Do it," Jen said. "We need to expose him for who he really is. Time isn't our friend here."

— 23 —

The political landscape had shifted, a tectonic change brought on by sweeping public demand for reform. Gone were the days of unregulated spending, when campaigns could drown opponents in a sea of money without a second thought. The new reality was a $5 billion spending cap per campaign. It was a sum so vast it still felt surreal, but compared to the blank checks of past elections, it forced a newfound discipline.

Vic Ross studied the spreadsheet in front of him, the numbers blurring after hours of scrutiny. Each row represented a critical choice: advertising, field offices, media consultants, and last-minute campaign pushes. The budget was finite, and as the final weeks loomed, he knew they were on track to hit the spending limit, dollar for dollar. The stakes had never felt higher.

Ethan Grant, his campaign manager, stood near the window, worry etched into his face. "We're almost there," Ethan said, pointing to the latest financial projections. "Both campaigns are going to max out in these last few weeks. Every choice we make has to be flawless, or we'll be out of fuel before the finish line."

Vic's jaw tightened. "No room for fucking error," he muttered. It was a far cry from previous campaigns when PAC money had flowed like a river and allowed for endless spending sprees. Now, with those funding sources severely restricted, every expenditure had to be meticulously justified. Even Vic, a seasoned player in the high-stakes world of politics, felt the pressure. The new rules are even the playing field.

Jen Morales, Vic's opponent and the architect of these very reforms, was no stranger to the financial strain. Her campaign had run on the energy of grassroots donations from the start, but that didn't mean it was easy. Every dollar had to be earned from a broad base of supporters, millions of small contributions adding up to something formidable. Yet, as the race entered the home stretch, her team felt the pressure of approaching the spending cap.

Late one evening, Jen sat in a strategy meeting with her top advisors.

The tension in the room was maxed out. They discussed the challenges of managing every cent and trying to make the most impact without running out of funds before election day.

Jen leaned back, her frustration evident. "You know what drives me nuts? I mean, really batshit crazy," she said, her voice heavy with irritation. "Ross's followers and his party don't really give a shit where the money comes from, who donates, or how it's used. They just care about winning. Meanwhile, we're expected to stay clean and transparent, and it feels like we're fighting with one hand tied behind our backs."

Nathan Carter, her former communications director, turned likely VP and nodded, a grim smile tugging at his lips. "It's the double standard," he agreed. "They bend the rules, play fast and loose, and no one bats an eye. But one misstep from us, and we're crucified."

Jen sighed. "I get it. It's why we're doing this—to change the system. But damn, it's exhausting."

The room fell silent, the weight of the campaign bearing down on everyone. Yet Jen's frustration only fueled her resolve. She knew that running a campaign rooted in integrity would always be harder. But it was a fight she believed in, even if it meant playing on a tilted field.

Despite the reforms, the new campaign finance era had opened unexpected avenues for influence. The elimination of traditional PACs and Super PACs left both campaigns scrambling to exploit the last major loophole: in-kind contributions and nonprofit consulting. These services—offered either for a fee, free or at heavily discounted rates— had become the new frontier in campaign strategy.

For Jen's team, this meant accepting discounted data services from sympathetic tech firms and leveraging volunteers from labor unions to canvas key areas. Even legal advisors, supposedly volunteering "pro bono" hours, offered expertise that would have cost a fortune on the open market.

"It's still legal," Nathan reminded Jen during a late-night discussion. "But it feels messy."

Jen agreed. "I never thought I'd be bartering favors like this. But when the rules are as strict as they are, we have to get creative."

On Vic's side, the story was much the same. His team secured in-kind contributions through free flights from a billionaire ally and discounted campaign tech from influential business leaders. Ethan, ever the strategist, had navigated these arrangements with finesse, but it left a bad taste in his mouth, yet it meant an end.

"It's all favors now," Ethan told Vic one afternoon. "You scratch my back, I'll scratch yours. It's not illegal, but it sure feels like we're dancing on the line—or that they're up my skirt." He laughed.

Vic frowned. "It's the game we're playing," he said. "Until the system changes again, we do what we have to do."

The $5 billion spending limit forced both campaigns to be ruthlessly efficient. Jen focused on targeted digital outreach and in-person town halls that resonated with voters. Every dollar spent was meant to forge a genuine connection to amplify her message of people-first governance. Her campaign had little room for glitz or excess, but it thrived on authenticity.

Vic's team took a different approach. They allocated funds for precise, data-driven ad campaigns and strategically crafted rallies, each designed to maximize exposure without waste. It was a well-oiled machine, but it was still strained under the new constraints.

As both campaigns barreled toward election day, reality hit home: both reaching the $5 billion cap in the final month, just as public interest reached its fever pitch, required a pivot to keep momentum. It was a race not just of ideals but of strategy, of who could outmaneuver the other.

Jen and Vic knew that the new financial limits had changed the game, but it hadn't leveled the playing field as they'd hoped. Power and influence still found ways to seep through the cracks. As the clock ticked down, both campaigns leaned on their remaining resources, making every dollar and every favor count.

Jen's campaign stayed focused, a beacon of hope for those who believed in reform. Vic's camp, battle-hardened and pragmatic, did whatever was necessary to maintain an edge. The stakes had never been higher, and the race had never felt more uncertain.

In the end, the campaign wasn't just about policy or principles. It was about survival in a new era of American politics, where ambition, no matter how carefully controlled, still came at a price.

— 24 —

The headquarters felt like a war zone. Jen Morales had barely slept in days. None of them had. There was no time for rest. Every minute counted. Every phone call, every volunteer, and every dollar raised was a step closer to victory or defeat.

It was down to the wire, and the stakes couldn't be higher.

We need more volunteers on the ground!" Nathan shouted, his voice raw from hours of issuing commands. "I don't care if they sleep at the office—we're knocking on every door, talking to every voter!" His rallying cry was met with cheers.

Jen watched as her campaign headquarters churned with frenetic energy. Volunteers and staffers rushed between tables, eyes glued to laptops and phones, fielding calls, strategizing outreach, and monitoring social media in real time. It was a battlefield of information, high emotions, and exhaustion, pushing everyone to the breaking point.

"We're holding on, shit, but barely," Nathan said as he turned back to Jen, his face pale with stress. "Vic's campaign has flooded the airwaves with attack ads. They've got ads running in every swing district, and we just don't have the cash to counter all of it."

Diego Castillo was sitting in the corner, furiously typing away at his laptop, his eyes dark and intense. "We're fighting back, microtargeting voters who haven't decided, blasting positive stories on social media to counter the hit pieces. But we can only do so much with the budget we have."

Jen felt the pressure deep in her chest, a weight that had been there for weeks but was now unbearable. "What are the numbers looking like?"

Nathan grimaced. "It's close. Too close. The polls are tightening, and we're losing ground in some key areas. Vic's dark money ads are starting to shift public perception. But our 8-minute response to negative information is working—it's had a huge impact, putting us close to even in the polls."

Jen nodded, trying to hold onto her resolve. The anger she felt—at Vic, at the dirty money fueling his campaign, at the overwhelming pressure to win—was gnawing at her. But she couldn't let it show. Not now.

"What about the volunteers?" Jen asked, her voice low but steady. "How are they holding up?"

Nathan rubbed his temples, exhaustion lining his face. "They're tired, but they're committed. We've got people on the phones 24/7, knocking on doors, talking to voters. But the tension is getting to them.

Everyone's on edge."

Diego didn't look up from his screen. "It's chaos out there. People are pissed. Vic's ads are designed to make people angry, and it's working. I've been monitoring social media, and there's a lot of backlash. People are frustrated with the whole system. We're seeing it in voter engagement. Some are pulling away, fed up with both sides."

Jen's chest tightened. "We can't afford to lose those voters."

Vic Ross, meanwhile, was riding the wave of dark money. His campaign headquarters was buzzing with excitement, fueled by the massive cash influx from shadowy quasi-PACs that had poured hundreds of millions into his final push in a manner that 9 years later would put several people in prison for decades.

The attack ads were relentless, blanketing the airwaves and social media. Every hour, new smears were going out, targeting Jen's integrity, background, and character.

Ethan leaned in during the strategy meeting, his tone a mix of irritation and admiration. "Our machine has perfected the in-kind loophole for services," he said. "No salaries, just clever workarounds—getting rents paid under a maintenance contract exception, which frees up a lot more money. It's likely only sustainable for this campaign, but for now, it's completely legal."

"Keep the pressure on," Vic barked, pacing the war room. "We need to keep hitting her, harder and harder. I want ads running 24/7 until Election Day."

Slater, standing near the digital command center, grinned as he watched the attack ads pour across every platform. "We've got every media buy locked down. Swing voters are seeing nothing but your face, Vic. Morales can't match our spending. She's drowning out there."

Rosa Delgado, however, wasn't celebrating. She sat quietly, watching the chaos unfold, but her instincts told her something was wrong. Vic was pushing too hard, too fast, relying on sheer volume and dark money to overwhelm Jen's campaign. But that wasn't always a winning strategy.

"The numbers are beyond close," Rosa said, her voice cutting through the noise. "Closer than they should be. **Morales is resilient**. She's holding on, and we're not gaining the ground we should be."

Vic glared at her. "We're goddamn winning. Don't start second-guessing now, Rosa."

But Rosa knew better. "We've spent 25 million attacking her, but she's still in this fight. That should worry you."

Vic's jaw tightened, but he didn't respond. Deep down, he knew Rosa was right. The race was tighter than anyone had expected, and with only a few days left, there wasn't much more they could do to shift public opinion. They were already throwing everything they had at Jen.

Vic leaned in, his voice low and commanding, the tension palpable. "From now on," he said, eyes locked on Slater, "limit who you talk to on the campaign. Keep your circle tight. I don't trust half the people working under us, and I can't afford any more leaks or whispers getting out." He paused, the distrust twisting his expression. "No one needs to know more than what's absolutely necessary. If anyone asks questions, shut them down. We have too many eyes on us, and I need to know you're not giving anything away." Slater nodded, feeling the weight of Vic's paranoia settle uncomfortably around them, knowing that the campaign had become a maze of secrets and mistrust.

Jen was out in the field, pounding the pavement alongside her volunteers. The campaign office had become a whirlwind of activity, but out here, it was real. She was shaking hands, talking to voters face-to-face, hearing their concerns, and feeling their frustrations. It was exhausting, but it was also energizing in a way that nothing else was.

"Look, I get it," Jen said, standing outside a local diner as she spoke to a small crowd of undecided voters. "I'm not here to make you promises I can't keep. I'm here to fight for you, to give you a voice. That's all I've ever wanted. I'm not taking dark money. I'm not selling out to the highest bidder; I actually care about the people. And that's what separates me from Vic Ross."

A woman in the crowd, arms crossed, shook her head. "How are we supposed to trust anyone in politics? All of you are the same."

Jen stepped forward, her eyes locking onto the woman's. "I understand why you're angry, know I hear you. I've spent my entire campaign fighting against the same system, trying to keep people like me—like us—out. But if we give up now, they win. Vic Ross is flooding this election with his dark money, blood money because he knows the only way he can win is by drowning out your voice. Don't let him. Don't let them take this from you."

The woman hesitated, her expression softening. "You do actually sound different from the others. But I still don't know."

"I am different," Jen said, her voice firm. "And I'm here because I believe in you. We can change this, but only if we fight together."

As the crowd began to warm to her, Jen felt a surge of hope. But there was still so much work to be done. The volunteers were stretched thin, working around the clock. Emotions were running high. Jen had seen some of her most dedicated workers break down in tears from sheer exhaustion, struggling to keep going.

At the campaign office, Nathan coordinated the chaos with a mix of brute force and raw adrenaline. "We need to reach every voter we can. I don't care if they've been called five times—we call them again."

The tension was palpable as he called every state campaign leader. Every moment counted, and every mistake could cost them the election.

Back at Vic's headquarters, the walls were closing in.

"Morales is gaining momentum," Slater muttered, his voice dripping with frustration as he stared at the latest polling numbers. "All this dark money, and she's still breathing down our necks."

Vic was furious, pacing the room like a caged animal. "We've outspent her 3-to-1. What more do we need to do?"

Rosa, ever calm, watched them both. "It's not about money anymore. It's about the message. Morales is connecting with voters in a way you're not. She's out there, face-to-face, while you're hiding behind ads and attack pieces."

Vic glared at her. "I've got better things to do than shake hands and kiss babies."

Rosa sighed. "That's why you're losing ground."

As the clock ticked down, Jen's campaign surged. Despite the flood of money and services into Vic's campaign, Jen held firm despite the relentless attack ads. Volunteers worked around the clock, fueled by nothing but passion and coffee. Exhausted but determined, they knocked on doors, made phone calls, sent texts, and posted on social media—all to sway just one more voter.

Jen could feel the anger in the air—the frustration, the hopelessness. But she also forced herself to feel glimmers of hope. **People were listening.** They wanted something different, something real. And in these last few days, that's what she was offering them.

It was all or nothing now.

— 25 —

The atmosphere inside Vic Ross's headquarters had shifted. The air was thick with tension and some desperation; the mood was dark. Vic paced the room, tension radiating off him in waves as the election numbers rolled in. With only a few days left, it became clear that the race wasn't going his way.

"We're in trouble," Slater said, glancing at Rosa Delgado, who was sitting across the table, staring grimly at her laptop. "The polling isn't moving like we expected. Morales's personal outreach is cutting into our base in several surprising states."

Vic's eyes narrowed, anger simmering just beneath the surface. "We've spent millions—*millions*—on ads. Why the fuck aren't we winning?"

Rosa didn't bother to look up. "Morales is playing a different game. She's out there, on the ground, connecting with voters. We've tried drowning her with dark money and attack ads, but she's still holding strong."

Slater leaned in, his voice lower. "We need to change the narrative, Vic. Shift the focus away from the numbers and create doubt, then create doubt and more doubt. We can't win clean; we need to lay the groundwork to challenge the election results; every campaign for the last 20 years has done this. It's our party SOP; everything is in place."

Vic's head snapped up, his jaw tightening. "What are you saying?"

Slater smirked. "We start seeding the narrative that the election is rigged—foreign interference, ballot tampering, widespread fraud, and Morales associates might have known about. If we can't win outright, we make sure the public doesn't trust the results, make the challenge painful, and hedge our bets. That way, when we take it to court, there'll be enough noise and doubt to back us up, and we'll get the states riled up, too."

Rosa crossed her arms, leaning back in her chair. "We'll need to stir up the base. Get them angry. Convince them that Morales is working with foreign powers; she's not the angelic politician that the election is being stolen right under their noses."

Vic's lips curled into a dark smile. **"And you think this will work?"**

"It'll work," Slater replied, his voice confident. "We've got an asset—a subsidiary of a tech company specializing in social media manipulation, and we've hesitated to use them. They've done work for overseas clients before, using the same tactics the Turks, Russians, and Chinese use to stir up chaos. We funnel some of our money through them and let them run wild. They'll use bots, trolls, fake accounts— everything. We can have them start planting stories about election fraud, foreign interference, all of it. The goal is to make people question the results before Election Day."

Vic's mind whirled as he considered the implications. The thought of losing—of being humiliated by Jen Morales—was unbearable. If he couldn't win outright, then destroying the public's trust in the election might be his only option.

"How far can we take this?" Vic asked, his voice low.

Slater paused. "Far enough that we can raise hell for weeks after the election if necessary. If you lose, we go straight to the courts and raise more money from your base. Play the victim, say the election was stolen. They'll eat it up."

Vic glanced at Rosa, who was watching him carefully. Her dark eyes narrowed slightly, a flicker of disapproval barely masked beneath her composed expression. Rosa knew Vic too well—she understood the ruthlessness that simmered just beneath his polished exterior, the way he calculated every risk and ignored the moral weight of his decisions. It wasn't that she was surprised; she had long since accepted that he was willing to cross any line to stay in power.

Should or shouldn't I do that? The train had left the station a long time ago, and in its place was a relentless drive to survive and win, no matter the cost. Rosa's lips pressed into a thin line, a silent acknowledgment that she couldn't change him but also a sign that she never stopped hoping he might make a different choice—just once.

"This needs to be goddamn airtight," Vic said, his voice cold and unyielding. The cigar in his hand burned down to a stubborn ember, and he jabbed it out in the nearby ashtray as if emphasizing his point. "I want ten layers between me and this operation. No one can trace it back to me. Fucking understood?" His steel-blue eyes locked onto the people around him, daring anyone to show hesitation.

"If you get this wrong," he continued, his jaw tightening, "we all go to prison. **No pardons. No second chances.**" The room fell silent, and the gravity of his words settled over them like a suffocating blanket. Vic knew the stakes, and he made damn sure everyone else did too.

Slater nodded. "Already handled. The subsidiary is a shell of a shell of a shell company—completely untraceable. We'll run it through a couple of intermediaries. No one will know it's coming from you."

Jen Morales was exhausted, but there was no time to rest. The campaign was in full swing, and every second counted. Her volunteers were still hitting the phones, knocking on doors, and engaging with voters face-to-face. But a new kind of noise was starting to filter through—something darker, something insidious.

"I'm hearing from some of our volunteers," Nathan said as he pulled up his phone, scrolling through messages. "Voters are getting confused and suspicious. There's talk about election interference, rigged ballots, and even foreign actors getting involved. It's all bullshit, but it's spreading."

Jen frowned, her exhaustion giving way to frustration. "Where's it coming from?"

Diego, sitting at his laptop, his fingers flying over the keys, looked up grimly. "It's coordinated. I've been tracking it for the past few hours. Fake accounts, bots, troll farms—they're all pushing the same message. Election fraud. Foreign interference. Claims that the election is being rigged in your favor."

Jen's stomach turned. "Vic's behind this; I know he is."

Diego nodded, his expression concerned. "It's him or someone working many ripples away from him," he said. "I can't trace it directly to his campaign, but it's too coordinated to be random. They're planting seeds of doubt, trying to discredit the election before it even happens." He paused, running a hand through his thick, dark hair, the frustration clear in the tension along his jaw. "I'll keep working on it," he added, determination tightening his voice.

The weight of the revelation hung between them, each of them knowing that in a game like this, where whispers turned into scandals, any wrong move could have devastating consequences.

Nathan cursed under his breath. "And if people buy into this, it will undermine the whole process. Even if you win, they'll say you stole it."

Jen leaned back in her chair, feeling the moment's weight pressing down on her. This wasn't just about winning anymore. Vic was trying to burn down the entire system if he couldn't come out on top.

"What do we do?" Jen asked, her voice steady but tense.

Diego's eyes darkened. "We fight back. I've already started

countering the misinformation, but it will be a tough battle. They've got a full-scale operation, using social media manipulation tactics that are hard to combat."

"Call Bill Prescott—I already talked to him!" Nathan shouted, urgency cutting through his voice.

Jen's mind raced, a whirlwind of strategy and resolve. "We need to get ahead of this," she said, her voice urgent but steady. "Call it out publicly. If we let this narrative grow unchecked, it'll poison everything."

She dialed Bill to brainstorm a response. "I refuse to become another Vic Ross," she said firmly. "Winning isn't worth it if it means losing who we are."

Her words cut through the tension, and the room went still for a moment. Jen knew the cost of fighting clean in a dirty game but refused to sacrifice her principles—even when the stakes were at their highest.

Vic's misinformation machine was in full swing.

The tech subsidiary Slater had engaged was doing precisely what they were paid for—flooding social media with fake stories, conspiracies, and outright lies. Bots were amplifying posts that claimed Morales was backed by foreign actors, that ballots were being tampered with, and that polling locations were compromised.

Vic's base was eating it up.

"This is exactly what we needed," Slater said, scrolling through the trending topics on social media. "Election fraud is trending. People are buying it. The more they believe the system is rigged, the better it is for us."

Rosa, who had been silent through much of the operation, finally spoke. "What's your endgame here, Vic? You're stirring up a hornet's nest. You really think you can control this once it starts?"

Vic smirked. "I don't need to control it. I just need it to be loud enough to cause chaos. Once the election happens, if I lose, we'll take it to the courts. We'll have enough noise to back up our claims, and my base will rally around the idea that it was stolen from me."

"Then what? And if you win?" Rosa asked, her eyes narrowing.

Vic's smile grew. "Then we let the chaos die or fuel it more. But either way, I'm staying in control."

As the coordinated "steal the election" narrative spread like wildfire, fueled by whispers and online disinformation planted by operatives working on behalf of Vic Ross's campaign, the consequences became brutally clear. What had started as political chatter was now causing real harm, and it was Hispanic communities bearing the brunt of it.

Fired up and emboldened by the lies, Ross' supporters began acting out. Store owners woke to find their businesses vandalized, graffiti accusing them of aiding some imagined conspiracy. Families faced harassment in public, getting shouted at and blamed for supposedly undermining democracy. The tension was so thick that in some neighborhoods, it became genuinely dangerous to walk the streets.

And then there was the rhetoric about the wall. Vic began promising to "rebuild the wall," playing to his base's nostalgia for a project that had been a mess from the start. The original wall, hastily constructed over a decade ago, had been riddled with problems: corners cut, corruption, and sections collapsing because of shoddy construction. It was a crumbling, ugly monument. Yet Vic talked about restoring it as if it were some grand act of strength, ignoring the fact that it had already cost lives and resources. And just like that, his words poured gasoline on an already dangerous fire.

When asked about the violence, Vic dodged accountability. "I don't control what people do," he'd say, brushing off the reports. He downplayed the attacks as misunderstandings or, worse, fabrications pushed by a biased media. He stuck to his message about "security and election integrity" and never once addressed the harm his words had caused. The campaign took the official stance of plausible deniability. Vic remained Vic—untouchable, unwilling to see how his game was hurting real people.

She'd believed in Vic once, truly believed he could be a force she would help win. But seeing the violence, knowing that real lives were being shattered, even in her own communities now, while Vic stayed cold and unmoved—**that was a breaking point**.

As Election Day drew closer, the battle was no longer just about votes. It was about truth, trust, and the integrity of the system itself. Jen's campaign was fighting a war on two fronts—trying to win over undecided voters while combating the flood of misinformation that was threatening to undermine the entire election.

Diego worked around the clock, coordinating with independent journalists and fact-checkers to counter Vic's team's lies. They were pushing back hard, but the volume of false information was staggering.

"Every time we shut down one false story, ten more pop up," Diego said, his voice tight with frustration. "They've got an army of advanced AI bots and a fake decentralized account network pushing this narrative. It's like putting out a wildfire with a garden hose."

Jen nodded, her face grim but resolute. "We keep fighting. We call out the lies, we push the truth, and we trust the voters to see through it. Do everything we can."

But even as she said it, Jen knew it wouldn't be that simple. Vic had set the stage for a battle that would continue long after the votes were counted. If he lost, he wouldn't go quietly. He would drag the election through the courts, scream about fraud, and rally his base to believe they had been cheated.

And that scared Jen more than anything.

— 26 —

Jen Morales sat in the back of the campaign SUV, her eyes locked on the notes she'd scrawled across her tablet screen. The car hummed along a Georgia highway, past stretches of pecan orchards and roadside stands selling fresh peaches. She knew the stakes couldn't be higher. Georgia and North Carolina were both swing states, and with only weeks until the election, every handshake, every speech, every connection had to count. Jen glanced at Nathan Carter, her running mate, who smiled reassuringly.

"Ready?" Nathan asked, sensing her tension.

Jen straightened. "Ready as I'll ever be."

Day One: Georgia

The SUV pulled into the parking lot of a packed community center in Savannah. Jen stepped out into the muggy heat, immediately feeling the weight of hundreds of expectant eyes. Supporters, curious independents, and skeptical locals crowded in, some holding signs, others simply watching. Jen had learned how to read a room, and this one felt like a room holding its breath.

She stepped onto the small stage, wiping a bead of sweat from her brow. "Good afternoon, Savannah!" she called, her voice bright and confident. "Thank you for coming out today. I know these are trying times, but I'm here to tell you that change is not only possible, it's within our grasp."

The crowd cheered, and Jen launched into her key talking points: healthcare, voting rights, and infrastructure. She made sure to address local concerns, like the threat of rising sea levels and how her administration would protect the state's coastal communities. A mother of two stepped forward during the Q&A session, her hands shaking as she took the microphone.

"My son has diabetes," the woman said. "He's ten, and we can barely afford his insulin. What will you do to make healthcare truly affordable?"

Jen stepped off the stage, closing the distance between them. "Healthcare is a right, not a privilege," she said, her voice unwavering. "I will work to cap the cost of life-saving drugs like insulin and hold pharmaceutical companies accountable. I propose to legislate caps so future administrations can't reverse for profiteering."

The woman's eyes filled with tears. "Thank you," she whispered.

Jen took a moment to squeeze the woman's hand before returning to the stage, feeling the room warm to her sincerity. But she knew this was only the first step.

Day Two: Rural Georgia

The second stop was far from the big city. It was a small town in rural Georgia where the economy had struggled for decades. The air felt heavy with humidity and the burden of lost opportunities. Jen stood on a hay bale-turned podium, addressing farmers and small business owners who had gathered beneath the shade of an old pecan tree. Many wore skeptical expressions; their arms crossed over sun-faded work shirts.

"I know Washington feels far away," Jen said, her voice breaking the stillness. "I know many of you have heard promises that never came true. But I'm not here just to talk—I'm here to listen and to fight for your future, much like Georgia's own, the late President Carter."

A grizzled farmer stepped forward, gripping his hat in one hand. His skin was weathered, and his voice carried the weight of a life spent in the fields. "I done seen politicians come through here my whole life," he said, his tone hard but not unfriendly. "What you gonna do to protect our land and our livelihoods? We barely makin' it as it is."

Jen took a breath, meeting his gaze directly. "You deserve policies that support—not undermine—your work," she began, her voice slipping into polished campaign mode. "We'll ensure our trade agreements are fair and invest in sustainable agriculture and rural fiber so rural communities can remain competitive in a global market and…"

She paused, catching herself. Then she started again, more plainly. "Look, I know you're dealing with rising costs on everything from diesel to fertilizer to farm equipment and building supplies. Those tariffs have been hitting you hard for years now. It's the same in New Mexico, my home state. We will work on reducing or even removing those tariffs to give you and others real economic relief. No fluff—just real savings that make it easier for you to keep your farms running and your families secure."

The farmer tilted his head, considering her words. "Mmm-hmm," he murmured thoughtfully. Around him, some folks nodded. Others muttered to each other, weighing her promises like a crop they weren't sure would take root. Jen couldn't tell if she'd convinced them, but she hoped she'd at least planted a seed.

As they left, Nathan touched her shoulder. "You're making headway," he said. "Slowly but you are getting the message through."

Jen offered a small smile. "Thanks. We'll see."

Day Three: North Carolina

North Carolina was a different beast entirely. They drove into Charlotte, where a crowd had gathered in a local park, spilling across the lawn into a sea of hopeful faces and skeptical eyes. Jen knew this city, a blend of old Southern tradition and modern ambition, would be pivotal. She walked onto the stage with Nathan at her side, feeling the moment's weight.

But she wasn't alone. Flanking her were some of North Carolina's most powerful women: the state's dynamic governor, a champion for education reform; the senior senator, a fierce advocate for healthcare and working families; and a congresswoman known for her tenacity and fight for local communities. Their presence was a testament to how much was riding on at that moment.

"Charlotte, thank you for coming out!" Jen began, her voice strong. "North Carolina is at a crossroads. Together, we can choose a future that works for everyone."

She spoke about investing in education, mentioning how underfunded schools could shape or shatter futures. The female leaders behind her nodded in agreement, adding weight to Jen's words. A high school senior stepped forward to ask a question. "My school doesn't have enough textbooks, and our classrooms are falling apart," the young man said, his voice cracking. "How will you fix that?"

Jen's heart ached at the desperation in his voice. She glanced back at the governor, who had fought similar battles, before turning to the student. "We need to prioritize our students," she replied. "I will increase federal funding for public schools, fight to raise teacher pay, and ensure every student, no matter their zip code, has the resources to succeed. And it's time we reestablish the Federal Department of Education," she added, her voice firm. "For over a decade, we've struggled without it, and our schools—and our kids—have paid the price. We need that leadership back to ensure every child has a fair shot."

The crowd roared its approval, and the women beside her clapped, visibly moved. But as Jen scanned the faces before her, she could see the exhaustion, too, the hope mingled with doubt. Later, she and Nathan sat on a park bench, listening to the distant hum of the crowd dispersing. The female governor and senator lingered nearby, talking quietly, strategizing for the long road ahead.

As Jen stood to head toward her group of SUVs, her gaze swept across the thinning crowd—and then she froze. There, walking toward her with a warm, familiar smile, was Laurie Anderson. Laurie, her college friend from Raleigh, who had always been a fearless writer and activist, poured her heart into making the world a better, more just place.

Jen's smile couldn't have been any wider. She felt the prick of tears but quickly blinked them back, overwhelmed at the sight of a friendly face from her pre-politics life. Laurie picked up her pace, and before Jen knew it, they were embracing, the hug fierce and full of unspoken words.

"Laurie," Jen said, her voice cracking. "God, it's good to see you."

"It's been way too long," Laurie replied, pulling back just enough to look Jen in the eyes. "You're out here changing the world—no surprise there. But you look tired, girl. Are they treating you okay?" She offered a half-smile, the kind that carried both warmth and worry.

Jen laughed, though it sounded almost like a sigh. "Tired doesn't even cover it. But seeing you here... it's like a shot of life."

Laurie's expression softened. "I wouldn't have missed this for anything. You know I had to come out and see you fight. Even if it means dealing with these crowds," she teased, gesturing at the dispersing supporters. "I still remember you giving speeches to five people back in college. Look at you now."

Jen chuckled, feeling a rare moment of pure joy. "Yeah, and you were the one who always told me I could do more. I'm not sure I ever thanked you for that."

Laurie waved her off, but then her smile turned sharp, her voice lowering to a fierce whisper. "No thanks needed. Just remember this: You fucking got this. The world, the country, and me—we all need you to win. And please, smile as you kick Vic Ross in the balls. I would say metaphorically, but I really mean right in the balls. He and his whole party are horrible for everything the country was built on."

Jen burst out laughing, the sound cutting through her exhaustion and filling the air with something genuine. "I'll keep that in mind," she said, her grin wide and real, feeling the weight lift from her shoulders, if only for a moment.

A member of Jen's team called for her, reminding her of the schedule, and Laurie squeezed her hand one last time. "You've got this," she repeated, her voice strong. "I'm rooting for you, always."

Jen nodded, her throat tight. "Thanks, Laurie. It means everything." As she turned to head toward the SUVs, she felt a renewed strength she didn't realize she had needed so badly.

— 27 —

His phone buzzed on the desk, a brief intrusion pulling him from his spiraling thoughts. He didn't have to look to know it was Slater. Vic let it go to voicemail, unwilling to deal with his strategist's intense gaze and sharper words. Not yet. He was desperate to hold on to a shred of control, to buy a few minutes before he had to face the disaster his campaign had become.

A knock at the door broke through his thoughts, followed quickly by the unwelcome sight of Slater walking in, his face hard. As usual, he didn't wait for permission. Slater rarely did.

"You've seen the latest numbers, I assume," Slater said flatly, taking a seat across from him, eyes glinting with a steely calm that always put Vic on edge.

Vic took a long sip of his drink, his jaw tightening. "Yeah, I've seen them. What the hell are we doing wrong? We were up by ten points last month. Now Morales is closing in, and if those swing states don't shift back, we're screwed."

Slater didn't flinch. "She's got momentum. The scandal didn't stick, and people are eating up her 'integrity and reform' message. We need to change the conversation. Make this about something else."

Vic slammed his glass on the desk, the Scotch sloshing over the rim. "You think I don't know that? We've been trying everything, and she just keeps coming back stronger. Every attack makes her more sympathetic. What do we do now?"

Slater leaned back, his eyes narrowing, fingers steepling as if he were savoring a private thought. "There are still options," he said, a hint of calculation in his voice.

Vic frowned, his wariness growing. "Like what?"

Slater's expression remained infuriatingly calm. "First," he said, "we must rethink the VP situation. Albright's arrest has been an anchor around your neck. Your team's managed to keep you afloat, but he's dead weight now."

Vic scoffed, though he'd considered the idea more than once. "You're saying I should dump him?"

Slater nodded. "Yes. The offer was floated for me to take the slot myself," he admitted, "but I declined. I know I'm not the best face to win over voters. Besides, I'd rather lock in a cabinet position where I can actually get things done—and, if things go south, ensure a pardon."

He leaned back, smirking. "We need a VP who can change the narrative and energize your base."

Vic's eyes narrowed. "So you're still angling to protect yourself," he said, voice edged with bitterness.

Slater's smile didn't waver. "Always. And if we want to survive this, you'd better start thinking the same way."

Vic stared into his glass, watching the Scotch swirl. The idea of replacing Albright felt desperate, almost humiliating, even though he'd thought about it a thousand times, and even had a list ready to go. It would be a public acknowledgment of weakness, a sign that his campaign was unraveling. Yet, with the numbers slipping and Morales's surging, how much worse could it get?

He gritted his teeth at the thought of her winning—a liberal, an anti-capitalist, a symbol of everything he had built his career to oppose. The idea twisted his stomach with a volatile mix of anger and fear. The old strategies weren't working. She was unyielding, transforming every attack into fuel and every setback into a source of strength.

Vic let out a bitter sigh. Maybe Slater was right. Maybe desperate times called for desperate measures, even if it meant sacrificing his pride and rewriting the script he'd clung to so fiercely. But the taste of that desperation left a burn worse than the Scotch.

"Who do you have in mind?" he asked, his voice low.

Slater's smile widened. "There are options. Senator Meyer has appealed in the Midwest, and Senator Whitmore could play well with the tough-on-crime crowd. Either would give you the image of control. No one needs to know you're scrambling."

Vic grunted, taking another drink. "And what? Morales just stands there while we play musical chairs with my VP. She's surging because she looks steady, and I look like I'm unraveling."

Slater didn't miss a beat. "That's where the second option comes in."

Vic raised an eyebrow, already dreading the answer. "Which is?"

"We stage an attack." Slater's tone was calm, like he was discussing an ad buy. "Nothing serious. A scare, enough to get sympathy. People rally behind a candidate who's 'under threat.' It's a classic tactic."

Vic blinked, unable to hide his shock. "You want me to get shot? What the fuck is wrong with you?" His voice came out harsh and incredulous, disbelief twisting his features.

Slater didn't even flinch. He leaned forward, his steely calm more unnerving than ever. "Not *actually* shot," he said, his voice as cold and smooth as polished steel. "A near miss. A staged attempt. Something to make you look strong and sympathetic. Something to shift the narrative, rally support with you, and put Morales on defense."

Vic stared at him, the idea churning in his gut, both horrifying and perversely tempting. **"You're out of your goddamn mind,"** he muttered, but he knew Slater well enough to understand he wasn't joking. Not even a little.

Slater shook his head, unphased by Vic's reaction. "Not shot. Just rattled. A controlled incident—a graze if we get lucky, perhaps. Something that puts you on the front page, looking like a fighter. The press would eat it up. They always do."

Vic shook his head, pushing himself up from the desk, his face flushed with a mix of disbelief and anger. "That's insane, Rick. That's a line even I won't cross. Didn't know I had a line, but you goddamn found it," he said, his voice tight with barely restrained fury. "I'm not some puppet for you to wave around in front of the media."

Slater's expression didn't waver, but a flicker of annoyance crossed his eyes. "Think about it," he pressed. "Desperation calls for bold moves, and this would make you untouchable. Sympathy, strength—it'd be a game changer."

Vic leaned forward, hands braced on the desk, his jaw clenched. "I said *no*," he growled. "I'm not risking my life or dignity for some twisted PR stunt. You work for me, Rick. Remember that."

Slater's lips thinned, but he said nothing. The room hung heavy with tension, and both men were locked in a silent war of wills.

Slater's gaze remained steady, a dangerous glint in his eye. "Think about it, Vic. Desperate times, desperate measures. You're looking at losing to her. If you want to win, you must be willing to do what it takes."

Vic turned away, his heart pounding. The idea of staging an attack was the sort of thing he'd once mocked his opponents for. But now, the truth was sinking in—he was slipping, and Morales was close enough to taste victory. Could he stomach a loss?

As he paced, he caught his *Candidate Service* agent standing in the doorway. She looked between him and Slater, her face unreadable but her posture tense, as though she'd overheard more than she'd intended. For a moment, Vic felt a flash of paranoia. Could he trust her? The agents were supposed to be discreet and loyal to their charge. But the idea of this "attack"—even a fake one—would change everything.

After a beat, she spoke, her tone neutral. "Mr. Ross, we'll need to discuss your security detail for the upcoming appearances. We've received reports of increased online threats."

Vic nodded absently, the conversation leaving a bitter taste in his mouth. The agent's eyes flicked toward Slater for a moment, her face unreadable.

"I need time to think," Vic said finally, his voice rough. "Give me a few days."

Slater stood, straightening his jacket. "Take the time you need, but not too much. If we don't shift the momentum soon, it'll be over. And everything we've worked for will be wasted. We might all end up in prison; keep that in mind."

Without another word, he left, leaving Vic with only his drink and his thoughts. His agent stayed back, watching him carefully.

She cleared her throat, her voice steady. "Sir, I'd advise against anything that could appear… staged. Any incident, no matter how well you think it's controlled, has risks."

Vic glanced at her, surprised by her insight, and for a moment, he considered dismissing her. But something stopped him. She had been by his side for months, quiet, steady, professional. He poured another drink, her caution echoing in his mind.

"Noted, and remember your secrecy clause," Vic said after a long pause. The agent nodded, satisfied, and left him alone with the Scotch and the empty, gnawing fear he couldn't seem to shake. Vic slumped back into his chair, running a hand over his face. He had always prided himself on being willing to push boundaries, but even he had his limits. Still, his mind kept circling back to the situation at hand, desperately searching for a way to regain control.

He thought about the layers of protection his campaign had built. The NDAs every agent signed were no joke—tested all the way to the Supreme Court, ironclad as contracts could get, any breach would mean prison time and financial ruin. It gave him a twisted sort of comfort. There were still ways he could shield himself, people he could use, people he could trust to carry out sensitive tasks and keep their mouths shut.

His gaze shifted to the list of loyalists he kept tucked away, those he knew he could depend on even when things got ugly. His options were dwindling, but he wasn't out of moves just yet. Not by a long shot.

He sank back into his chair, staring out over the dark cityscape. As the alcohol burned its way down his throat, the question clawed at him: *What if Morales actually won?* If she took this from him, everything he'd built would be for nothing. His legacy and his career would all be shattered by a liberal woman who had no business challenging him.

He had spent his entire life preparing for this, climbing his way to the presidency, always with a clear path. Losing had never been an option. But now, as the polls tightened and the walls closed in, it was no longer a distant threat. Losing was dangerously, terrifyingly real.

And for the first time, he didn't know if he could handle it.

— 28 —

She stood at the edge of the small rally stage, the sun dipping low behind the mountains, casting the desert in warm hues of orange and red. Her campaign had taken her to places like this—towns most politicians only flew over, places where people still shook hands, where they still believed change was possible. And today, for the first time in weeks, Jen felt something she hadn't felt in months: hope.

The crowd was massive, and it needed to be at this stage. They were cheering, holding up signs with her name, and hanging on her every word. She could feel their energy, the way it fed her own. For too long, she had been fighting just to stay in the game, dodging the constant mud that Vic Ross and his team had thrown at her. But now, the tide was turning. The polls were tightening, and with every new report, she was closing in on him.

She smiled, waving to the crowd as they chanted her name. Nathan Carter, her running mate and longtime confidant, sidled up beside her with his trademark grin.

"Starting to feel real, huh?" he said, his voice low, so only she could hear.

Jen nodded, her heart swelling. "Yeah. I think we've got a real shot, Nathan."

"You don't think Ross is going to come back swinging?" Nathan asked, more seriously now, his eyes scanning the crowd. "He's been quiet the last few days, too quiet."

Jen shrugged. "Let him. The more desperate he gets, the more he shows the world who he really is."

Nathan chuckled, glancing over his shoulder as the crowd began to disperse. "You really believe that, or is that just campaign rhetoric?"

Jen turned to him, her smile soft but steady. "I believe it. He's a man on the edge, and people can see it. We just have to stay on course."

Nathan raised an eyebrow. "We stay on course, sure. But don't think for a second that means Ross won't try to burn everything down on his way out."

Meanwhile, across the same town, Vic Ross was staring at his television like a man watching his life unravel. His eyes were bloodshot, his tie loosened around his neck, and the room around him was littered with the detritus of too many late nights and too many drinks. Scotch bottles. Empty takeout containers. The remains of what had once been his campaign war room now felt more like the bunker of a man under siege.

On-screen, the latest poll numbers flashed. Morales was closing in, her gap shrinking with every day that passed. And no matter what his team threw at her, she just kept coming. Unstoppable.

Vic slammed his glass on the table, liquid splashing over the edge.

"She's a goddamn idealist!" he shouted to no one in particular. "People don't want that! They want reality. They want—"

"They want someone who's not falling apart on live TV," Slater's voice cut through the room, cool and unflappable as always. He stood in the doorway, arms crossed, a look of faint amusement on his face.

Vic glared at him. "You're enjoying this, aren't you? Watching me fall apart."

Slater shrugged, stepping further into the room. "If you weren't so drunk, you'd see what I see. She's gaining, yes. But we can still turn this around."

"Turn it around?" Vic spat. "How, Rick? You want me to get shot, remember? That's your big plan, you prick."

Slater's smile was thin, humorless. "It worked before, and not saying you need to take a bullet, but we need to shift the narrative. You're losing control of the story, Vic. And that's why you're losing ground."

Vic's eyes narrowed, his mind spinning. He'd been thinking about Slater's plan more than he cared to admit. A staged attack. It was reckless, dangerous even. But it had worked for candidates in the past. A small scare, nothing serious, could generate headlines that would bury Jen's rise in sympathy votes for him.

"We need something bigger," Vic muttered, pacing the room like a caged animal. "The VP idea isn't enough. We need something that puts me back in the spotlight and makes people remember why I'm the best option. Why they need me."

Slater raised an eyebrow. "So what are you saying?"

Vic stopped pacing, turning to face Slater fully. His eyes were wide, manic. "We do it."

Slater's expression didn't change, but his eyes gleamed with something like satisfaction. "Are you sure?"

"Yeah, I'm sure," Vic said, his voice almost trembling with the force of his own desperation. "But it has to be controlled. It can't be anything too serious—just enough to make people pay attention. Something that puts me back in their minds."

Slater smiled, a slow, deliberate smile that made Vic's skin crawl. **"Consider it done."**

Vic sat down heavily, his hands shaking as he reached for the bottle again. He didn't want to think about what he agreed to. All he knew was that he couldn't lose. Not to her. Not to a woman, and especially not to a woman like Morales.

Back in Morales' campaign headquarters, the mood was light, almost celebratory. Jen sat with her team in the war room, staring at the latest reports. Things were looking up. She could feel it—this slow, steady build of momentum. For the first time in a long time, they weren't just playing defense. They were on the attack.

Grace Howard, her sharp-tongued longtime volunteer turned communications director, leaned over the table, tapping on the polling numbers. "We're gaining in the Midwest, rural votes are trickling in, and the swing states look better. Ross is faltering a bit."

Jen smiled, a mix of exhaustion and hope coursing through her. "That's great news. But we can't get comfortable. He's going to hit back hard."

Grace snorted. "Let him. The guy's a wreck. I saw him on TV the other night, it looked like he hadn't slept in days. If this keeps up, he'll implode on his own."

Nathan chuckled from across the room, leaning back in his chair. "Ross has never dealt with real pressure like this before. He's been playing politics his whole life, but this? This is a real fight. And he's not handling it."

"I'm not counting him out yet," Jen said, her voice firm. "He's dangerous when he feels cornered."

Grace nodded, but her smile didn't falter. "Don't worry, we've got him. He's unraveling, and everyone can see it. All we need to do is stay steady and stay the course. People are tired of his brand of politics. They want change."

Jen nodded, but something in her gut still twisted. She couldn't afford to get too hopeful, not yet. Vic Ross was a snake; snakes could still strike when backed into a corner.

Across town, Vic Ross stood in front of the mirror in his bathroom, staring at his reflection. His face was gaunt, his eyes bloodshot. He looked older than he remembered, the stress of the campaign etched into every line and crease. The man in the mirror didn't look like a president. He looked like shit and a man losing control.

He splashed water on his face, trying to sober up, but the alcohol still buzzed in his veins. His heart pounded, the adrenaline from his decision earlier still coursing through him. He was going to go through with it. Slater was setting it up now—a staged attack, something small but dramatic.

It felt like madness, but at that moment, madness was all he had left. He couldn't lose. He wouldn't lose. Not to Morales. The very thought of her winning, of him having to stand on that stage and concede to her, made him sick.

"This is what it takes," he muttered to his reflection. "This is what it takes to win."

As he stared at his own face, he didn't notice how thin his voice sounded, how close he was to breaking.

— 29 —

The dimly lit room in Vic Ross's campaign headquarters was filled with the sharp clicks of fingers on keyboards, phones buzzing nonstop, and the low hum of too many exhausted staffers working late into the night. It had been this way for weeks—an unrelenting grind to keep Vic afloat in the face of Morales' unexpected rise. But tonight, something was different. Something was wrong.

Vic's phone buzzed on his desk. He ignored it, still nursing the remnants of a hangover from the night before. The constant stream of bad news had been chipping away at him, and the Scotch he'd downed to keep his nerves steady was doing less and less to calm him these days. But this buzz was different. Persistent.

Another buzz. Another. Then, the screen lit up with a message from his cybersecurity team – **Urgent, you need to see this.**

Vic's stomach tightened as he reached for the phone. A sense of dread settled over him. He clicked on the message, and immediately, his blood ran cold.

"We've been hacked."

His head pounded. The room seemed to spin briefly, but the words on the screen were unmistakable.

A second message followed. "It's bad. We're being held for ransom. They want fucking money!"

Vic dropped the phone, his hands shaking as his mind raced. Hackers. The campaign had been hacked. His campaign. How the hell had this happened? How had they let this happen?

Storming out of his office, he found Slater and several senior staffers huddled around a laptop, their faces lit by the blue glow of the screen. They looked up as he entered, eyes wide with panic.

Slater met Vic's gaze with his usual ice-cold demeanor. "They got in through someone's phone. One of the interns. They accessed campaign emails, text messages… everything."

Vic's heart pounded in his chest. "Everything?"

Slater nodded. "Everything."

Vic clenched his fists, his body buzzing with a mix of fear and fury. He slammed his hand down on the table, making everyone jump. "How the hell did this happen? We were supposed to have the best cybersecurity in the game!"

"It was a mobile breach," Slater said, barely flinching. "They came in through someone's unsecured personal phone."

"Vic's voice was rising, his face flushing with anger. "You're telling me some intern's phone cost us our entire campaign? What the fuck?!"

"Not necessarily." Slater's voice remained calm, maddeningly so. "But it's bad. They're demanding $1,119,999.99 within the next three days, or they'll release everything."

Vic froze. He stared at Slater as if the man had lost his mind. "Are you saying we're going to pay these bastards?"

"No, well, yes," Slater said coolly. "But we need to think strategically. We need to see exactly what they have and plan for the worst. If we play this right, we can control the narrative."

Vic grabbed the nearest chair and sank into it, running a hand over his face. His mind raced. "Control the narrative? Control the fucking narrative? Slater, you were born saying, "Control the narrative,"

What could be in those emails? Those texts?" He paused, his eyes narrowing as he leaned forward. "What about the personal stuff, Rick? What about the deals?"

Slater didn't flinch. "It'll all come out unless we're smart."

Meanwhile, elsewhere, Nathan sat in his car, staring at the message on his phone: **"Transfer confirmed—IT's handled; cleaned."** His jaw tightened as he read it, the words reverberating like a warning. Without hesitation, he deleted the app from his burner phone, ensuring no trace remained. For a long moment, he gripped the steering wheel, his mind racing. He wasn't sure how far this would spiral—or if he'd be caught in the fallout.

Vic stood abruptly, pacing back and forth like a caged animal. "Goddamn it. And Morales? Is she dealing with this?"

"She's been ready for this for months," Slater said, his voice clipped. "Her campaign's been talking about cybersecurity since day one. She fortified her digital walls like no one before after the incompetent Russians breached them."

Vic slammed his fist against the wall. Morales had anticipated this, while his own team had let their guard down. The thought of her sitting in her cozy little headquarters, secure in the knowledge that her campaign was clean, made his blood boil.

"Get someone on this now," Vic growled. "I want to know who did it. I want them found, and I want them stopped. You hear me?"

The next morning, things went from bad to worse. Vic's possible VP pick, Senator Tom Whitmore, had already proven to be a liability, but today, he managed to outdo himself.

Whitmore had gone off script at a rally in front of a crowd of fervent supporters. He always did, but this time was different. Standing at the podium, he began making casual remarks about Vic's policies, weaving in a dangerous mix of charm and subtle defiance. He criticized Vic's aggressive foreign policy approach, hinting that "strength can be shown without recklessness." The crowd hung on his every word, but there was an unmistakable edge to his rhetoric, a simmering discontent he seemed eager to ignite.

Then, in a moment that left even the most seasoned campaign staffers stunned, Whitmore crossed a line no one could have anticipated. He made an unbelievable comment, referencing a "strategy" from history that had kept order, speaking in an almost admiring tone. The reference was unmistakable—a jaw-dropping nod to the authoritarian control tactics used by the Nazis. The crowd, hungry for strongman rhetoric and patriotic fervor, erupted in wild applause, the roar deafening. They didn't seem to care about the dark implications—only that someone spoke with bold, unfiltered confidence.

Whitmore, oblivious or unconcerned, kept talking, riding the crowd's energy. But everyone in the campaign knew this moment was a disaster. Jen heard about it and knew she couldn't afford to leave the comment unchallenged.

Behind the stage, Vic stood frozen, his face a mask of barely contained rage. He could feel the anger boiling over. How many times had they discussed this? How many times had he told Whitmore to stay on message and to toe the line? But here he was, in front of the cameras, publicly undermining Vic on key issues—and, for God's sake, referencing Nazi strategies. What a fucking mess, yet again.

The media ran with it instantly, turning the moment into a firestorm. Outlets across the spectrum lit up, analyzing, condemning, and dissecting Whitmore's words. Within hours, it became a viral spectacle, overshadowing everything else Vic's campaign had planned for the day. As the chaos unfolded, it was clear that Whitmore's off-script remarks had created a scandal Vic couldn't easily shake—and might not survive unscathed.

"Senator, are you saying you don't fully support Ross's tax plan? What about his foreign policy approach—do you think it's too aggressive unless done like Nazi Germany?" a reporter shouted, the microphones closing in.

Whitmore, ever the fool, tried to backpedal. "No, no, it's not that I don't support Vic," he said, laughing awkwardly. "I just think we need to have more conversations about these things, you know? Vic and I… well, we don't always agree on everything, but that makes this partnership strong."

Later that evening, in the privacy of Vic's office, Whitmore groveled like a man begging for his life.

"Vic, I didn't mean it like that," Whitmore stammered, his face pale with desperation. "You know how it is, right? I was just trying to—"

"Shut up," Vic snarled, standing with his hands clenched into fists. "You're a goddamn disaster, Tom. Do you realize what you've done? Do you have any idea how much damage you've just caused?"

Whitmore's eyes were wide, his mouth working, but no words came out. He had seen Vic angry before, but never like this.

"I've got a campaign hanging by a thread," Vic continued, his voice rising. "A goddamn hack that could destroy us at any moment, and you're out there disagreeing with me like we're running two different campaigns!"

"I—" Whitmore began, but Vic cut him off again.

"You've been screwing up from the start, and now you've given the media exactly what they want—a divided ticket with me and a Nazi lover. How the hell am I supposed to fix this, Tom? How?"

Whitmore's voice cracked as he muttered, "I'm sorry, Vic. I'm so sorry, and I'll fix it and apologize publicly. I'll go on record, I'll do interviews, I'll—"

"You'll do nothing," Vic spat, his voice trembling with fury. "You'll shut up, and you'll stay out of the public eye until I decide otherwise. You've embarrassed me for the last time, Tom."

Whitmore's eyes watered, his hands trembling as he clutched his briefcase. "I—I'll fix it. I swear."

Vic turned away, his hands gripping the back of his chair so hard his knuckles turned white. "Get out, Tom. Before I say something, then kill you, sort of like you've done to my campaign. Leave."

Whitmore hesitated, but one look at Vic's face told him there was no point in arguing. He slunk out of the office, leaving Vic alone with his rage.

As the door clicked shut, Vic sank into his chair, grabbing the bottle of Scotch from his desk. His hand shook as he poured himself another glass. Everything was falling apart. The hack. The ransom. His own possible VP turning on him in both policy and common fucking sense. Even if you like Nazi whatever, you don't tell people, goddamnit. Morales gaining ground every day.

And now? Now, he was forced to change again, scrambling to salvage his campaign from the brink of disaster. Another incompetent VP pick, another crisis threatening to unravel everything he'd built. Vic clenched his fists, the frustration mounting with each passing second. The campaign felt like it was teetering on the edge of collapse, held together by a threadbare web of damage control and increasingly desperate measures.

How had it come to this? He'd built a platform on strength and invincibility, but every time he clawed his way back to control, something—or someone—ripped it from his grasp. The mistakes, the scandals, the rogue comments—it was all spiraling, and Vic was beginning to feel like he was fighting a losing battle, the walls closing in from every side.

He downed the drink in one long swallow, the burn barely registering anymore. His mind raced, scrambling for solutions, for any way out of this mess. He needed to regain control. He needed to stop the bleeding.

And fast.

But how?

Vic grabbed the bottle, pouring another drink with unsteady hands. As he stared at the amber liquid, one thought echoed through his mind: **Whatever it takes.**

He slammed the glass down and snatched up his phone, firing off a message to Slater: **"Get Jok Industries CEO to pay the ransom TODAY, off the books!"**

— 30 —

Vic Ross sat behind his desk, his head swimming with a cocktail of rage, paranoia, and Scotch as his campaign crumbled. His possible VP, Senator Tom Whitmore, was the latest in many disasters. Whitmore's position had become untenable after the public gaffe at the rally. His latest screw-up had pushed the campaign to the brink, and now Vic was ready to cut him loose.

But how?

And now? Now he was forced to change again, scrambling to salvage his campaign from the brink of disaster. Another incompetent VP pick, another crisis threatening to unravel everything he'd built. Vic clenched his fists, the frustration mounting with each passing second. The campaign felt like it was teetering on the edge of collapse, held together by a threadbare web of damage control and increasingly desperate measures.

Thank God he had waited to announce the VP past the 40-day rule. That small act of restraint had bought him a lifeline. The idea had come up in one of their late-night strategy sessions—quietly swapping out the possible VP with someone stronger, someone who could get the base excited again. But removing Whitmore in the middle of a campaign wasn't simple. There had to be a reason, a story. And in the world of politics, nothing was too sacred to be sacrificed for the right narrative.

Vic gritted his teeth. How had it come to this? He'd built a platform on strength and invincibility, but every time he seemed to regain control, something—or someone—knocked it out of his grasp. The mistakes, the scandals, the rogue comments—it was all spiraling, and Vic was beginning to feel like he was fighting a losing battle, the walls closing in from every side.

Slater leaned against the wall, arms crossed, watching as Vic paced the room. His calm demeanor grated on Vic's nerves, especially given the chaos they were in. The polling numbers weren't just slipping; they were plummeting. Morales was gaining ground in states Vic had never worried about before. This wasn't supposed to happen. Morales was never supposed to be a threat.

"We need him gone," Vic muttered, rubbing his temples as the pressure of the decision weighed on him. "But it has to be clean. We can't have a scandal. Not with the hack hanging over us."

Slater's expression remained unreadable. "I've been thinking about that. There's a way to make him disappear without it looking like we're pushing him out."

Vic raised an eyebrow. "How?"

Slater pushed off the wall and walked over to the desk. He leaned down slightly, lowering his voice as if what he was about to say required secrecy. "We stage a medical event. Something serious. We make it look like Whitmore's health permanently forces him out of the campaign."

Vic stopped pacing, his mind racing with the possibilities. "A medical event?"

"Heart attack. Stroke. Whatever feels plausible," Slater said with a shrug. "It's not hard to set up. We bring in a doctor on the payroll and make it look convincing. Whitmore steps down for his health, we issue a statement and boom—he's gone. The media and public buy it, and we replace him with someone more capable. Clean. No scandal. No backlash."

Vic stared at Slater, his heart pounding. The idea was dark, manipulative—but it could work. Whitmore was a weak link, and they needed him gone. But faking a medical event? It felt like a new low, even for him.

"And Whitmore?" Vic asked quietly. "He goes along with it?"

Slater's smile was thin. "He doesn't have a choice. He's screwed up too many times. We clarify that this is the only way to protect his reputation. He'll take it."

Vic sat down heavily, rubbing his face. His mind raced through the potential fallout. It was twisted, but it could save the campaign. Still, something about it didn't sit right with him. Faking a man's medical emergency to win an election? He poured himself a glass of Scotch, his hand trembling as he raised it to his lips.

"I'll talk to him, give him no choice in the matter," Vic said, finally, the words coming out slow and reluctantly. "Set it up."

It didn't take long for Whitmore to agree. When Slater presented the plan, the senator protested at first—his objections barely lasted thirty seconds. "You can't be serious," he'd sputtered, but the defiance quickly crumbled under the weight of Slater's unwavering stare. A few direct threats, a reminder of the catastrophic damage Whitmore had already done to the campaign, and his resistance evaporated.

The plan was simple, if grotesque: a staged heart attack at Whitmore's home or maybe a speaking event. Just believable enough to sideline him permanently, sparing the campaign from further embarrassment. Whitmore swallowed his pride, nodding numbly as he realized he had no other choice. The senator's reputation would be shattered, but at least he'd avoid a harsher political or personal downfall.

Slater's expression remained ice-cold. "It's better this way," he said, his voice devoid of sympathy. And just like that, the machinery of the campaign ground forward, prepared to manufacture yet another cover story to save Vic's sinking ship.

The wheels began turning immediately. Within hours, they had a doctor on the payroll, ready to certify the "incident" when it happened. Statements were drafted and ready to be released after the news broke. Whitmore's exit was inevitable; within days, Vic would be free of the albatross around his neck.

But a new complication arose just when Vic thought they'd managed to pull off the perfect maneuver.

It came in the form of a rumor. One of Slater's operatives—a man whose job it was to keep tabs on everyone close to the campaign— brought it up in a private meeting late that night.

"Tom's talking to someone," the operative said, his voice low. "He's been meeting with a ghostwriter. Someone he trusts. There's talk of a book."

Vic's stomach dropped. He turned slowly to face the man. "A book?"

The operative nodded. "Yeah. From what I've gathered, it's about everything that's happened during the campaign. He's planning to tell his side of the story, spin his gaffes, maybe even drag you through the mud to save his own skin."

Vic's vision blurred for a moment, a white-hot rage flooding his system. A book? After everything they'd done for Whitmore, after they'd crafted this clean exit for him, the bastard was going to turn on them.

Slater was silent, watching Vic carefully. "It's bad," he said finally, his voice tight. "If he writes that book, it's over for you. Everything could come out. The deals. The hack. Every decision you've made."

Vic slammed his fist on the desk, the glass of Scotch nearly toppling over. "We can't let that happen. He can't be allowed to——"

"There's a solution," Slater interrupted, his eyes narrowing. "But it's...extreme."

Vic froze, his breath catching in his throat. He knew what Slater was about to suggest, and he wasn't sure he wanted to hear it.

Slater's voice was quiet, almost cold. "We could make it look like Whitmore took his own life. A final act of desperation. The pressure of the campaign got to him. The heart attack was too much. The man couldn't handle the shame."

The room was silent momentarily, the words hanging in the air like a loaded gun.

Vic stared at Slater, his mind reeling. "Are you out of your mind? We can't kill him, Rick!"

Slater didn't flinch. "We wouldn't kill him. It would be staged. suicide, his own poor choice. It would solve all our problems. He wouldn't be around to write the book, and you'd come out of this looking sympathetic. The media would rally behind you."

Vic felt sick. The idea was too dark, too twisted even for him. But as he sat there, staring at his drink, the panic began to creep in. If Whitmore really were planning a book, if those emails and text messages came out, his career would be over. The thought of losing to Morales, of having his entire life's work destroyed by one weak link, was unbearable.

"I can't," Vic muttered, shaking his head. "I won't do it."

But even as he said the words, a part of him was already considering it. His grip tightened around the glass. If Whitmore turned on him, he was finished. Everything would be ruined.

Slater watched him carefully. "Think about it, Vic. If that book comes out, you're done, and we might all end up in prison at some point. This is the only way to ensure he doesn't turn on you."

Vic didn't respond. He couldn't. He poured himself another drink instead, trying to drown out the voice in his head that told him Slater was right.

A week later, Vic found himself far away from the chaos of the campaign, holed up in his private cabin at Lake Tahoe. The fresh mountain air did little to soothe the storm inside him, and neither did the company.

He had flown in an adult entertainer for the weekend—an old habit he indulged in whenever the pressure became too much. She was beautiful, paid to be discreet, and exactly what he needed to escape the nightmare his life had become. But this weekend was different. Vic was on edge, spiraling deeper into paranoia with every passing hour.

As the two of them lounged on the deck, a soft breeze blowing off the lake, Vic lit a cigar, staring blankly at the water. The woman, whose name he'd already forgotten, looked up at him through half-lidded eyes.

"You seem tense," she said, her voice smooth, practiced.

Vic gave a dry laugh. "You have no idea."

She smiled, leaning closer, her hand brushing his leg. "I've got something that might help. Take the edge off."

Vic raised an eyebrow, "Blow or hand job?"

She laughed as she pulled a small pill bottle from her purse. "Adderall," she said, popping one of the pills into her mouth with practiced ease. "Helps with focus, you know? Keeps the mind sharp." Her grin turned sly. "And it gets you past most drug tests."

Vic smirked, caught off guard by her candor, but she just shrugged, unbothered. The campaign trail was brutal, and everyone had their coping mechanisms. Still, the casualness with which she admitted it made him wonder just how many corners people were willing to cut to keep up in this relentless game.

Vic hesitated for a moment, then reached for the bottle. He'd heard about it before—politicians, CEOs, and athletes all used it to keep going when the pressure got too intense. He was under more pressure than any of them. What could it hurt?

He swallowed the pill dry, feeling a strange mix of anticipation and guilt settle in his gut. It wasn't like this was his first time dabbling in stimulants—hell, he'd done speed in the past, and more than his fair share of dick pills too. A prude he was not.

But here, on the campaign trail, the stakes felt higher, the desperation more palpable. The pill promised clarity, focus, and a way to keep pushing forward in this brutal, high-stakes race. Yet beneath that rush of anticipation was a gnawing sense of self-awareness, a whisper reminding him just how far he was willing to go to stay on top.

As the sun set over the lake, Vic stared out at the water, his mind buzzing with possibilities. Adderall was already kicking in, sharpening his thoughts, giving him a razor-sharp clarity he hadn't felt in weeks. He loved the feeling—everything seemed clearer, every solution more within reach.

Sure, everything was falling apart: the campaign, the polling numbers, the scandals that refused to die. But there was still time to fix it. He just had to be willing to go further than anyone else, push the boundaries harder, and play the game dirtier.

Vic's pulse quickened with the thought. Maybe, just maybe, salvaging his future meant doing things he'd never imagined himself doing. Things that would make even the most cutthroat of his allies hesitate. Because winning was everything, and if he had to cross lines he'd once thought sacred, well... he'd already crossed so many. What were a few more?

— 31 —

He sat in the dim light of his office, the glow from his computer casting long shadows across his face. His eyes were bloodshot, his skin sallow. Vic hadn't slept well in weeks, not since the poll numbers had started to turn. Worse still, the money was drying up. The reality that his once-unshakable campaign was running low on funds gnawed at him. This wasn't supposed to happen. He was supposed to be untouchable, unstoppable.

Jen Morales, meanwhile, was enjoying her best fundraising month yet. Reports had come in just that morning—her campaign had raised more in the last thirty days than in the entire previous quarter via the nonprofit channels. Grassroots donations were pouring in, and the media couldn't stop talking about it. The story was everywhere: ***"Morales campaign set a new record."***

It made Vic sick to his stomach. He'd spent his life building wealth, trading on the idea that he was the financial genius America needed. Yet here he was, scrambling for cash.

Slater's voice cut through his thoughts on speaker as Vic leaned against the desk, tapping his phone. "We're going to need to make up ground, Vic," Slater said, his tone as hard as ever. "We're starting to look in the coffee cans for cash—the coffers are almost dry. If we don't raise serious money in the next two weeks, we're finished."

Vic turned away from the lake, the clarity from the Adderall merging with a pulse of anxiety. Money had always been the lifeblood of the campaign, and now the reserves were dangerously low. He knew Slater wasn't exaggerating; if the funds dried up, so did his shot at salvaging everything he'd worked for.

Vic clenched his jaw, considering the implications. "We'll find the cash," he muttered, more to himself than to Slater. But even as he said it, the adrenaline pumping through his veins made him wonder how far he was willing to go to make sure of it.

Vic's jaw clenched. "I'm well aware of that, Rick. What do you think I'm doing, sitting here twiddling my thumbs right up my own ass?"

Slater didn't flinch. "We need ideas. Big ones," he said, his voice low and unyielding. "Your network's tapped out—people are tired of hearing the same old pitch. The fundraising rules are fucking us up, and your donors aren't used to this level of transparency. They don't like being put under a microscope."

He paused, frustration etched across his face. "Meanwhile, Morales is raking it in. She's got a narrative, a cause people believe in. Nonprofits are funneling support her way, and she's made herself look like something new and exciting. A real movement. You? They see you as the establishment—old news, part of the problem. We need something to change that perception fast, or we're dead in the water."

Vic's pulse quickened as Slater's words sank in. Adderall made everything feel sharper and more urgent, and the pressure was suffocating. He had always relied on his reputation and connections, but now they felt like anchors dragging him under. Morales had hope and momentum; he had history and baggage. If they didn't come up with something game-changing—and soon—everything he'd built would crumble.

Vic's hands curled into fists. The *establishment.* That word made his blood boil. He wasn't some washed-up old senator or career bureaucrat. He'd built his life on inherited wealth and turned it into an empire. At least, that's what he told himself. He had been born with money, yes, but he liked to think he'd made it grow through his own ingenuity. Though, if he was honest, it was more luck than skill. He'd made a few fortunate investments, leveraged his family's connections, and somehow managed to package it as his personal genius.

But the campaign needed cash now, not clever branding.

Slater swiped on his phone, then texted a screenshot to Vic, his eyes narrowing with calculated intensity. "We've lined up some opportunities," he said. "First, you're doing fifty one-on-one meet-and-greets. We're charging $150,000 a head. Should bring in around $7,500,000, all funneled through a nonprofit, all by the book."

Vic rubbed his temples, feeling the weight of every dollar they needed to pull in. But Slater wasn't finished.

"And listen," Slater added, his voice dropping lower. "Certain donors are bringing hard cash. We don't have a choice anymore. $7.5M legit, $10.7 million in bags. It's risky as hell, but if we don't push this, we're finished."

Vic swallowed, the tension crawling up his spine. Slater heard the hesitation and pressed on. "Look," he said, voice hard, "if you win, we've got pardons lined up if we ever get caught. Safety nets. But if you lose, for the twentieth goddamn time, I am someone's bitch in federal prison, and so are you. We're all doing time. You think they'll go easy on us? You think the feds will look the other way?" He shook his head. "We don't have room for second thoughts. This is it, Vic. It's a win, or it's prison."

Vic's mouth went dry. The stakes had never felt so high, the consequences so crushingly real. Every decision was a gamble with his freedom, future, and life. And with Slater's words echoing from the speaker, he knew just how thin the line between victory and ruin had become.

Vic groaned. He hated these meet-and-greets—the forced smiles, the endless small talk, pretending to care about what the donors had to say. But the campaign was hemorrhaging money, and he had no choice.

"Fine," Vic muttered. "What else?"

"You've been approached by a company to do something... different. They want to mint a special edition silver coin—your face on one side, the American flag on the other. Uncirculated, collector's item. They'll pay $10 million up-front, plus 15% of all sales. It's personal money, but you could loan it to the campaign if it comes to that."

Vic blinked, disbelief etched across his face. "A coin? Are you serious?" He let out a bitter laugh, running a hand through his hair. "I'm now even more of a whore. Fuck me!"

Slater didn't even flinch but was glad a phone was between them. He'd seen Vic at his breaking point before, and this wasn't far from it.

But the brutal truth was, there was no time for pride, no room for indignation. Vic's shoulders sagged slightly, the weight of it all pressing down harder than ever. Everything—the fundraising, the shady cash deals, the relentless pressure—had turned him into something he hardly recognized. But there was no backing out now.

"As serious as it gets," Slater replied. "It's tacky, sure. But patriotic memorabilia sells, especially to the crowd you're trying to energize. Think of it as a way to make a quick million, with more to come. You're essentially selling your image."

Vic put his head in his hand and felt a headache coming on. A silver coin with his face on it. Jesus. But $10 million up-front was no small thing. The campaign might be in trouble, but his personal wealth was still substantial, having grown over the years from a series of fortunate investments. He could afford to loan the money to his campaign if needed.

And that was the other thing that gnawed at him. People talked about his wealth as if it had been carefully cultivated through hard work and brilliance, but he knew better. He'd been lucky, born into a fortune, and had only grown through a few decent investments. But luck could only get him so far. He packaged it as a genius, of course— his public persona required that. But behind closed doors, Vic Ross knew his success had come more from privilege and good fortune than any real skill.

He sighed, reaching for the Scotch on his desk. "Fine. I'll do the coin. God help me."

Slater grinned. "I knew you'd see reason. Call you later with details."

By two mornings later, no more Lake Tahoe, wheels were in motion. Vic's campaign schedule had been packed with private meet-and-greet events, each one more grueling than the last. They were exhausting, soulless affairs where he had to stand in some wealthy donor's mansion, schmoozing with people who barely knew anything about politics but loved to feel important.

The first event was in two days. Vic grimaced at the thought of it.

Then there was the coin. The idea still felt ridiculous—his face plastered on a silver disc, being sold as a patriotic keepsake to people who thought owning it made them more American. But the money was real, and the company behind the coin had already wired the $10 million to Vic's personal account. He could tap into it if the campaign needed an emergency cash injection.

The shifts in campaign fundraising had been drastic, but not all unwelcome. The chaos forced them to pivot, tapping into unconventional sources and leveraging discreet back channels that hadn't been considered before. It wasn't just about survival—it was an opportunity. If handled correctly, these new avenues could open lucrative doors, creating alliances with power players who value discretion as much as results. Vic thought to himself, if they played their cards right, this mess could become more than a crisis.

Vic leaned back in his chair, staring out the window as the city skyline glimmered in the afternoon sun. The money would keep the campaign afloat for now, but it wouldn't solve the real problem. Morales was outpacing him not just in fundraising but in momentum. Every day, it seemed like her lead grew, while his campaign felt like it was stuck in quicksand. His stomach churned as he thought about it— losing to her. Jen Morales. It was unthinkable.

A woman. A liberal minority woman with no national money before the start of the campaign, no less. Vic's grip tightened on the arm of his chair. How had she, of all people, become a real threat?

Slater had been right about one thing, though: people loved Morales's narrative. She was new, fresh, a candidate of hope and change. It reminded Vic too much of another election not too long ago when people rallied behind a different kind of change. He'd scoffed at it back then, thinking it was a passing phase. But here it was again, breathing down his neck, threatening everything he'd worked for.

His phone buzzed. A message from the fundraising team.

First meet-and-greet set for tomorrow night. 15 guests. It should net an extra $1,225,000.

Vic grimaced but replied, "Got it."

He closed his eyes, trying to push the anxiety away. This was temporary. The meet-and-greets would raise enough money to keep the campaign going for a few more weeks, and if the coins sold well, there would be even more to fall back on. He could still turn this around.

But somewhere in the back of his mind, a dark thought whispered that it wouldn't be enough. Morales was pulling too far ahead, and she had captured the country's imagination in a way he never could. He had spent his life controlling the narrative—his own and everyone else's—packaging himself as the visionary America needed, as the man with the answers. Yet no matter how he spun it, how much he poured into the campaign coffers, the tide seemed to be turning against him.

And for the first time in his career, Vic Ross wondered if he might actually lose.

He stared at the Scotch on his desk, the amber liquid catching the faint light of his office. He had money. More than he could ever spend in a lifetime. His inheritance, carefully disguised as self-made wealth, had given him a cushion most could only dream of. But no amount of inherited fortune, no silver coins stamped with his face, and no endless parade of private meet-and-greets with wealthy donors would save him if he lost this election.

Lately, losing has felt more real than ever.

The Scotch sat untouched. His hand didn't reach for the glass like it usually did. Not anymore. Not since he'd found something better—something that didn't drown his mind in a haze but instead gave it razor-sharp focus. He hadn't slept more than three hours a night in weeks, but thanks to his new friend, Adderall, he didn't need to. The pills kept him going, kept the dark cloud of exhaustion from pulling him under. They kept him sharp, alert, and ready to fight another day.

Vic had been introduced to Adderall on a whim. What had started as a weekend of blowing off steam in Tahoe—a hazy, indulgent escape from the relentless pressure of the campaign—had turned into something far more dangerous. "A couple of pills to stay sharp," she had said, her voice playful but convincing, her smile smooth and knowing.

Vic had laughed at first, brushing it off as something for sleep-deprived college students, not a man vying for the highest office in the country. But desperation is a powerful motivator. The weight of speeches, strategy sessions, and the constant feeling of running on empty had eroded his better judgment. And something about her confident, almost seductive assurance had convinced him to try.

The effect had been immediate. A clarity he hadn't felt in years. The mental fog that had plagued him lifted, and suddenly, his thoughts—once racing and tangled—were ordered and precise. Hell, his dick got hard all by itself for the first time in fifteen years, a bizarre and unexpected side effect he almost found amusing. The exhaustion that had been clawing at him for months vanished, replaced by a laser-like focus that felt like a superpower.

Sleep became an afterthought. The pills pushed him through endless nights of strategy meetings, hours of poring over poll numbers, and grueling fundraising events. He didn't need rest; he needed action. Three hours of sleep a night was more than enough now. Adderall kept him sharp, and he felt unstoppable for the first time in ages. But deep down, he knew there was a cost—a line he'd crossed that he couldn't uncross.

But the trade-off was slowly becoming apparent. The clarity came at a cost. There were nights when his heart raced so fast he thought it might pound out of his chest. His hands would shake, and there was a gnawing pit in his stomach that wouldn't go away, no matter how much he ate or drank. The paranoia, always lurking at the edges of his mind, grew sharper, too. The pills kept him awake, but they also kept his fear awake—the fear that Morales was too far ahead, that his money wouldn't be enough, that the walls were closing in on him.

He felt it now, sitting alone in his office—the gnawing fear, the creeping certainty that even with all his money, connections, and so-called genius, he might not be able to turn this around. He leaned forward, rubbing his temples, willing the dizziness to ease.

But the dark thoughts only got louder.

What if this was it? What if, after everything, he ended up a failure? A punchline? The man who couldn't beat some idealistic woman who had no business being in the same race as him. The man who couldn't hold onto the narrative, who let it slip through his fingers like water, leaving nothing but shame behind?

He reached for the pill bottle on his desk, shaking out two more Adderall. His hand trembled as he swallowed them dry. He told himself he needed them, that they were the only thing keeping him from losing control. The focus would come back. It had to. He'd stay awake as long as it took, plan as hard as necessary, and claw his way back into the lead. He had to.

The only side effects from the drug were dizziness, sleeplessness, and almost shitting himself daily, so far anyway.

But even as he stared out the window at the dark city skyline, Vic felt something he hadn't felt in years: the cold, creeping sensation of defeat. It was still a whisper, quiet and distant, but it grew louder daily.

For the first time, Vic Ross felt like the walls were closing in on him. And this time, he didn't know how to stop them.

— 32 —

Jen Morales leaned back in her chair, rubbing the back of her neck. The tension that had knotted her muscles for months was starting to loosen, but the campaign was far from over. The polls were closing in her favor, donations were flowing, and the momentum that her team had hoped for was finally becoming a reality. But one thing was still eluding them: the debate.

"He's dodging us," Grace Howard, her communications director, said with a frustrated edge to her voice. She was pacing the room like a caged animal, her sharp eyes scanning the map of swing states plastered across the wall. "We've pushed for it for weeks, but Ross keeps weaseling from any real conversation about debating you. If he keeps this up, we'll never get him on stage."

"He's scared," Nathan Carter, her running mate, said from the other side of the room. He had his feet propped up on the table, scrolling through the latest polling data. "He knows you'd wipe the floor with him. That's why his team is stalling. They don't want to risk you showing him up."

Jen exhaled slowly, feeling the weight of the race press down on her. Things were going well, but she wasn't naïve. Ross wasn't going to make this easy. Every step forward in the polls had been hard-fought, and while she knew the public was turning against him, she could feel the danger of overconfidence creeping in. They had to keep pushing. She had to keep pushing.

"We need that debate," Jen said, sitting up straight. "We've gained ground, but the public must see us on stage together. They need to see the contrast, and more importantly, they need to see him sweat."

Nathan grinned. "Oh, he'll sweat all right. Once you're standing there calmly answering questions and he's floundering, the voters will see who's the real leader."

Grace stopped pacing and faced them. "The problem is he's playing it safe. He knows that if he keeps dodging, his base will stay with him, and he won't lose ground in key areas. We need to push him into a corner."

Jen frowned. "We've already tried negotiating the debate rules with his team, but they keep throwing up roadblocks. What else can we do?"

Grace's eyes lit up with the kind of fierce determination that always made Jen wary but impressed simultaneously. "We take it public. We start framing the narrative that *he's* the one avoiding you. Go on every network, give interviews, and clarify that you've been ready to debate for months, but Ross has been hiding behind his handlers. He hates being seen as weak, and once the media runs with that angle, he'll have no choice but to agree."

Jen leaned back, considering the idea. It was risky. If they pushed too hard, Ross could double down on avoiding the debate, making it look like they were the desperate ones. But if it worked—if they could force Ross to confront her on stage—it could be the game-changer they needed.

"I like it," Nathan said, sitting up straighter. "If we control the narrative, we control the debate. We can frame him as a coward, afraid to face the future of this country. He won't be able to resist. His ego's too big for that."

"Exactly," Grace agreed. "We'll start with a few targeted interviews, plant the seed in the media's mind, and watch it grow. When we're done, Ross will beg to debate you just to prove he's not scared."

Jen nodded, feeling a surge of confidence. "Let's do it. If he wants to play games, we'll show him how it's done."

Grace was already texting the media team. "Consider it done. Ross won't know what hit him."

Two days later, the headlines started rolling in.

—Why Won't Ross Debate Morales? Is He Afraid to Face Her on Stage?

—Morales Pushes for a Debate, but Ross Stays Silent.

—Is Ross Dodging a Debate with Morales? What is wrong with him?

Jen watched as the media narrative began to shift. Every interview she gave, every soundbite her team released, played into the idea that Ross was hiding, avoiding her. The press quickly picked up on the angle, and soon, it was everywhere.

The pressure was mounting, and Jen could feel the momentum building even faster now. People were talking about the debate as if it was inevitable, and Ross looked weaker every day he refused to commit.

Her campaign was firing on all cylinders. The fundraising continued to surge, her team was motivated, and the public was rallying behind her.

Jen paused for a moment. "Nathan, can you check in with Diego and the tech team? They've been unusually quiet, and I want to know what's going on over there."

Let me know if you'd like further tweaks!

But she couldn't shake the feeling that Ross had something up his sleeve. He wasn't the type to let himself be pushed around, and Jen knew better than to underestimate him. They were close to securing the debate, but they weren't there yet.

And in politics, nothing was certain until it happened.

By the end of the week, the pressure on Ross had reached a boiling point. News outlets were running stories about his reluctance to debate Morales, and social media was filled with mocking posts about his "fear" of facing her.

Finally, after days of silence, Ross's campaign issued a statement.

—**"We are pleased to confirm that a debate between Governor Ross and Ms. Morales will occur later this month. Details to follow."**

Jen allowed herself a small smile as she read the statement. They had him.

"Get ready," Grace said, standing behind her. "You're about to tear him apart on live television."

Jen took a deep breath. The debate was on, and now all she had to do was win it.

— 33 —

Vic Ross stood at the edge of the stage, the bright lights casting harsh shadows across his face. The crowd's roar reverberated around the rally arena, but his mind was elsewhere. His campaign speeches had become automatic by now—well-practiced lines delivered with just enough confidence and fire to stir the base. But today, he wasn't thinking about his words. Today, he was thinking about the end of Tom Whitmore's political career and life.

The heat from the stage lights bore down on him as he glanced to his left, where Whitmore stood, nervously clutching the edges of the podium. The man was sweating more than usual, his face pale and drawn. He looked like he was on the verge of collapse—and that was exactly what Vic needed.

Tom Whitmore had become a walking disaster for the campaign. His missteps in interviews, bumbling remarks at rallies, and, worst of all, his public disagreements with Vic on key issues had made him a liability—a weak link that needed to be cut loose before the entire campaign collapsed.

Whitmore shuffled nervously, glancing out at the crowd, clearly dreading the few words he'd been asked to deliver today. Vic shot him a brief, tight smile, but it didn't reach his eyes. Whitmore had no idea what was coming. He thought today was just another rally, but Vic knew better. This would be Whitmore's last public appearance as his possible running mate. After today, he would be gone from the campaign—permanently.

Vic could still hear Slater's voice from earlier that morning, calm and unflinching as ever: *"Everything's set. The heart attack will happen right after the rally. Paramedics are in place. It'll be over quickly, and Whitmore will be out."*

It was a simple plan—almost too simple, Vic had initially thought. But the more Slater explained, the more sense it made. A staged medical emergency was the cleanest way to remove Whitmore from the ticket without causing a scandal. The public would buy it, and Vic would get a fresh start with a new, more competent VP.

Vic was thankful they weren't killing him—at least not yet. He snapped back to the present, his polished smile widening as the crowd cheered, responding to his latest remark. His words flowed effortlessly, the practiced rhythm of his speech automatic, but his mind was elsewhere, locked on Whitmore.

Standing just off to the side of the stage, Whitmore looked visibly shaken. His hands trembled as he clutched his notes, the pages crumpling under his nervous grip. His face had paled, and sweat beaded at his temples, betraying his growing panic. Vic could see it clear as day: Whitmore's time was running out.

Vic's gut twisted, a mixture of relief and ruthless calculation. The fallout from Whitmore's blunders had brought them to the brink, and now, even with the senator barely holding himself together, the show had to go on. But Vic knew one thing for sure: when it was time to cut ties, he'd do it without a second thought.

The speech dragged on, each minute bringing them closer to the moment Vic had been waiting for. As he neared the end of his remarks, he glanced once more at Whitmore, who was now sweating profusely, his face an unhealthy shade of red.

The speech's final lines came out, and the crowd applauded. Vic stepped back from the podium and gestured for Whitmore to take the microphone. The senator looked terrified, but he moved forward nonetheless, clearing his throat nervously as he began to speak.

"Thank you, everyone, for coming out today," Whitmore began, his voice shaky. "It's been an honor................alongside Governor.......in this campaign... and, uh... we've worked hard to bring you all a vision for the future of this great country."

Vic barely listened. Instead, he watched Whitmore like a hawk, waiting for the moment it would all fall apart. The plan had been precise—Whitmore would falter at the halfway point of his speech. His hands would go to his chest, his knees would buckle, and then he would collapse on stage in front of the entire crowd. The paramedics, already in position, would rush in, and just like that, Whitmore would be removed from the race due to a severe "health condition."

As Whitmore rambled on, Vic noticed the man's face was growing redder by the second. His breathing became labored, and he stumbled over his words.

Any second now.

Suddenly, Whitmore's hand shot to his chest. His face contorted in pain, and his legs buckled beneath him. The crowd gasped as Whitmore collapsed onto the stage, clutching his chest as if he were in excruciating pain.

"Tom!" Vic shouted, rushing to his side, playing the part of the concerned running mate. He knelt next to Whitmore, who was writhing on the stage, his breaths coming in shallow, ragged gasps. "Get help!" Vic shouted.

The paramedics—strategically positioned in the front row—jumped into action, rushing onto the stage with a stretcher. The crowd was in an uproar, some standing in shock, others pulling out their phones to record the chaotic scene.

Vic knelt beside Whitmore, gripping his shoulder with just enough pressure to make it look sincere. "Hang in there, Tom. You'll be okay."

Whitmore's eyes were wide with panic, and for a moment, Vic wondered if the man actually believed he was having a heart attack. The plan was supposed to be convincing, but the fear in Whitmore's eyes made Vic uneasy. What if something went wrong? What if Whitmore actually—

"Step back, sir," one of the paramedics instructed, and Vic obliged, moving away as they loaded Whitmore onto the stretcher. The crowd watched in stunned silence as Whitmore was carried off the stage, the ambulance's flashing lights visible in the distance.

Vic stood and turned to face the audience, his expression somber. "Ladies and gentlemen, please keep Senator Whitmore in your prayers. He's been a loyal friend and a tireless public servant, and we hope for a speedy recovery."

The crowd applauded softly, unsure of how to respond. But the cameras were rolling, and the scene would dominate the news cycle for the next several days.

Vic felt a strange sense of relief as he walked off the stage. It was done. Whitmore was out of the race, and now, Vic could move forward with selecting a new running mate—someone stronger, someone who wouldn't embarrass him at every turn.

Later that evening, back at campaign headquarters, Vic poured himself a drink, the tension from the day slowly beginning to melt away. Slater walked in, his face a mask of satisfaction.

"Everything went off perfectly," Slater said, scrolling through his phone, a smug grin spreading across his face. "Whitmore's officially out. The stress and panic attack today looked just like a heart attack. Honestly, I thought he was fucking dying for a second." He let out a short, humorless laugh, shaking his head. "But the media's already running with the heart attack story. We'll get a sympathy boost from this, no question."

Vic let out a slow breath, relief washing over him, though a cold pit of guilt lingered beneath it. The plan had worked—better than he'd dared to hope. Whitmore was out, sidelined without further scandal, and the narrative spun in their favor. But even as he nodded at Slater's update, Vic couldn't shake the nagging feeling that they'd crossed yet another line.

Vic took a long sip of his drink. "Good. I need that sympathy bump. How soon can we get the final list of VP candidates interviewed?"

"Already in progress," Slater replied. "We'll have a list ready by tomorrow. Some strong contenders can step in and energize the base. People who won't be liabilities."

Vic grunted in approval, but as he swirled the Scotch in his glass, a nagging thought crept into his mind. Yes, Whitmore was out of the race, but that didn't mean he was out of Vic's life. The man knew too much—too many secrets about the campaign, the deals, and the hacked emails. Whitmore wasn't exactly known for his discretion; if he decided to speak out, it could spell disaster.

"He's going to talk," Vic muttered, staring into his glass. "I know it."

Slater raised an eyebrow. "What do you mean?"

Vic looked up, his expression dark. "Whitmore. He's going to spin this whole thing. Paint himself as the victim. He'll make it seem like I pushed him too hard, and he'll use this heart attack as his excuse to take me down."

Slater leaned against the desk, crossing his arms. "You think he's planning something?"

"I know it," Vic said bitterly. "He's a loose end. We need to make sure he doesn't become a problem."

Slater was silent momentarily, his expression hardening as he considered the implications. Then he nodded slowly, his eyes narrowing. "We'll keep an eye on him," he said, his voice low and even. "If he becomes a threat, we'll deal with it. He and his family have been warned."

Vic felt a chill run down his spine. Slater's casual way of "dealing with" problems never failed to unsettle him. It was a reminder of just how deep they were in this game, how far they'd already gone—and how much further they might still have to go.

Vic didn't respond. He finished his drink and poured another, the weight of the situation pressing down on him. He had rid himself of Whitmore, but the danger hadn't passed. If Whitmore decided to go public with anything, Vic's campaign—and his entire career—could implode into a million pieces, but he didn't want to kill anyone either.

As the night wore on, Vic stared out the window, watching the city's lights flicker in the distance. He had crossed a line today, and he knew it. But there was no turning back now, his only hope was to win the presidency.

— 34 —

Half-asleep in his leather chair when the phone rang, piercing the late-night silence, Vic jumped. His office was dim, the only light coming from the flickering glow of the television playing muted news reports. An empty glass of Scotch sat on his desk, next to a crumpled speech he'd barely bothered to read before the rally earlier that day. His hand reached for the phone, his stomach tightening when he saw the name on the screen.

Slater.

Vic took a deep breath and answered.

"Vic, we've got a problem," Slater's voice came through, steady but with an unmistakable undercurrent of tension.

Vic sat up, suddenly wide awake. "What kind of problem?"

"Whitmore's talking," Slater said flatly. "He did end up meeting with a ghostwriter. Word is, he's working on a spill my guts, tell-all book."

Vic's heart skipped a beat. He shot to his feet, his hand gripping the back of his chair so tightly his knuckles turned white. **"A book?"** he barked, his voice laced with disbelief and rising anger. "Are you kidding me? After he was *explicitly* warned off?"

Slater looked up from his phone, his jaw tightening. "Yeah, it looks like Whitmore's playing the martyr. Leaked rumors about a tell-all. We don't know how much he's planning to spill yet, but if he goes through with it, this could sink us."

Vic's pulse pounded in his ears. The room felt suffocating, the weight of betrayal crushing down on him. They had taken every precaution and issued every warning, and now Whitmore had the audacity to make a move like this? It was a disaster waiting to happen— and Vic wasn't sure how much more he could handle.

"I wish I were," Slater replied. "The details are fuzzy, but from what we've gathered, Whitmore is painting himself as the victim of the campaign, blackmail, and violent threats. He's spinning this heart attack as a result of the pressure you put on him. He's positioning himself as the man who was pushed too hard and ultimately sacrificed for your ambition."

Vic's blood boiled. "That son of a bitch! I gave him an out! I saved him from the embarrassment of being dropped from the ticket. He's going to throw me under the bus after everything we did for him?"

"It gets worse," Slater continued, his expression darkening. "He's been talking to the media off the record. Nothing's been published yet, but the narrative is already forming. The heart attack is gaining him sympathy, and he's spinning it to make it sound like you exploited his health. Even if it wasn't real," Slater added, his jaw clenching, "what a prick, using *our* game against us."

Vic's grip on the chair tightened, his face contorting with fury. "If this book comes out," Slater finished, his voice dropping to a near whisper, "it'll destroy you. Everything we've worked for—gone."

Vic felt a surge of panic rising in his chest, but he swallowed it down, trying to think clearly. Whitmore had managed to turn their own strategy into a weapon, and now they were teetering on the edge. "We need to shut this down," he said, his voice hard. "Whatever it takes."

Slater nodded, his eyes glinting with that ruthless, calculating focus Vic had come to depend on. "I'm already on it," he replied. "We'll make sure Whitmore knows just how much he has to lose."

Vic's mind raced, piecing together the disastrous consequences that could come from Whitmore's betrayal. The heart attack had been a carefully calculated move to get Whitmore out of the race without stirring up controversy, but now, it seemed like the perfect setup for Whitmore to paint himself as a martyr. The press would eat it up—possible *VP candidate's health threatened and sacrificed for ruthless political gain.*

"What's the damage?" Vic asked, his voice tight with barely contained rage.

"It's bad," Slater said, his tone grim. "He knows about the hacked emails, the side deals with our financial backers, the promises we've made that we can't deliver on. He's got enough to sink you, Vic. And if he releases that book, everything you've built will go up in flames."

Vic ran a hand through his hair, pacing the length of his office. "We need to stop him. We can't let him get away with this. If that book comes out, I'm done."

Slater was quiet for a moment, then he spoke, his voice lower than before. "There's a way to stop it."

Vic stopped pacing, his heartbeat thudding in his ears. "What are you suggesting?"

Slater took a breath. "We make it look like Whitmore couldn't handle the pressure. The stress of the campaign, the heart attack—it all became too much for him. He's already been framed as a man struggling with his health. If we push it just a little further, we can make it look like he... couldn't take it anymore."

Vic froze, the full weight of what Slater implied crashing down on him. **"Faking a suicide?"**

"It's clean," Slater said calmly, his tone matter-of-fact. "No one would suspect a thing; Russians do this weekly. The media will report it as a tragedy—a man who gave his all for the campaign but was ultimately brought down by the stress. You'll get a wave of sympathy, and Whitmore will be gone. No book. No interviews. No threats."

Vic's stomach churned. The idea was monstrous. A staged heart attack was one thing—Whitmore had been willing to go along with that, and no one got hurt. But this? This was something else entirely. This was cold, calculated, and final.

"Jesus, Rick," Vic muttered, dragging a hand down his face. "We can't just make someone disappear like that. For God's sake, we're not the Russians."

"It wouldn't be on us," Slater said smoothly. "We'd plant the seeds, make it look like his choice. The stress got to him, and he couldn't see any other way out in his weakened state. No one would ever question it."

Vic shook his head, trying to clear the fog of panic and disgust that was clouding his thoughts. He had done a lot of things in his political career—things that would horrify the average person if they knew. But this was different. This wasn't just bending the truth or playing dirty to win. This was faking someone's death, taking control of another person's fate.

"I can't do that," Vic said quietly, more to himself than Slater. "We can't do that."

Slater's voice remained calm. "I am not excited about killing either. Think about it, Vic. If Whitmore talks, everything you've worked for is gone. All those deals, all the promises you made—it'll all come out. You'll be buried in scandal, and Morales will take the election by a landslide. Is that what you want?"

Vic stared at the floor, his heart pounding in his chest. He could see the headlines already—***Ross's campaign blows up, VP candidate releases explosive tell-all.*** Everything he had built, every strategic move he had made, and every lie he had told to get this far would all be for nothing if Whitmore released that book.

His eyes closed, the fear clawing at him like a living thing. He imagined the humiliation, the public downfall, the disgrace that would follow him for the rest of his life. He could already hear his enemies' jeers, sneering laughter, and smug, triumphant looks on their faces. He could picture Morales and her camp gloating over his destruction, painting him as a villain whose empire had finally crumbled.

The thought of losing everything—his power, his reputation, the life he'd fought tooth and nail to build—was unbearable. And beyond the humiliation was the even darker possibility: prison. His throat tightened at the idea of being stripped of everything, reduced to a powerless figure behind bars. He couldn't let it happen. Not now. Not ever.

Vic opened his eyes, his heart pounding. No, he told himself. He had to act. There were no more lines he couldn't cross; there was only survival.

"Vic?" Slater's voice broke through the haze of Vic's thoughts.

Vic exhaled, feeling the weight of the decision pressing down on him. He didn't want to do this. He didn't want to be the kind of man who would agree to something like this.

But then again, he hadn't wanted to be a lot of things. And yet here he was.

Finally, in a voice barely above a whisper, he said, "Read this." His hand trembled as he grabbed a notepad and scrawled four words: *I don't want to know.* Slater's eyes met his, unflinching. A silent understanding passed between them.

Slater gave a slight, almost imperceptible nod, grimly acknowledging the unspoken directive. Vic swallowed hard, his pulse hammering in his ears. Without another word, he moved to the kitchen stove. His heart thudded as he lit a burner, holding the paper over the flame.

The words were gone, and the directive was reduced to ashes, but the implications still hung heavy in the air. The weight of it pressed down on him, a crushing reminder that he had chosen to be willfully ignorant of whatever dark acts would come next. There was no turning back.

Vic sank back into his chair, the room spinning around him. The decision had been made. Whitmore would be taken care of, and Vic would be free of the threat that had been looming over him for weeks.

But the relief he had expected to feel didn't come. Instead, there was a gnawing sense of dread—a visceral, bone-deep horror that he had crossed a line he could never uncross. Killing people. The word echoed in his mind, heavy and unrelenting, a stain that no amount of justification could wash away.

His hands trembled as he poured himself another drink, the Scotch sloshing over the rim of the glass. He lifted it to his lips, desperate for anything to steady his nerves, but the burn of the alcohol did nothing to dull the nausea twisting in his gut. Suddenly, a violent wave of sickness overtook him, and he doubled over, vomiting all over the polished hardwood floor, the sound loud and jarring in the silent room.

Vic wiped his mouth, feeling stunned, almost betrayed by his own body. He stumbled back, leaning against the counter, breathing heavily as he tried to collect himself. The acrid taste lingered, bitter and foul, clinging to the back of his throat no matter how hard he swallowed.

He staggered to the window, staring out at the city lights flickering in the distance. The world outside continued on, oblivious to the darkness he had let seep into his life. He had done a lot of things in his career that he wasn't proud of—deceptions, betrayals, backroom deals—but this... this was different. This was a bridge he couldn't come back from, and its weight felt suffocating.

He was in too deep now. There was no turning back.

— 35 —

The cold, clear air of Lake Tahoe whipped against Vic Ross's face as he stepped out onto the deck of his private cabin. The crisp night sky was dotted with stars, and the moon reflected off the lake's still water. It should have been peaceful. The isolation, the calm—everything about this place was designed to offer an escape. But Vic couldn't find peace. Not tonight.

His hands shook as he fumbled with the bottle of Scotch, pouring himself another drink. He had lost count of how many he'd had by now, but it wasn't doing the job. The alcohol wasn't taking the edge off, wasn't silencing the buzzing in his head. It wasn't killing the gnawing thought that had been eating away at him since he'd told Slater to proceed with the plan.

Whitmore's going to be dead.

Fuck.

Vic took a long drink, the Scotch burning as it went down. He wasn't sure what felt worse—the anger or the fear. Both had been battling inside him for weeks and now they collided, pulling him in opposite directions. He'd done things—dark things, things he couldn't tell anyone. But this? This was beyond politics. This was making someone fucking die.

A chill ran down his spine despite the heat from the fire inside the cabin. Vic leaned forward, gripping the edge of the deck railing, staring out at the lake. He tried to focus on the sound of the water lapping against the shore and tried to ground himself in the cool night air, but his thoughts kept spinning. The deal had been struck. Slater was handling everything, but the decision was his.

It's not murder. It's just... protecting myself. Anyone would do it.

The thought bounced around in his mind, hollow and pointless. Vic wanted to believe it, wanted to think that faking Whitmore's suicide or heart attack wasn't the same as killing the man. But deep down, he knew it didn't matter. If Whitmore ended up dead because of him, he might as well have pulled the fucking trigger himself.

"Fuck," Vic muttered under his breath. He slammed the glass down on the railing, the sound of it shattering in his hand barely registering through the haze of alcohol and adrenaline pumping through his veins. He winced at the sharp sting of the glass cutting into his palm but didn't bother to check the damage. His head was too full of everything else.

Behind him, the sliding glass door of the cabin opened with a quiet hiss. He didn't turn. He already knew who it was. The woman he'd brought with him for the weekend—a hired distraction, someone to take the edge off while everything else in his life spiraled out of control. She was good at her job—professional, beautiful, and utterly uninterested in the mess that was his campaign. That's why he'd brought her. He didn't need someone asking questions or giving a shit.

"You, okay? Maybe my lips around you would help?" Her voice was soft, but he could hear the practiced professionalism behind it.

Vic let out a humorless laugh, still staring out at the water. "Do I *look* fucking okay?"

He didn't turn to see her reaction, but he could hear the slight shift in her tone as she walked up beside him. "You seem... tense. Let me help."

"Tense doesn't fucking begin to cover it," Vic muttered, running a hand through his hair. "I've got more problems than I know how to deal with, and none of them are going away any time soon."

"Maybe I can help," she offered, her voice sweet, her tone detached.

Vic finally turned to look at her. She was standing next to him, leaning casually against the railing. Her long dark hair hung loose around her shoulders, and her expression was calm, almost amused, like she'd seen this kind of meltdown before. And maybe she had. He wasn't the first powerful man to fall apart in her company, and he sure as hell wouldn't be the last.

"How the fuck could you help?" Vic scoffed, his voice cracking under the strain. He shook his head, a bitter laugh escaping his lips. "You don't know what's going on. You don't know the half of it." His hands clenched and unclenched, the tension coursing through him like a live wire.

He could feel himself unraveling, his composure slipping further every second. The gravity of what he had done—of the lengths he was willing to go to win—was sinking in, suffocating him. He was melting down by the minute, the realization hitting him like a sledgehammer. Every desperate choice, every line he had crossed in the name of power, now felt like a crushing weight he could no longer bear.

She smiled, that same detached professionalism still in place. "I might not know the details, but I've got something that'll help with whatever's happening in your head."

Vic raised an eyebrow as she reached into her bag and pulled out a small, familiar pill bottle. She shook it lightly, and the sound of pills rattling inside made Vic's pulse quicken. He knew what it was before she said a word.

Vic stared at the bottle, his breath catching in his throat. He'd been using it for weeks now, ever since their last encounter. At first, it had been a way to stay awake, to power through the endless meetings and strategy sessions without needing to sleep. But now? Now it was something else. It was the only thing that kept the chaos at bay, the only thing that made him feel like he was still in control.

He grabbed the bottle from her hand, popping six pills into his mouth without hesitation. He swallowed them dry, the bitter taste lingering on his tongue.

Within minutes, he felt the familiar rush—the sharpness, the clarity, the drug pumping through his veins. His heart raced, his mind buzzing with a thousand thoughts, but they were clear now and organized. He could focus. He could think.

The woman smiled, satisfied with his reaction. "Better?"

Vic nodded, though he barely registered her presence anymore. His mind was spinning, but it wasn't uncontrollable this time. He felt alive. Awake. The pills worked, sharpening his senses and quieting the noise.

"You want to know the problem?" Vic said, his voice low but steady. "I'm fucking surrounded by people who want to see me fail. That's the problem. Everyone's waiting for me to screw up, waiting for me to fall apart so they can swoop in and tear me down."

The woman nodded as if she understood, though Vic doubted she really cared. That didn't matter. He wasn't talking to her; he was talking to himself, letting the words pour out now that the pills had kicked in.

"I've done everything right," Vic continued, his voice growing louder. "Everything. I've outmaneuvered every opponent and played the game better than anyone. And yet, here I am, dealing with idiots like Whitmore trying to drag me down."

The anger in his voice was rising, and he could feel his pulse quickening, his body humming with energy. Adderall was kicking in hard now, feeding his rage and sharpening the edge of his thoughts. He slammed his fist down on the railing again, this time more to release tension than anything else.

"He thinks he can ruin me with some fucking book. He thinks he can just waltz off into the sunset and destroy everything I've worked for?" Vic's voice was venomous. "Not a fucking chance. He's going to pay for this."

The woman stayed quiet, watching him with detached interest as Vic ranted. He barely noticed her, his thoughts tumbling out faster than he could catch them.

"Morales thinks she's going to fucking win this thing, too," Vic spat. "She thinks she's the future, that people actually want to hear her preachy bullshit. She's nothing. Just a goddamn idealist who's never had to make a hard decision in her life. She has no idea what it takes to win. No idea what it's like to carry the weight of an entire country on your back."

Vic downed the last of his Scotch, his hand shaking as the adrenaline surged through his system. His mind raced, planning and strategizing, his thoughts darting from Whitmore to Morales and back again. The pills were doing their job, making him feel invincible like he could take on the world and come out on top.

"They all want me to fail," Vic muttered, his eyes narrowing as he stared out at the water. "But I'm not going to. I'll do whatever it takes.

I'll fucking burn this entire campaign down if I have to. They want me to play nicely, to stay within the lines, but that's not how you win. You win by doing whatever it fucking takes."

The woman finally spoke, her voice soft and soothing, cutting through the thick tension in the room. "So, can I take your pants off now?" she said, a playful smile curving her lips.

Vic blinked, momentarily caught off guard by the unexpected change in tone. The absurdity of it almost made him laugh, but the smile she wore had a way of diffusing the chaos swirling in his mind. For a brief, surreal moment, the weight of his world seemed to lighten, though he knew it wouldn't last.

Vic grinned a dark, dangerous smile. "I'm going to win."

Vic's phone buzzed, breaking through the haze of adrenaline and alcohol. He pulled it from his pant pocket lying on the ground and glanced at the screen.

It was a text from Slater. Just three words:

Good night, sir.

Vic's heart skipped a beat, the weight of those words sinking in. Whitmore was gone. Dead. The heart attack had taken its toll, and the stress of the campaign had finally pushed him over the edge—at least, that's how the media would spin it.

Fuck.

He stared at the phone, the reality of what he had done settling in. Whitmore was dead because of him. Slater had handled the details, sure, but the decision had been Vic's. He had given the order.

The woman noticed the change in his demeanor, tilting her head curiously.

Vic didn't look up. He couldn't. He just stared at the phone, his pulse racing, his mind buzzing with the same thought repeatedly.

I fucking did this.

He shoved the phone back into his pocket and turned to the woman, forcing a smile. "It's nothing."

She gave him a knowing look but didn't press. Instead, she reached for his hand, guiding him back toward the cabin.

"Come on," she said softly. "Let's forget about work for a while."

Vic followed her inside, but his mind was still on the phone, Whitmore, and the line he had just crossed.

As the door slid shut behind them, Vic felt a surge of adrenaline, sharper than before. His heart raced, his body humming with nervous energy. Adderall and Scotch buzzed in his system, making him feel like he was vibrating from the inside out.

He had done it. Whitmore was gone. The book would never come out, the threat was eliminated, his campaign was safe, and he had to win to protect himself.

But as he stood in the cabin, staring at the woman who was supposed to be his distraction, Vic felt something else creeping in—something darker, a sense of inevitability.

— 36 —

The campaign war room was tense with anticipation. Jen Morales sat at the head of the long conference table, her fingers drumming lightly on the polished wood as her team pored over the latest polling data. With just days left before the election, everything hinged on tonight's debate—her last chance to tip the scales and shift public opinion in her favor.

Nathan Carter, her running mate, leaned back, glancing over his notes. "So, we're finally getting Ross on stage?" His tone was measured, but his voice had a clear urgency. Everyone in the room knew how crucial this moment was.

Jen's communications director, Grace Howard, tapped her pen against a thick folder of debate prep materials. "Ross's team couldn't delay any longer. With only a week before Election Day, they had no choice but to agree," she said, her voice taut with a mixture of relief and urgency. "We're locked in for StreamUp tonight."

StreamUp, one of the country's largest and most influential streaming media channels, had become the go-to platform for political debates among younger, tech-savvy audiences. Known for its high viewership and interactive features, the channel offered a unique format that could amplify—or completely derail—a candidate's message. The stakes were enormous, and Grace knew that tonight's performance could shape the campaign's final days.

Jen nodded, casting a quick glance at the debate terms on the table. Her team had fought tirelessly to finalize every detail. After weeks of stalling and maneuvering by Ross's camp, the moment was finally here. Ross couldn't avoid her now.

"StreamUp is risky," Jen said, her gaze sweeping over her team. "We're going straight to a digital audience, younger and harder to predict. But it's also our chance to reach undecided voters directly."

Grace smiled, nodding. "Exactly. And we'll each get a five-million-dollar payout from the campaign finance fund by doing the debate. That alone will help us reinforce your message in these final days."

Jen turned to Nathan. "What's your take?"

He tilted his head thoughtfully. "It's unconventional, but so is this election. Ross's team is betting on that payout to finance a last-minute media blitz. But we can use it just as well."

Jen nodded, feeling the weight of the debate settle over her. "Then we're all in. Let's finalize our strategy and make sure we're ready for anything Ross throws our way."

Just outside the door, Candidate Service agents were at their posts, a quiet but steadfast presence as they coordinated every security detail. Agent Ramirez, who had been with Jen since the primaries, was particularly vigilant. She was constantly scanning the room, her earpiece buzzing with the latest security updates from their control center.

Ramirez leaned into the room, nodding to Grace before catching Jen's eye. "We're securing all your access points on the StreamUp platform and monitoring any potential threats or online chatter. You'll be fully protected throughout the debate."

Jen nodded in acknowledgment, grateful for the silent, watchful presence of her protective detail. In such a high-stakes setting, knowing that her team's security was in the hands of professionals allowed her to focus solely on the message she wanted to deliver.

Across town, Vic Ross sat alone in the back of his campaign car, staring out at the darkened streets. He felt a faint, almost bitter taste of victory on the horizon for the first time in weeks. His new VP pick had delivered a much-needed boost in the polls, and Ross was once again neck-and-neck with Morales. But it wasn't enough. Not yet.

His head throbbed as he scrolled through his phone, news headlines flashing past. The sleepless nights, the endless pills, the constant barrage of strategies and calculations—it was all catching up to him. In his pocket, a small bottle of pills pressed against his leg, his only lifeline these days.

"How's the debate shaping up?" Vic asked, turning to Slater, who was seated next to him, engrossed in his own notes.

Slater looked up, studying Vic's face for a moment before

responding. "We're set. Morales's team agreed to StreamUp. We'll have a large, engaged audience—perfect for targeting undecided voters."

Vic nodded, though his thoughts were racing. He could already see the stage, feel the lights, and imagine himself delivering each rehearsed blow. But deep down, a gnawing anxiety clawed at him. It was more than just nerves; it was the creeping fear that the campaign was slipping out of his control and Whitmore.

"And the five million?" Vic asked, needing to feel like he still held some leverage.

"We'll use it for an all-out media blitz in the final days," Slater replied, his tone pragmatic. "Flood every platform with ads in every battleground state. Go until nothing is left."

Vic exhaled and leaned back, letting the words wash over him, hoping they'd drown out the dark cloud of doubt that had taken up residence in his mind. For the first time in his career, he felt truly soulless, hollowed out by the compromises and lies, by the endless games he'd played to stay on top. It was a hard thing to admit, even only to himself. The ambition that had once fueled him now felt like poison, corroding whatever scraps of integrity he might have had left.

He closed his eyes, desperate for a reprieve from the gnawing emptiness, even if only for a moment. But no matter how he tried, he couldn't shake the feeling that he had lost something essential— something he might never get back.

Agent Roters, stationed just outside the car, watched Vic with a sharp, discerning gaze. She'd been shadowing him throughout the campaign, and the toll it was taking was obvious. Over the past weeks, she'd noticed his reliance on the pills and the haunted look in his eyes. Roters and her team had increased their security measures, knowing the pressures could drive any candidate to the edge.

As Vic's car pulled up to the debate venue, Roters followed closely, communicating in low tones with her fellow agents stationed around the building. Every entrance and exit were fortified, and the StreamUp platform's security was monitored in real time. She knew that while Ross's biggest threat tonight was his opponent, there were plenty of others watching from the shadows, ready to exploit any slip.

Inside the debate prep rooms, each candidate's team buzzed with last-minute instructions. Jen's team gathered around her, finalizing their approach.

"Keep calm, stay on message," Grace advised, pacing the room.

"Ross will come out swinging, but we're here to keep you above the fray. Let him show his temper; you stay collected."

Jen nodded, fingers clenched tightly in her lap. She'd watched Ross carefully throughout the campaign—he was ruthless, relentless. But lately, rumors about his health and erratic behavior had started circulating, and her team was banking on that.

Meanwhile, Ross's prep room was in a state of controlled chaos. Vic paced restlessly, mumbling strategies under his breath, his gaze flickering with a manic intensity. His new VP sat nearby, quietly observing as Vic worked himself into a fury.

"We need to go after her record—make her look unprepared," Vic muttered, running a hand through his hair. "She's not strong enough to lead."

"You're ahead in the polls," Slater reminded him, his voice low. "Hold your ground. Don't overplay it."

But Vic wasn't listening. The adrenaline and pills had him wired, ready to tear into Morales on stage. He could already envision himself emerging victorious, the press calling him the clear winner. But somewhere beneath the bravado, a small voice of doubt echoed, no matter how hard he tried to ignore it.

As the candidates took their places on stage, Candidate Service agents moved into position, alert and watchful. Ramirez and Roters, each assigned to Jen and Vic, respectively, kept a close eye on their surroundings, prepared to respond to any threat. Every aspect of the StreamUp platform's security was managed, ensuring neither campaign would face unexpected disruptions. Ramirez stood just beyond the stage's edge, her gaze steady on Jen, ready to respond to even the faintest sign of trouble.

In the shadows, Roters tracked Vic, her earpiece buzzing with live updates from the team monitoring the online chatter and physical security. She had come to know his unpredictable rhythm and sudden shifts in demeanor. Tonight, she could sense a dangerous energy in him—a mixture of desperation and exhaustion that made her uneasy.

As the moderator began the debate, the tension in the room was palpable, a silent force pressing down on everyone. Each word, each gesture, was being scrutinized by millions online, and both candidates knew that any misstep could be fatal.

Ross began by requesting prayers for the Whitmore family, his tone measured, almost solemn. But as the debate unfolded, the dynamic shifted. Jen held her ground with practiced ease, her answers calm and composed, just as her team had prepared her.

Vic, however, leaned forward, his words sharp and forceful. He interrupted Jen repeatedly, driving his points with a fervor that edged on hostility. From opposite sides of the stage, Roters and Ramirez exchanged a brief, knowing glance, both acutely aware of the mounting pressure.

Finally, as the debate drew to a close, both candidates delivered their final remarks. Jen's voice was steady and confident, her words measured and hopeful, striking a chord with those looking for change. Vic, on the other hand, delivered a fiery closing, his voice rising with each sentence, his rhetoric full of force but edged with desperation. His body language betrayed him: hands gripping the podium a bit too tightly, shoulders tense, each gesture reflecting his fraying patience and simmering frustration.

The energy in the room shifted, a tangible current that left the audience murmuring with mixed reactions. As the candidates exited the stage, Roters, one of Vic's senior agents, caught sight of him. The exhaustion was etched into Vic's face, the strain visible in the way he moved, and he was a bit unsteady on his feet. The debate had taken a heavy toll, and for the first time, Vic looked every bit as worn and vulnerable as he felt.

In the wings, the other agents remained on high alert, ready to move with each candidate to their secure exits. Ramirez met Jen with a brief nod of reassurance while Agent Roters took her place beside Vic, guiding him silently to his car. She could see the strain etched into his expression, the thin veneer of control barely holding. It was only a matter of time before something broke.

As they left the venue, the night's results still reverberated through the campaign, both candidates knew that this debate had set the stage for the final sprint.

— 37 —

The midday sun hung high in the sky, baking the pavement as the campaign bus rolled into the parking lot of a community center on the city's edge. Parked front and center was a brightly colored taco truck, its side adorned with smiling faces and slogans about "bringing everyone to the table." The smell of grilled meat wafted through the air, and a small crowd had already gathered, camera phones out, ready to capture the moment.

Vic Ross eyed the scene from his seat on the bus, arms folded across his chest. His expression was less than amused. "Remind me again why I'm doing this?" he grumbled, turning to Rick Slater, his campaign manager and the mastermind behind today's event.

Slater barely glanced up from his phone, his fingers still swiping through a flurry of campaign updates. "We've gone over this, Vic," he said, his voice clipped. "You need to connect with both minority and blue-collar voters, especially undecided women. This taco truck stunt makes you look like a regular guy. You know, rolling up your sleeves and getting your hands dirty with the locals."

Vic's face twisted with doubt, but Slater pressed on, undeterred. "Trust me, it'll play great on social media. People eat this stuff up," he continued. "Photos of you serving tacos, chatting with families, laughing like you don't have a care in the world—instant relatability. It's the kind of imagery that sells empathy, even if you have to fake it."

Vic exhaled sharply, the idea feeling as hollow as the rest of his campaign theatrics. But in a game where perception was everything, he knew he couldn't afford to argue.

Vic scowled. "It's ridiculous. I'm not some reality TV contestant. This isn't how you win elections."

Slater finally looked up, his expression calm, controlled, and full of calculated confidence. "This is exactly how you win elections," he said, his voice steady. "Polls are tight, and we're losing ground with minority voters. You running a taco truck shows you're relatable. You're not just a guy in a suit; you're someone they can trust."

Vic forced himself to nod, though the word *relatable* lingered like a bad joke. Right. Relatable. As if posing at a taco truck for a photo op could somehow bridge the chasm between him and the voters he'd failed to connect with. But Slater's plan left no room for doubt: optics over authenticity, strategy over sincerity.

In the background, Ethan and Riley moved quietly, working to smooth out potential hiccups before they became problems.

He took a deep breath, grabbed his sunglasses, and stepped off the bus. A cheer erupted from the crowd, and the familiar blinding flashes of cameras greeted him. He raised a hand in a practiced wave, plastering on the politician's smile he'd perfected over the years. He was used to playing this game, but today felt different—manufactured in the worst way.

As he approached the taco truck, two middle-aged Latina women in aprons greeted him. "¡Hola, Señor Ross! We are so happy to have you here!" one of them exclaimed in a thick accent. She smiled warmly, her eyes twinkling with excitement.

Vic nodded stiffly, the smile never quite reaching his eyes. "Happy to be here. So, what do I need to do?"

The women eagerly ushered him to his spot, where the grill was pork and chicken sizzling, tortillas were being flipped, and ingredients were lined up in neat trays. "Don't worry! We will show you everything," one said, handing him an apron that read *Mi Casa, Su Casa* in bold letters. "It's easy. Even a president can do it!" She laughed, and the crowd joined in.

Vic smiled again, though inside, he was cringing. He slipped on the apron and positioned himself behind the grill, feeling the heat from the burners rise against his face. The first few minutes were fine. The women guided him through the steps, showing him how to flip the tortillas and pile the toppings into tacos. It was straightforward enough, and for a brief moment, he thought this might be better than he had anticipated.

Then came the rapid-fire instructions—spoken in fast, heavily accented Spanish. Vic's brow furrowed as he tried to keep up, the language barrier quickly becoming problematic. The two women kept pointing, laughing, and correcting him as he clumsily assembled the tacos, their accents thick and difficult for him to follow.

"Cuidado, Señor Ross!" one of them called out when he nearly dropped a plate of carne asada, her tone playful. The crowd laughed, and phones snapped pictures at every awkward fumble. Vic's jaw tightened. He could already picture the memes flooding the internet later.

"This is a nightmare," he muttered under his breath, feeling the weight of the cameras on him. The women, oblivious to his frustration, continued to chatter and guide him, but their enthusiasm only made it worse. It was obvious to everyone watching that this was not where Vic belonged, and no amount of taco assembly would change that.

"Smile," Slater's voice drifted in from behind the crowd. "You're killing it."

Vic glanced over at him, his patience wearing thin. "This is ridiculous," he whispered through clenched teeth, his smile now a strained grimace. "I'm not a damn line cook. I'm running for president, for God's sake."

Vic wanted to rip off the apron and storm back onto the bus, but he knew the cameras were still rolling, capturing every forced smile and gesture. The last thing he needed was another scandal about how out of touch he was with ordinary people. So he gritted his teeth and kept working, dropping cilantro onto tacos with a practiced motion. Each sprinkle of the green herb made him want to gag. He was one of those people for whom cilantro tasted like soap, and he had a special, visceral disdain for it.

But he pushed through, squeezing lime and nodding at the locals, plastering on a smile as if he was having the time of his life. Inside, though, he simmered with resentment, cursing the whole charade and the herb that mocked his every move.

After what felt like an eternity, the event finally wrapped up. The crowd began to disperse, and Vic wasted no time in yanking off the apron and tossing it onto the counter. He wiped his hands on a napkin, barely containing his anger. "This was a circus, Slater, you fucking idiot," he snapped, his voice low but seething. "Who even thought this was a good idea?"

Slater, ever the pragmatist, shrugged. "It's all about the optics. Voters love this kind of thing. You just made yourself look accessible, like someone they can trust. Trust me, by tomorrow, this will be trending for all the right reasons."

Vic wasn't convinced. He climbed back onto the bus, his face flushed with frustration. He could already feel his phone buzzing in his pocket—notifications piling up from his social media feeds. He pulled it out and scrolled through the first few headlines:

Vic Ross Tackles Tacos! Out of His League? Ross's Taco Truck Struggles Go Viral!

And then came the memes. Clip after clip of him fumbling tortillas, his forced smile plastered awkwardly across his face, circulated like wildfire. The hashtags were relentless: #TacoFail, #RossDoesntGetIt, #RossSucksTacos. His attempt at looking relatable had turned into a social media spectacle, and the internet was having a field day.

Vic groaned, the sound deep and frustrated, and threw his phone onto the seat beside him. The whole stunt had backfired spectacularly, making him look even more out of touch than before. Each mocking post felt like a knife in his already battered campaign, and the laughter echoing across social media was a bitter reminder of just how badly he'd miscalculated.

The whole stunt had been an embarrassing charade, and now, instead of looking relatable, he was the punchline of the day.

— 38 —

Vic Ross stood in the elevator of his building, his reflection staring back at him from the gleaming chrome walls. The smooth hum of the elevator was soothing in a way—one of the only things left that still felt predictable and controlled. He adjusted his tie absentmindedly, his fingers running over the fabric, more out of habit than care. His eyes were bloodshot, the dark circles under them deeper than they had been even a week ago. He hadn't slept more than three hours a night in months. Sleep was a luxury, one that his campaign couldn't afford.

Vic stepped into the dimly lit hallway leading to his penthouse as the elevator doors slid open. The quiet echoed around him, a sharp contrast to the chaos of the outside world. The moment the doors closed behind him, it was as if the weight of the city fell away. But the pressure—the pounding in his head, the tightness in his chest—remained.

The campaign had finally agreed to the late debate terms. It had taken weeks of back-and-forth negotiations, and now, just two days before the debate, Vic was back in D.C. for a brief break, or at least that's what his team had insisted on calling it. "Just a couple days in the city to clear your head," Slater had said, as if Vic had the luxury of taking time off to relax.

His penthouse felt cold, even sterile, despite the view of the Capitol stretching out below him. The sleek, modern furnishings—a black leather couch, sharp-edged glass coffee tables, and abstract art that was more about making a statement than personal taste—reminded Vic that this place was more a symbol than home. He rarely spent time here except to work or drink alone, staring out over the city he had once felt completely controlled. Now, everything felt fragile.

Vic poured himself a Scotch from the decanter on the bar cart, his hand trembling just enough that he noticed. He hated noticing things like that, weakness. The small things slipping away. He took a long sip, letting the burn settle in his chest as he moved to the window. The Capitol dome gleamed under the streetlights below. A symbol of power, of the world he'd spent his life navigating with precision. But it was a world he no longer trusted. His paranoia had been creeping in for weeks, and even as his new VP boosted the polls, Vic felt the ground shifting beneath him.

Just a little further ahead, he reminded himself. Ross had gained three percentage points in the last week—an unexpected yet welcome bump from the media attention around his new running mate. He was ahead of Morales for the first time in weeks, albeit by a slim margin. It was enough to give him a taste of victory again, a reminder of the control he'd once held with such ease. But the pressure of holding on was more than he'd expected.

The debate in two days would be his chance to solidify the lead, to pull ahead just enough to secure the win. And yet, Vic felt more unsteady than ever. Adderall was keeping him sharp—or at least that's what he kept telling himself. The number of pills had continued to grow each week, but he reassured himself he'd quit after the election. Just a few more days, then he'd put it all behind him.

"I'm not a junkie," he muttered under his breath, gripping the edge of the campaign bus seat. "I don't live under a bridge. I am not an addict." The words were a mantra he repeated to steady himself, a flimsy shield against the gnawing guilt that came from relying on pills to keep him functioning.

He could feel the familiar buzz coursing through his veins, a heightened sense of clarity and control—if only temporary. The pills gave him the focus to get through the relentless pace of speeches, meetings, and public appearances. With the election so close, he knew he couldn't afford to slow down or slip up, no matter the cost. But deep down, he could feel the strain, a tension creeping in that even Adderall couldn't mask.

He reached into his pocket, pulling out the small pill bottle that had become his constant companion. The donors—people who owed him favors or simply too afraid of losing access to power—had been quietly supplying him with a steady stream of the pills for weeks now. Vic had convinced himself it was necessary. How could anyone expect him to keep going without it? To stay sharp, stay ahead?

Popping another nine pills into his mouth, he swallowed them dry, ignoring the bitter taste. He needed the edge. His team was prepping for the debate downstairs, ready for a late-night strategy session, but

Vic needed a few more minutes alone, a few more minutes to find his focus.

"I haven't eaten in days," Vic muttered to himself, running a hand over his face. "I figure it's the pills, but no time to fix all of this until it's over." The words hung in the cramped silence of the campaign bus, an uncomfortable reminder of how far he'd let things go.

Everything was paused until the election: his health, sanity, and future. Adderall was keeping him moving and sharp, but the side effects were piling up. His body felt off-kilter, strung out, and neglected, but there was no room in his life to slow down or adjust—not now, only when it was over.

He took another sip of Scotch and turned his gaze back to the Capitol, the city sprawled out beneath him like a chessboard. He used to enjoy moments like this—standing here, looking out over the symbols of power, knowing they were within his grasp. But tonight, there was something else there, a tightening in his chest that no amount of Scotch or pills could shake.

Downstairs, Vic's debate prep team was gathered in the sleek conference room of his penthouse. The table was strewn with papers—research on Morales's past debates, talking points for the big night, and a detailed dossier on her recent campaign strategy. Slater stood at the head of the table, his phone in one hand, tapping it nervously against his leg as he waited for Vic to join them.

"Is he okay?" one of the junior strategists asked, glancing toward the elevator.

Slater didn't answer right away, his eyes fixed on the debate notes in front of him. Vic's behavior had been erratic, to say the least. The pills were clearly starting to take a toll, but no one dared mention it. "He's better than ever," Slater said after a long pause. "He is the best of the best when it counts."

But even as the words left his mouth, Slater wasn't sure if he believed them. Vic hadn't been sleeping, and the sharp, controlled precision he was known for had been slipping, replaced by bursts of anger and paranoia. The team had been walking on eggshells for weeks, trying to keep things running smoothly without setting him off.

The elevator dinged, and Vic stepped into the room, looking more composed than Slater had expected. His suit was perfectly tailored, as always, but the tension in his posture was obvious. Still, Vic Ross was a master of appearances.

"We don't have time for small talk," Vic said, taking his seat at the head of the table. He glanced at the papers spread before him, but his mind was already jumping ahead to the debate. "Let's get started."

The room settled into a quiet intensity as Slater flipped through the latest polling data. "We're up three points. The new VP has given us the bump we'd predicted and needed, and we're slightly ahead of Morales in key swing states. But the debate is crucial. It's going to be close no matter what at this point."

"How close?" Vic's voice was sharp, his eyes narrowing with an intensity that made Slater hesitate.

"We don't know," Slater admitted, his voice strained. "It's all about turnout. We're in trouble if they show up 5-6% more than expected. If not, we're looking good." He took a deep breath, the weight of uncertainty pressing down on him. The margins were razor-thin, and everything hinged on factors they couldn't fully control.

Vic's jaw clenched, the tension coursing through him like a live wire. He hated being at the mercy of something so unpredictable, and the waiting was shredding his nerves. Every percentage point felt like the difference between victory and ruin.

"Closer than we'd like," Slater admitted, showing him the breakdown. "Morales has strong favorability in the younger demographic, especially after announcing her policy shift toward climate action. That crowd will be watching the debate on StreamUp and Zingerich."

Vic glanced at the numbers but waved them off. "We've handled worse. She's weak on experience, and that's where we'll hit her. Let her come across as the idealistic dreamer. I'll remind everyone what it takes *actually to* run a country."

The strategy was sound: focus on Morales's inexperience, chip away at her idealism, and hammer home Vic's years of experience. It had worked before, and it could work again. They would paint Morales as someone with lofty dreams but no real understanding of how to navigate the harsh realities of leadership, while Vic would present himself as the seasoned, steady hand the country needed.

But there was one unpredictable element: the debate's unconventional platform—StreamUp. The social media streaming channel catered to a younger, highly engaged audience that didn't consume politics like traditional voters did. Having used it before, the team felt cautiously optimistic. StreamUp had a reputation for making debates go viral, with every moment scrutinized, clipped, and dissected in real time. The platform could transform a single soundbite into a sensation or turn a minor stumble into a meme shared millions of times.

Both campaigns would play to a crowd more volatile and unpredictable than the conventional media audience. Candidates in the past had managed to shift the polls by several percentage points after a strong—or disastrous—appearance on the platform. It was a high-stakes gamble: one electrifying moment could energize Vic's struggling campaign, but one wrong phrase could ignite a firestorm he couldn't put out.

"Thank you, everyone," Vic shouted, his voice straining to sound upbeat and confident, though it came off as oddly forced. He was trying to rally his team, but even his words of encouragement felt brittle under the weight of what was coming.

Vic's team had prepped hard for this moment, knowing that one misstep on StreamUp could become an overnight sensation, a viral fiasco that would haunt his campaign. Every answer and gesture had been rehearsed and analyzed; his responses were fine-tuned for an audience that could turn on a dime. Yet they also believed a strong performance could ignite the desperately needed momentum. It was a high-stakes gamble, and Vic could feel the pressure mounting like a physical force pressing down on his chest.

But he told himself the strategy was solid. The talking points were honed to perfection, and his confidence was bolstered by weeks of intensive prep. Even so, as he adjusted his tie and stepped toward the stage, he couldn't shake the feeling that he was walking a razor's edge, one viral moment away from triumph—or disaster.

Slater knew Vic needed to be at his best, but as he looked at him now—his eyes glassy, his focus too sharp, almost manic—he wasn't sure the man sitting at the table was the Vic Ross who had dominated the political landscape for years.

"Stick to the plan," Slater said, forcing himself to stay calm. "No need to overreach. Hit her on the experience about the economy, foreign policy, and national security."

Vic nodded, but the tension in his jaw betrayed him.

The prep session dragged on late into the night. Vic's team rehearsed potential questions, practicing how he would handle Morales's attacks and how to counter any unexpected challenges. Vic, fueled by Adderall and adrenaline, powered through, barking out responses and pacing the room between practice runs. The longer the session went, the more restless he became.

At one point, Vic stopped mid-sentence, his hand gripping the back of his chair, eyes narrowing at the team around him. "This isn't enough," he muttered, his voice low but sharp. "We need more. She will come at me harder than we're preparing for."

Slater exchanged a glance with one of the other strategists but kept his voice steady. "We've covered every angle. You just need to stay on message."

But Vic wasn't listening. His mind was already racing ahead to the debate, to the pressure of the stage lights, to Morales standing across from him, poised and ready to challenge him in front of millions. His confidence was there—fueled by the recent poll bump—but it was a brittle kind of confidence, one that teetered on the edge of collapse.

"Enough for tonight," Vic said suddenly, cutting off the conversation. He stood up, brushing past the team as he made his way back to the elevator. "I'll handle it from here."

"Why are you here, Jen?" Vic's voice was flat and weary as he stepped off the elevator, his eyes fixed somewhere far beyond her image. He didn't wait for an answer, didn't even look back. The elevator doors slid shut behind him, sealing him off from everyone, even from himself.

Slater stood nearby, watching in tense silence, the weight of the next 48 hours pressing down on him like a suffocating blanket. He'd seen Vic unraveling for weeks now, the cracks in his composure growing wider with every setback, every moment the campaign slipped further out of control.

He didn't trust Vic's stability. Not anymore. The once-unflappable powerhouse had become unpredictable, and Slater knew that a single emotional misstep could cost them everything. With only two days until the debate, the stakes had never been higher—and the man he relied on to hold it all together was teetering on the brink.

Upstairs, Vic poured himself a drink, then another, the penthouse as quiet as a tomb. The Scotch was smooth and rich, but it did nothing to calm the gnawing dread twisting in his gut. He stood at the floor-to-ceiling window, the glass cool against his forehead as he stared out at the Capitol dome, gleaming in the night.

Suddenly, a wave of nausea surged through him, and he doubled over, barely catching himself on the windowsill as he puked. The Scotch splattered onto the polished marble floor, tinged with streaks of blood. He wiped his mouth with a trembling hand, the metallic taste lingering in the back of his throat.

Straightening up slowly, he tried to steady his breathing, but the raw burn in his gut only seemed to worsen.

— 39 —

He stepped off the private jet onto the tarmac with a bit of a smirk, the flash of cameras greeting him like blinding sunlight. For weeks, he'd been traveling on commercial flights and private shuttles, pandering to the "woke" crowd that his campaign manager insisted he appeal to—trying to appear as the everyman while his billionaire pockets told a different story. He had even leased out his own jet, paraded as an eco-friendly choice, like some fucking environmentalist. He was done with that now.

Vic had finally had enough of the charade. He wasn't like Morales. He wasn't going to pretend to be something he wasn't. He had money, and he was going to use it. He was, above all, the regular-guy bullshit. So today, he arrived in Atlanta for the debate with *his* jet—*his* statement of power. The crisp logo of his campaign was plastered on the side of the plane, and he was back in his element. The jet was more than just transportation—it symbolized the wealth and control that had made him who he was.

The plane gleamed in the southern afternoon sun, and as Vic stood on the steps, waving to the cameras, he felt a surge of energy—an adrenaline-fueled high he hadn't felt in weeks. He straightened his suit, brushing imaginary dust from his lapel, and then, inexplicably, he waved to the crowd.

Only, there was no crowd: just reporters, camera crews, and a few security staffers. But in Vic's mind, they were there—supporters, throngs of them, cheering his name. He waved again, lingering on the steps for the cameras, smiling wide like he was addressing a stadium packed with screaming fans.

"Thank you! Thank you!" he shouted, his voice rising above the hum of the cameras. "You're all incredible!"

Slater, standing at the base of the stairs, exchanged a glance with one of the staffers, his expression hard to read. Vic had been acting strange for weeks, but this? This was another level. Still, no one dared say anything. Slater had stopped trying to rein him in—it was like trying to stop a freight train.

Vic's eyes gleamed as he gave another wave to the invisible crowd before finally descending the steps. He ignored the waiting questions from the reporters, instead pushing past them with a dismissive flick of his hand. He didn't have time for their nonsense. He had bigger things to worry about.

More than he wanted to admit, the lack of sleep was starting to take its toll. He could feel it creeping into his mind, like a fog blurring the edges of reality. His body was tired, but his mind wouldn't stop. Adderall kept the wheels turning but at a price. He couldn't remember the last time he had slept more than a few hours. The few moments of rest he did get were shallow, broken by the constant hum of his thoughts.

Lately, those jigsawed thoughts have become fixated on something unexpected: **a comic book**.

It had started as a way to pass the time on one of those unbearable commercial flights. One of the staffers had left it on his seat—a stupid-looking comic book with some dark villain-turned-superhero on the cover. Usually, Vic would have tossed it aside, annoyed by its triviality. But something about the cover had caught his eye—the shadowy figure, the gleaming red eyes. The hero wasn't your typical good guy. He was dark, shady, and morally ambiguous. But the people *loved* him.

Vic had become obsessed. He carried the comic everywhere, flipping through the pages during downtime, reading and rereading the same scenes. In the story, the hero—if you could even call him that— wasn't bound by the same rules as everyone else. He took what he wanted, made his own decisions, and didn't care what anyone thought. The people adored him for it, even though he was, at his core, a villain.

It resonated with Vic in ways he couldn't explain, even to himself.

As he settled into the back of his black SUV, the comic tucked into his briefcase, he leaned back against the cool leather seats and closed his eyes. The debate was tonight, but his mind wasn't on Morales or the talking points his team had drilled into him. It was in the comic— the dark hero, the villain who everyone loved despite his flaws.

Life imitates art.

Vic smirked to himself. He was that hero. The antihero, the man who did what needed to be done—unapologetic, ruthless, and unstoppable.

The SUV sped through the streets of Atlanta, weaving between traffic with the urgency of a campaign running out of time. But Vic's mind was elsewhere, caught in a blur of thoughts and half-formed plans. The debate was important, sure, but it wasn't the endgame. No, this was just another step in his inevitable rise to power. He would crush Morales tonight, just like he'd crushed every other obstacle in his way.

But beneath that veneer of confidence, something darker twisted. His biggest fight wasn't with Morales or the media—it was with his own unraveling sanity. The scotch, the pills, the endless pressure: they were all chipping away at his control. His hands fidgeted in his lap, betraying the storm inside him, as he forced himself to believe that he could keep it together, if only long enough to make it through the next few critical hours.

The debate venue was electric, filled with reporters, campaign staff, and the hum of anticipation. StreamUp, the platform hosting the debate, had set up an innovative stage—simple, stripped of the pomp and circumstance of traditional debates. This was designed for the people, the digital age, not the old guard media networks. Vic hated it.

He missed the grandeur of a real debate stage, the formalities, the history. But StreamUp had been chosen for one reason: $5 million for each campaign, thanks to the new campaign finance regulations. And as much as he despised pandering to the social media crowd, Vic wouldn't turn down that money.

In his dressing room, Vic paced, adrenaline coursing through him as the pills kicked in. His debate team briefed him and reviewed the strategy one last time, but their voices were like distant echoes. He could see them, hear them, but their words weren't registering. He was too keyed up and focused on the image in his mind—the comic book villain, the hero who bent the rules, who did whatever he wanted.

"You stick to the plan, we win this," Slater said, though Vic barely heard him. "Hit her hard on experience. Make her look unprepared for the real world. This isn't a time for idealism."

Vic nodded, his jaw tight. "Goddamnit, I've got it," he said, more to shut them up than anything else.

But as the clock ticked closer to the debate, Vic felt his mind drifting, the edges of reality blurring again. He could see himself on the stage, not as Vic Ross, presidential candidate, but as the dark hero from the comic book. He'd come out swinging, relentless, taking what was his.

"You're going to crush her," Vic muttered to himself, his fingers gripping the edge of the dressing table.

"What was that?" Slater asked, glancing nervously over.

"Nothing." Vic stood, shaking off the haze. "It's time. Let's get this over with."

Vic stepped onto the stage, the lights hot and blinding as the cameras focused on him and Jen Morales. The moderator's voice echoed in the background, introducing the candidates, and laying out the rules, but Vic wasn't listening. He was watching Morales, sizing her up. She looked composed, calm—too calm. He would tear that calm apart and expose her to the fraud she was.

Oddly turned on by Morales, Vic shifted uncomfortably in his seat, forcing himself to focus on anything but the lingering image of her from the last debate prep footage he'd watched. It was maddening—his rival, the woman threatening to undo everything he'd built, and yet here he was, battling his body's unwanted reaction. He clenched his jaw, frustration flaring as he willed himself to regain control.

Damn pills, he thought bitterly. Adderall, combined with the stress and the restless energy coursing through his veins, had been messing with his mind and his impulses in unpredictable ways. He exhaled sharply, trying to compose himself, forcing his attention back to the fight ahead—the debate, the campaign, the battle he couldn't afford to lose. But the distraction was one more crack in his already fragile composure.

The first few questions came and went in a blur. Vic answered mechanically, hitting his marks and throwing in a jab here and there. But the more Morales spoke, the more agitated he became. Her answers were measured, thoughtful, and polished. The audience was eating it up, and Vic could feel his grip slipping.

His heart pounded in his chest, the lack of sleep catching up to him as the adrenaline and pills pushed him to the edge. He was losing focus, his thoughts swirling.

"You're out of your depth," Vic snapped at one point, interrupting Morales mid-answer. "This isn't some idealistic fantasy. This is real life. And you're *not* ready."

The moderator tried to regain control, but Vic kept going, his voice rising. He waved his hand toward the empty space beyond the cameras, where he imagined his supporters were watching, cheering him on.

"You think you can handle the pressure of running a country? You can barely handle a debate," Vic growled, his eyes narrowing as he leaned forward. "I'm the one who's built something here. I'm the one who's earned this."

Morales, to her credit, didn't flinch. She waited for Vic to finish his rant before calmly continuing with her point, making him look even more unhinged in comparison.

The audience watching at home couldn't see the cracks forming, but those in the room could. Slater, Ethan, and Riley shifted uncomfortably backstage, watching as Vic's carefully controlled facade began to crumble. This wasn't the plan. Vic was losing his grip, letting his ego, exhaustion, and obsession take over.

But Vic didn't care. In his mind, he was the dark hero—the one who could break the rules, the one who could tear his opponent apart and still come out on top.

As the debate dragged on, Vic's focus wavered. He was rambling now, barely staying on topic, interrupting the moderator, cutting off Morales at every opportunity. But instead of looking strong, he looked desperate and frantic at times.

By the time the debate ended, the damage was done. Morales had held her ground while Vic had spiraled, his erratic behavior on full display for the world to see.

As the streaming ended and the stage lights dimmed, Vic stood there momentarily, dazed, unsure of what had just happened. He could hear Slater calling his name, but it sounded distant, as if it were coming from underwater.

He had won, hadn't he? He was the hero, the one who had come out on top. But as he looked at his team's faces, the tight, worried expressions, the uneasy glances, something told him that this wasn't the victory he had imagined.

— 40 —

Vic Ross slammed his phone onto the polished marble counter, watching it skid across the surface before clattering to the floor with a sharp crack. His hands trembled—not just from adrenaline but from the rage and paranoia that had been simmering for days. The debate had been a disaster, and now this—he couldn't even use his goddamn phone without feeling like someone was watching, listening, waiting to strike.

"They hacked me!" he shouted into the empty room. "Those fuckers hacked me again!"

He wasn't sure who "they" were anymore—Morales's team? The media? Someone inside his own campaign? It didn't matter. In Vic's unraveling mind, everyone was a threat, every ally a potential enemy.

Once his fortress of control, the penthouse felt like a prison now. Every shadow seemed to hold unseen eyes, and every piece of tech was a potential vulnerability. The fallout from the debate had been brutal, with reporters tearing into his performance. His team claimed minimal damage and that the polls hadn't moved significantly, but Vic didn't believe them. They were lying, softening the blow to keep him from snapping.

He paced the room, his mind spinning in a thousand directions, every thought crashing into the next like a chaotic storm. His fingers tangled in his hair, disheveling his once-pristine appearance. "Fuck, fuck, fuck," he muttered under his breath, his voice raw and desperate.

Nothing felt safe anymore, and no one felt trustworthy. Everyone was a liability waiting to implode, and the weight of the campaign—its lies, betrayals, and impossible stakes—had become suffocating.

In the adjoining room, Rick Slater, his campaign manager and confidant, waited silently. Usually, Slater's presence calmed him, but tonight, even he was part of the paranoia. Vic couldn't trust him—not fully.

Grabbing the landline—a relic in the digital age, but one of the few devices Vic trusted—he jabbed in Slater's number, too wary to confront him face-to-face.

"I need a new cybersecurity team," Vic barked when Slater answered. "Four hours. I don't care who they are or how much it costs. Get me the best."

"Vic—"

"No, shut up and listen!" Vic's voice cracked, his panic spilling into fury. "My phone's compromised. My fucking life is compromised. I can't do anything without feeling like they're watching me." His voice dropped, colder now. "And you—you've been behind the intrusion, haven't you?"

Slater's silence was damning in Vic's ears. The accusation had escaped before he could stop it, but now that it was out, he doubled down. "Cocksucker," Vic hissed, his knuckles white as he gripped the receiver. "You're fired."

A tense silence followed, the weight of his words hanging between them like a blade. Slater's voice, when it finally came, was measured but sharp. "Vic, you're losing it."

Vic's rage erupted again. "Don't you dare talk to me like that! Morales's team is coming for me, and I must be ahead of them. Fix this!"

Slater exhaled, and the sound was static on the line. He knew better than to argue. "Fine," he said finally. "But firing your own team isn't going to solve anything."

The phone clicked as Vic ended the call, his manic frustration bubbling over. He stormed across the room, his movements erratic, knocking over a glass of Scotch that shattered across the floor. He didn't even notice the mess.

In the adjacent room, Vic's running mate, Dean Harkness, sat at a table reviewing notes for their upcoming appearance. The man barely looked up as Vic stormed in, but Vic wasn't interested in waiting for pleasantries.

"We need to talk," Vic growled, slamming his fist onto the table.

Dean flinched, looking up slowly. His expression was calm, and measured, but Vic could see the hesitation in his eyes—the doubt. "What's the problem, Vic?"

Vic leaned forward, his voice low but venomous. "The problem is you're not fucking loyal to me, that's the problem."

Dean frowned, his tone remaining steady. "Vic, I've been doing everything—"

"Bullshit!" Vic cut him off. "You're not doing everything for me. You're doing it for yourself. I see how you talk to the press and act in front of the cameras. You're already positioning yourself for something bigger."

Dean straightened, his calm cracking. "I'm doing my job. You're the one dragging us down with this—this paranoia. The polls are up because I'm here, and you know that, Vic. Come back to reality."

Vic's laugh was sharp, humorless. "The polls are up because of me. Don't ever forget that."

Dean stood, his voice rising. "This isn't helping, Vic. You're unraveling, and the team sees it. I see it."

Vic froze, his mind spinning with rage and suspicion. "If you're not 100 percent for me," he muttered, his voice cold and clipped, "then you're against me. And I don't have room for enemies in my camp."

Back in his office, Vic sat in the dark, staring at the Capitol dome glowing in the distance. His paranoia spiraled, his thoughts twisting into dangerous shapes. He needed to regain control—to remind the public that he was the only one who could lead them.

Then the idea came to him.

It was initially subtle, creeping in like a whisper, but it grew louder with each passing moment. He needed something dramatic, something to make voters rally to him. Over the past two decades, political theatrics had become almost expected. Bomb threats, staged attacks— each election cycle seemed to bring its share of incidents. Every time the candidates in question emerged with a "sympathy bump," their resilience was admired, and their polls surged.

Nothing serious, Vic thought. Just a scare. Something to make them sympathize. Something to make them believe in me.

His hand hovered over the phone as the idea solidified. Controlled chaos. Theatrics.

Vic dialed Slater.

"Rick," he began, his voice low and conspiratorial. "I've got an idea."

Slater's hesitation was immediate. "Vic, what are you talking about?"

"Something big," Vic said, turning toward the window. "Something that'll remind people what's at stake. You've seen it happen before. Hell, it happens every cycle now."

Slater's voice dropped, cautious. "You're serious."

Vic's gaze hardened, his reflection glaring back at him. "Dead serious. We control the narrative, the details, everything. It'll work."

For a long moment, Slater didn't respond. Then: "You're asking for disaster, Vic."

Vic's grip tightened on the phone. "I'm asking for results. Get it done."

He hung up, standing in the silence of the darkened room. The campaign wasn't about winning anymore. It was about survival.

— 41 —

Delgado hadn't set foot in Vic Ross's penthouse in weeks. She'd been watching the campaign from a distance, noting how his behavior had grown increasingly erratic and how the fallout from his public stunts was now impossible to ignore. Last night, Slater had called her, desperation unmistakable in his voice. He never sounded desperate, which was what convinced her to come back. Rosa had always been Vic's fixer, the one who could handle the worst situations without flinching. But this time, something felt different.

When she stepped off the elevator and into the cold, minimalist expanse of the penthouse, tension hit her immediately. The silence was thick and uncomfortable, like the calm before a storm. Rosa had always disliked Vic's penthouse—the sharp-edged furniture, the black leather couch, and the abstract art that spoke more of wealth than warmth. It was a space built to exude control, reflecting Vic's success. Now, it felt hollow.

Slater met her at the door, looking more exhausted than she'd ever seen him. Stress etched his features, and he managed a terse nod. "Thanks for coming," he said, his voice barely above a whisper. "I don't know how much more of this we can handle."

Rosa nodded curtly, eyes scanning the space. "Where is he?"

Slater glanced toward the closed office door at the far end of the room. "In there. He's been on the phone all morning, ranting about cybersecurity and demanding a new team. He's convinced everyone's hacking him."

Rosa raised an eyebrow. "And are they?"

Slater shook his head. "No, he's paranoid, Rosa. He's spiraling fast, and nothing we do seems to make a difference."

Rosa's eyes settled on the door, her gaze thoughtful and calculating. She'd known Vic for years by reputation—his ruthlessness, ambition, and uncanny ability to claw his way to the top. But only in the past few months had she seen him firsthand, watched him weather scandals, crises, and countless political storms. Men like Vic were familiar to her: relentless, cunning, and willing to do whatever it took to win.

Her clients always came out on top because she knew how to control the narrative and timing and twist the system to their favor. It was a game she played expertly, a power she wielded without hesitation. But this? The tension in the room, the way Vic was coming unglued, the frantic desperation in his voice—this felt different. The familiar tools of spin and media manipulation wouldn't be enough to save him if he fully unraveled.

Rosa felt a rare flicker of unease. She'd managed chaos before, but something about this moment made her wonder if Vic had gone beyond the point of control.

"I'll talk to him," she said, her tone firm.

She approached the office door, pausing for a moment before knocking. From the other side, Vic's voice rose and fell in agitated bursts, muffled but unmistakably angry. She knocked twice and then opened the door without waiting for a response.

Vic was pacing behind his desk, his phone clenched in one hand, a mess of papers strewn across the desk in front of him. His usually pristine suit was rumpled, his tie half-loosened, and his hair looked like he'd been running his hands through it for hours. A half-empty glass of Scotch teetered on the edge of the desk.

"I don't care what it costs!" Vic shouted into the phone, his face flushed. "I need a new cybersecurity team now. You have four hours. If they're not here, you're fired."

He slammed the phone down, his breaths coming in quick, shallow bursts. When he turned and saw Rosa standing in the doorway, his expression softened slightly, a fleeting look of relief crossing his face.

"Rosa," he said, his voice strained. "Done staying away. Where the hell have you been?"

Rosa crossed her arms, her gaze drifting over the chaos on Vic's desk—scattered notes, empty coffee cups, and a bottle of half-drunk Scotch. The disarray perfectly reflected the man spiraling in front of her. "Watching you burn this campaign to the ground from a safe distance," she said, her voice dry and cutting. "You're a goddamn train wreck."

Vic's head snapped up, eyes narrowing at the bluntness of her words. But Rosa didn't flinch. She had seen enough in her career to know when a ship was sinking, and right now, she wasn't sure if she should try to salvage what was left or jump off before the inevitable implosion.

Vic let out a bitter laugh, shaking his head. "Nice to know

someone's enjoying the show."

"I'm not here to watch," she said coolly. "I'm here because Slater called me. He thinks you're about to implode and cost the election. Frankly, I agree."

"They hacked me, Rosa," he said quietly, his voice tinged with paranoia. "I know it. My phone, my emails—someone's watching everything I do."

Rosa frowned, stepping closer and picking up the glass of Scotch from his desk. "Who's 'they'?"

Vic spun around, eyes wild. "I don't know! Morales's team, the media, and maybe even someone on the inside. Everyone's out to get me."

Rosa placed the glass firmly back on the desk, her gaze steady. "Vic, listen to yourself. There's no hacking, no conspiracy. You're fucking losing it, man."

Vic's eyes flashed with anger, his jaw clenching. "You think I'm crazy? You think I'm making this up?"

Rosa met his glare without flinching, her expression unyielding. "I think you're scared, and yes, getting a bit batshit crazy," she said bluntly. "And when you're frantic, you start looking for enemies."

Vic slammed his fist on the desk, the impact sending papers flying and rattling the glass bottle of Scotch. "I'm not scared—I'm pissed," he snapped. "This election was mine, Rosa. *Mine.* And now everything's falling apart."

Rosa held her ground. She'd seen Vic furious before, but this was different. This was desperation—raw, unchecked, and spiraling into something dangerous. His rage wasn't just anger; it was the panic of a man losing his grip on the one thing he thought he could control.

"You're going to lose more than the election if you don't get your head straightened out," she said, her voice calm but unrelenting. "You're losing your team, your reputation, your legacy. Slater is barely holding it together. And as for your VP?" She paused, letting the gravity of her words sink in. "He's halfway out the door."

Vic's face fell, the reality crashing into him like a wave. The fortress he'd built was crumbling, and he was running out of time to salvage what remained.

His face darkened. "Dean's a snake. He's positioning himself."

Rosa arched an eyebrow. "He's doing his job, Vic. He's trying to keep this campaign from crashing like the rest of your team. But you're making it impossible."

Vic's hands clenched, his knuckles white. "If he's not with me, he's against me."

Rosa sighed, frustration finally breaking through. She fixated on him with a hard stare and said,

Vic blinked, momentarily thrown off balance. "What did you say?"

Without missing a beat, she stepped closer, her voice steady and unyielding. "I said, get your shit together or lose this election. Did you hear me that time?"

His face twisted with frustration, his gaze narrowing. "You think you can talk to me like that? You work for me."

"Fuck you, I don't," Rosa replied, her voice icy. "If you keep acting like this, you'll run this campaign into the ground, and the people who've backed you for years. Get your head out of your ass before it's too late."

They locked eyes, a tense silence stretching between them. Rosa had been the one to pull him back from the edge, a steady voice of reason in a storm of ego and ambition. Even in the short time they'd worked together, she'd become the expert at fixing the unfixable, weaving sense out of his chaos and giving his messes a veneer of control. But this time, something felt different. The cracks in his composure ran deeper, and she could see the madness simmering beneath the surface.

She wasn't sure she could pull him back this time. Some things were unfixable, even for her. Rosa had always prided herself on finding a way, no matter how dire, but watching Vic teeter on the brink, she felt a rare and unwelcome doubt creep in.

And that doubt felt like a warning, a reminder that sometimes, even the best damage control couldn't save someone determined to self-destruct.

A day earlier, in Santa Fe, Jen Morales sat at her kitchen table, savoring a rare moment of calm. She'd returned home for a few days to recharge before the final push. The debate had gone well, even better than her team expected, but she knew better than to let her guard down. Vic Ross was unpredictable, and anything could happen with only days left until Election Day.

Agent Ramirez, a familiar and steady presence by now, stood watch by the door. She had been with Jen since early days and was one of the few people Jen could rely on to keep her grounded. Ramirez kept an eye on her, always assessing any potential threat and keeping security airtight, knowing how critical these last days were.

Jen glanced at Ramirez with a small smile. "It's almost hard to believe we're this close."

Ramirez nodded, her face softening slightly. "You're almost there, Ms. Morales. Just a few more steps."

But even with her agent's quiet reassurance, Jen couldn't shake the sense that the final days would bring challenges she hadn't anticipated.

— 42 —

Rosa crossed her arms, her patience fraying as Vic ranted about the comic book villain-hero he had become obsessed with. "Enough with the fucking comic books, Vic," she snapped, her voice cold and sharp. "You're freaking everyone out with that nonsense. They care about the election."

Vic glared at her but said nothing. His mind was buzzing too fast to respond. Later, when he was pacing the office, Rosa quietly gathered every comic she could find—the ones stashed in his desk, scattered across the couch, and piled near his bed—and threw them into the trash. He noticed, of course, scowling in her direction, but she kept her gaze steady. "You don't need distractions," she said firmly, not giving him room to argue. Vic huffed in displeasure but, moments later, moved on to the next thought in his spiraling mind. As chaotic as he was, he liked Rosa was in charge again, and without the comics cluttering his space, his focus—however scattered—felt more manageable.

The tension in Vic Ross's penthouse was suffocating. The polished floors and sleek, minimalist decor, once a testament to Vic's control over his world, now felt like a stage set for his unraveling. Rosa Delgado had done everything she could to reel him back in, but it wasn't working. His paranoia had taken root, twisting reality until everything was a threat. Everyone was out to get him—or so he believed.

Vic stood at the window, his hands clenched into fists. His reflection in the glass looked ghostly, hollow-eyed, and pale, a shadow of the man he once was. The election was days away, and despite the campaign's best efforts to recover from the debate, the polls remained stagnant. Morales was holding steady, and worse, his team was doubting him.

Rosa sat on the couch, her gaze sharp as she watched his pace, her patience fraying. Slater had just left after a tense strategy session, and the room still buzzed with the argument that had erupted before he stormed out. Slater had been trying to hold the campaign together, but Vic's erratic behavior was tearing it apart. They'd gone from being a well-oiled machine to barely holding on, and now, even Slater was talking about contingency plans. Plans for losing. Vic wouldn't hear it. He was *not* going to lose.

"You've got to stop this, Vic," Rosa said, her voice steady but firm. She wasn't afraid of him, and that was the problem. Vic wanted people afraid, especially now. "You're saying the whole world is conspiring against you, but it's not. It's just a bad strategy and nonsense."

Vic turned to her, his eyes wild. "Bad strategy? You think this is about strategy, Rosa? No. This is bigger than that. They're rigging the whole thing, all of them—Morales, the media, the *system*. I can feel it."

Rosa shook her head, exasperated. "You sound like a lunatic. Do you realize how crazy you sound? You've spent your entire career controlling every move, every narrative, but now you're losing it."

Vic slammed his fist against the glass, rattling the entire windowpane. "Losing it? I'm the *only one* who sees what's really happening! They will steal the election if we don't stop them."

Rosa stood, crossing her arms. "You don't see anything clearly anymore. You're spiraling, and you're dragging the campaign down with you, and by the way, who is them?"

Vic's heart raced, his head pounding with the familiar, frantic rhythm that had become his constant companion in these final weeks. He hadn't slept more than a few minutes for days. Even the pills were starting to wear thin. His mind buzzed with a thousand thoughts, none of them coherent, none very lucid and stable.

"I need something," Vic muttered, half to himself. "I need something big. Something that'll flip everything in the last days."

Rosa narrowed her eyes. "What the hell are you talking about?"

Vic's gaze flickered to her, his face twisted with a manic intensity. "I've been thinking… maybe it's time for a stunt. Something drastic."

"Like what?" Rosa asked warily, sensing the danger in his tone.

Vic's lips curled into a twisted smile, and he started pacing again, his steps quick, erratic. "I've seen it work before, you know. Candidates pull some stunt, something crazy, and people rally behind them. Sympathy, fear, whatever—it works. I just need something that'll make me *the* story."

"Are you hearing yourself?" Rosa stepped closer, her voice low but sharp. "What are you planning? You're talking like a fucking maniac."

Vic's head snapped toward her, his eyes alight with a dangerous intensity. "Maybe... maybe something like that, maybe. Remember years ago? That candidate who got shot at during a rally. It played up perfectly. The hero factor—the people's champion. They milked it for everything it was worth, and the polls swung in her favor overnight. That's what I need."

Rosa's stomach dropped. Her expression froze for a moment before she found her voice. "Are you seriously suggesting that you stage an assassination attempt?" She stepped closer, her voice rising with disbelief. "Do you have any idea how insane that sounds?"

Vic paced the room, his steps quickening as his breathing grew heavy. "It's not insane—it's smart. It'll make me untouchable. It's strategy." He smirked, a flicker of arrogance in his eyes. "No one attacks the guy who's just been 'shot at.' They'll brand me as a fighter, a survivor. The media will eat it up."

"*No,*" Rosa said firmly, stepping in front of him, and blocking his path. "This isn't a stunt, Vic. This is crazy. And even if you did pull it off, it could go wrong in a million ways. You're talking about putting your life at risk."

Vic glared at her, his face tight with anger. "You're supposed to help me. Fix things. That's your job."

"I'm here to stop you from destroying yourself," Rosa shot back, her voice rising. "And right now, you're doing a damn good job of that on your own."

For a long moment, they stood there, tension crackling in the air between them. Vic's mind was racing, his thoughts dark and spiraling. He couldn't shake the feeling that everything was slipping through his fingers, that the election—the *power*—was being stolen from him. He needed control. He needed to win.

"I'm not going to sit here and watch you commit political suicide, possibly hurting someone," Rosa said, her tone hard. "If you go through with this, you're on your own. You think you're paranoid now? Wait until you have the FBI breathing down your neck because someone gets hurt in your little stunt."

Vic's eyes darkened. "What did you just say?"

"You heard me," Rosa replied, unflinching. "You want to pull something like this? You'll have to do it without me. Because I'm not going down with you."

Vic's rage boiled over, and he stepped toward her, his fists clenched. "You walk out on me now, and you're done. You hear me? *Done.*"

Rosa stared him down, her gaze unwavering. "I'm already done, Vic. You just don't realize it yet."

Downstairs, while Vic raged in the penthouse, his campaign was on the verge of collapse. Slater, frustrated and running out of options, met with the remaining senior staff in the war room to discuss damage control. They had tried everything—shifting the narrative, doubling down on policy ads, even some subtle smear attempts on Morales— but nothing was moving the needle. The debate debacle was still hanging over them, and with only a few days left, it felt like they were out of moves.

"The polls haven't budged," one of the strategists announced, staring at the latest data with a mix of disbelief and relief. "Morales is holding steady. We're not losing ground, which, honestly, feels like a miracle."

Vic's shoulders sagged slightly, a momentary reprieve from the relentless anxiety pressing down on him. But the news didn't feel as hopeful as it should have. He knew staying in place wasn't enough— not with how close the race was. He needed momentum, a game-changer, something to put him ahead for good.

Still, the room took the news as a small victory, a brief pause from the chaos, even if the relief was temporary.

Slater sighed, talking to himself. "Vic's talking about pulling some kind of stunt. I don't know how long we can keep this campaign afloat if he keeps spiraling like this."

Slater hesitated in silence. The whole room fell into a tense silence. Everyone knew the campaign was teetering on the edge of disaster.

— 43 —

Two days out from the election, both campaigns were in overdrive, fighting tooth and nail in the swing states that would decide everything. The rules had changed, the entire system had shifted two elections ago when the Electoral College had been reduced to just

20%, with the popular vote now making up 80% of the final vote. The new rules meant both candidates had to rethink their strategies—no longer could they simply rely on key states. It was all about mobilizing the masses and getting the largest swaths of voters in the states with the most population.

With the introduction of online early voting, turnout shattered every record. Forty million had already cast their ballots, and it was the highest participation in history. The game was different now. The stakes were higher on election day.

Vic Ross was heading to Texas, a state that had become even more crucial with its massive population and the weight it now carried in the new system. His team had pulled every resource into focusing on this state and a few others like Florida, Pennsylvania, and Ohio. But Vic wasn't entirely present. His erratic behavior had intensified, his thoughts scattered, to say the least, the constant barrage of hundreds of pills, and his growing paranoia.

He no longer trusted his team fully. Rosa was the only one who had any influence over him, and she was gone.

Ross sat in the back of his jet, staring out the window at the clouds, his mind already calculating the next move. Texas. He needed to win Texas. He was starting to think that if he could turn Texas, he could actually pull this off. The online voting turnout had thrown everything into chaos, making traditional polling harder to read.

"How's Texas looking?" Vic asked, not looking at anyone in particular.

Sitting across from him with his tablet open, Slater cleared his throat. "We're seeing extremely high turnouts in Dallas and Houston. Morales's campaign is pushing hard there, but we're still within striking distance. It'll come down to the suburbs and rural areas. You've got two rallies tomorrow."

Vic nodded, though his thoughts drifted again. Every moment felt like a countdown; every move had to be perfect. "We need more TV ads," he muttered. "Hit them hard. Emphasize the change she wants—people don't like it. Make it clear she's too extreme."

"We've already got saturation," Slater replied cautiously. "We're spending everything we've got on digital ads too. The numbers are high."

Vic didn't care about the details. All he saw was Morales gaining ground, inching closer with every passing day, and it was driving him deeper into desperation. His hands trembled slightly as he leaned forward, his eyes wild with barely contained panic. "Just get it done," he snapped. Then, almost as an afterthought, his voice softened. "Please."

The *please* hung heavy in the room, an unexpected crack in Vic's usual armor of arrogance and command. Slater froze, his blood running cold. All the time he'd known Vic, he had never heard him plead. It was a terrifying sound, a sign that the man who had once been so unshakeable was on the verge of completely breaking.

Slater swallowed, suddenly unsure if even the best-laid plans could save them now.

Meanwhile, in Florida, Jen Morales was executing her own strategy, though with far less chaos. She had managed to keep her campaign running like a well-oiled machine despite Vic's attempts to derail it. Florida, with its massive population and swing status, was critical to her win. The new 80-20 rule made it all about population centers, and Florida's diverse electorate made it a challenge.

Her campaign had invested heavily in ground games and digital ads, but the human touch was making the difference. Morales had spent the past week bouncing between rallies in Miami, Orlando, and Tampa. Early voting numbers were strong in the urban areas, and the goal was to ensure that rural counties didn't tip too far in Vic's favor.

"We're making up ground in Miami-Dade," her campaign manager, Tony Vargas, reported during their flight from Tampa to Miami. "But we need a bigger push in the panhandle. If we can turn those undecided voters there, we'll lock this big ass ole' state up."

Jen nodded. She knew the numbers as well as anyone. The sheer volume of early votes cast through online platforms had changed everything, and with more voters having already made up their minds, they were focusing on the last undecided few. It felt strange knowing that a massive portion of the electorate had already voted, and yet the campaign had to act as if there were still millions to convince.

"How's Texas?" Jen asked, aware that Vic was likely gunning for it as well.

Tony glanced at his phone. "Neck and neck, but Vic's unraveling is hurting him. The debate fallout hasn't really moved the needle, but his behavior on the trail is starting to raise eyebrows. We've been pushing hard on his instability."

Jen exhaled slowly. She hated running negative ads, but she knew it was necessary in this environment. Vic's behavior had become unpredictable, and they were using it to plant doubts in the minds of undecided voters. Times were different now—elections weren't just about promises. They were about perception, and Vic was crumbling in the public eye.

Privately, because Jen genuinely cared about people—even her fiercest political opponents—she found herself worried about Vic. There was something off about him lately, something she couldn't quite put her finger on. His erratic behavior, as he seemed to teeter on the edge of control, had begun to unsettle her.

As someone familiar with addiction, she suspected drugs of some kind, though she never voiced her suspicions, not even to her closest advisers. It felt invasive, too personal, and she had no proof. But the concern gnawed at her. Despite the brutal nature of their campaign, she couldn't help but feel a pang of empathy, wondering if the pressures of their world had driven Vic to a breaking point. Even with everything on the line, **she hoped he wouldn't unravel completely**.

The last two elections under the new electoral rules had shifted the landscape. With 80% of the outcome based on the popular vote, both candidates had to maximize turnout everywhere. It wasn't enough to win the swing states anymore—they needed sheer numbers. That's where online voting had come in, a new tool that had shaken the old way of thinking. Early voting, now available exclusively online, had already captured millions of votes. The campaigns had to navigate a world where voters were no longer bound by Election Day, and this new dynamic was driving turnout to unprecedented levels.

Vic hated it. He couldn't control it or strategize around it in the same way. His usual tactics—smear campaigns, fear-mongering, massive rallies—felt less effective when people could quietly cast their votes from a mobile phone weeks in advance. He didn't trust the system, and it gnawed at him.

"Online voting is rigged," he muttered to Rosa during one of their late-night strategy sessions. "It's too easy to manipulate."

Rosa who was in his head only, oddly didn't respond. He was picking on himself now. "It's the system we've got, he heard."

Vic tapped on the table, and the pounding in his head and voices worsened. Everything felt out of reach. His own team had lost faith, and Rosa had left him, the only one keeping the operation from completely falling apart. But he wasn't sure how much longer he could take it.

"We're going to win Texas," he said, almost as if convincing himself. "That's how we take this back."

As the final week of the campaign wore on, the energy on both sides was palpable. The media was in a frenzy, tracking every move, every misstep, and every rally. Both candidates worked tirelessly to flip the final undecided voters in the population-dense states that now held even more sway under the new electoral rules.

Vic's rallies became more erratic. He pushed his team harder, ignoring their warnings and demands for caution. Every speech became a mix of populist rhetoric and veiled threats about the integrity of the election. The closer it got, the more desperate his tone became, but he was starting to get names, places, and details wrong.

Jen, on the other hand, kept her campaign steady. She focused on turnout, pushing the idea that every vote mattered, and that this new system allowed every individual voice to be counted like never before. But even she couldn't shake the nerves as the final days ticked down. It was too close for comfort, and she knew Vic could pull some last-minute stunt.

With days left, the battle for the country's soul had become an all-out war, and neither side was ready to concede an inch.

Two days before the election, the scene in New York was chaotic. It was one of Vic Ross's final rallies, held in the heart of the city—a population center he needed to turn the tide. The crowd was massive, with thousands packed into the plaza, waving signs, cheering, and eager to catch one last glimpse of their candidate. Vic was in the middle of one of his fiery speeches, laced with his usual rhetoric about strength and leadership. **And then, pop-pop-pop, shots rang out.**

The sound cut through the air like a whip. For a split second, there was silence—stunned, eerie silence. People screamed and scattered, pushing and shoving as they tried to get away. Panic spread through the crowd like wildfire, and before anyone could process what was happening, another shot echoed through the plaza.

Vic's security team reacted immediately, pulling him down and shielding his body as they dragged him off the stage. The *Candidate Service*—a new federal protection agency for incumbents and top federal candidates—moved in like a well-rehearsed drill, forming a tight perimeter around Vic as they rushed him to safety. It wasn't the Secret Service but these folks were the next best thing.

Vic hit the ground hard, his hands scraping against the rough pavement. Blood smeared his palms from the fall, but none of the bullets had hit him. The gunfire, which seemed so close, had missed. As far as anyone knew, he had barely escaped an assassination attempt.

His breathing was ragged, his mind racing as the chaos around him unfolded.

But something shifted in him—an idea flickered. *This could work.*

In a dark, undisclosed location, the CEO of an elusive black-ops contractor known only as ***Last Call*** watched the scene unfold through an encrypted feed. No one in the organization knew her real name—she operated solely under the codename "Last Call," and her reputation was as cold as her methods were effective. Her team never missed their mark, and precision was their religion.

The three shots fired that evening were never meant to hit Vic Ross. Instead, they were meant to graze the fine line between threat and terror, to create the illusion of a close call and the aura of manufactured danger. The attack had been meticulously planned and orchestrated with precision. Every angle, every bullet's path, calculated to spark fear but leave no actual harm to Vic Ross or any bystanders.

Last Call never worked directly with clients, only through shadowy, untraceable intermediaries. Every transaction was facilitated in Bitcoin, routed through a labyrinth of anonymous wallets, ensuring no digital footprints. Officially, the organization didn't exist, and those who tried to prove otherwise usually ended up as cautionary tales.

The phone on her sleek, minimalist desk buzzed—a secure line ringing once, signaling success. It was done. The contract had been executed flawlessly. She (Last Call) tapped a tablet, confirming the remainder of the payment: an obscene sum of Bitcoin dispersed into countless anonymous accounts. The job was complete.

Vic Ross's name had just been catapulted back into the national conversation, wrapped in a shroud of fear and intrigue that no one would forget. And somewhere, *Last Call* watched it all with detached satisfaction, already planning the next contract.

Vic's body buzzed with adrenaline as his security detail lifted him from the ground. His team surrounded him, voices shouting over the chaos, but his focus was singular. As they tried to rush him to safety, Vic saw something—a private security officer's gun, visible in its holster as the man worked to keep the crowd back.

In one impulsive motion, Vic grabbed the gun from the guard, his mind already spinning with its optics. He raised the weapon, adopting a defensive position, his face a mask of steely determination. He turned toward the stage, toward the frenzied crowd, aiming the gun toward… nothing in particular. Cameras flashed wildly, capturing the moment in perfect clarity. It was a hero's pose.

The media was already swarming, and every major social media platform was blowing up with live footage of the event. People were screaming about the gunshots, about the attack, about how Vic Ross had been targeted. But what they would remember—what every social media feed would carry—was the image of Vic, holding the gun, standing tall, looking every bit like the man who had just defended his team and his supporters from imminent danger.

Slater called Rosa, his voice numb and almost broken. "What happened?" he asked, his words heavy with confusion and dread.

Rosa's response was short, her tone clipped and final. "I don't know," she said, her voice cold and distant. There was a beat of silence, then she added, "Don't ever call me again." The line went dead, leaving Slater staring at his phone, the weight of her words sinking in.

He lowered his hand, feeling the shock settle deeper into his bones. Rosa was completely gone—cutting ties, distancing herself from whatever storm had just been unleashed. With a sickening twist in his gut, Slater realized that they were all teetering on the brink of something uncontrollable, and he was quickly running out of allies.

Within hours, the story had reached every corner of the globe. **"Attempted Assassination of Presidential Candidate Vic Ross"** was splashed across every major network. There were blurry videos from bystanders showing Vic grabbing the gun, looking like he was ready to defend his staff from the unknown assailant. The narrative spun out of control, and speculation spread like wildfire.

Who was behind it? A lone wolf? A domestic terrorist? A foreign state? With each passing hour, the story grew darker. Analysts speculated wildly, and whispers of North Korean or Iranian involvement began to circulate—fed to the media by unnamed sources. There was no evidence, but evidence didn't matter. The narrative mattered, and the narrative was working in Vic's favor.

By the next day, polls had shifted dramatically. Vic Ross had surged by 4 percentage points, now holding a 3-point lead over Morales. The shift was particularly strong among young voters and independents, a demographic that had been hard to capture. Social media was flooded with images of Vic's heroic pose, and he became a viral sensation, especially among younger voters who saw his quick reaction as evidence of his strength and leadership under pressure.

The attempted attack became *the* story, eclipsing everything else in the news cycle. Headlines and social media exploded with theories and speculation, each outlet scrambling to piece together the fragments of a narrative that seemed to have no clear answers. Political commentators debated the implications for days, and the public was riveted. Sympathy and outrage poured in from all corners of the country, and Vic Ross was suddenly back in the spotlight, this time as a near-victim of a shadowy, unsolved threat.

No one was ever caught or charged. There wasn't even a suspect for law enforcement to interview. The incident had been meticulous precision that left no fingerprints, no discernible trails. It was as if the attack had been a ghostly illusion, a crime with no perpetrators.

Vic had pulled off one of the biggest three-card Monte moves in history. What should have been a disastrous moment became a masterstroke of distraction and manipulation. The narrative of the campaign had shifted, and for now, the desperate chaos that had threatened to consume him was masked by a newfound aura of resilience and intrigue. His enemies were thrown off balance, and Vic's campaign surged with momentum in the final days, all because the real game was played where no one could see.

Vic's desperation had gone beyond strategy. He was playing a dangerous game, one that could have gotten real people killed. And he was willing to do it all just for a few percentage points in the polls.

The next morning, she met with Vic one last time. He was riding the high of his surge in the polls, feeling invincible. His hand was bandaged from the fall, and he wore it like a badge of honor, bragging to anyone who would listen about how he had stood his ground.

"I'm gone; we'll never talk again," Rosa said bluntly, her voice cold and final.

I'm not sticking around to see how this ends; guilty or not guilty, I don't care. Take the win, but I don't exist going forward."

Vic opened his mouth to argue, but Rosa silenced him with a sharp glance. She slid an envelope across the desk, the signal transaction code for the final payment. One last, untraceable move. Vic wouldn't dare talk—he couldn't.

She turned and left without another word, leaving Vic standing alone in his office, staring after her. He was numb, he felt... nothing.

As the media continued to speculate about the source of the attack, law enforcement and intelligence agencies scrambled in a so-called "manhunt." But there was nothing to find: no shooter, motive, or trail to follow. The investigation stalled, but the public didn't care. The damage—or the victory, depending on how you saw it—had already been done.

Vic Ross had become the story. He was a candidate who had survived an assassination attempt, who had stood his ground, gun in hand, ready to defend his people. It was the perfect image for a nation consumed by fear and chaos, and Vic knew it.

The attack had worked. With just 24 hours left, the race was tighter than anyone could have predicted, but he definitely pulled ahead.

— 44 —

Far away from the lights and cameras of Vic Ross's campaign, hidden from the frantic media frenzy and the fake manhunt, Last Call remained a ghost. The name belonged not just to the black ops' contractor but to the woman who had built it—a CEO known only by her codename. She moved like smoke through the world's most elite, high-stakes arenas: politics, bedrooms, boardrooms, and the dark underbelly of sports empires. No one knew her true identity. No one who mattered, anyway. And those who did? They were either dead, loyal, or bound by fear.

Her real name had been wiped from every system decades ago. Her legend, though, lived in whispers among the powerful, those who needed things handled that no legitimate firm would touch. Her clientele was a rotating gallery of the world's most elite and corrupt: heads of state, Fortune 500 CEOs, sports magnates, and politicians willing to trade everything for a shot at the top.

This wasn't her first rodeo, nor was Vic Ross her most high-profile client. Last Call's operations were infamous among those in the know, and the jobs she'd taken over the years would have shocked the world—if anyone ever found out. Some of her work read like conspiracy theories, except it was all terrifyingly real.

She had orchestrated the downfall of a tech billionaire who stood in the way of a trillion-dollar merger by leaking falsified documents about the CEO's involvement in an international scandal. The man had resigned in disgrace, his life ruined by lies no one could disprove. The merger went through the next week, untouched by the wreckage left in her wake.

Her clients never spoke of her, and if they did, they spoke in hushed tones, knowing that any breach of their relationship would result in violence toward them as their family. No one violated the agreement.

Vic Ross was capitalizing on the attack in every way possible. He had spent the last day doing what he did best—controlling the hero narrative, pushing out last-minute misinformation on Morales, and turning the entire story into a spectacle. His wounds, minor as they were, had been paraded to the press as badges of courage. His bandaged hand, the only real injury from the event, was a constant feature in every interview, and the story had grown wilder with each retelling.

"What we saw in New York," Vic said, his voice low and serious during one of his many interviews, "was an attempt to silence me, to silence *us*. But I'm still standing. We're still standing."

The crowd cheered every time. His numbers had jumped dramatically. Every news channel ran stories about the so-called "manhunt," claiming involvement from foreign actors like North Korea or Iran, though there was no evidence. It didn't matter—people believed what they wanted to believe, and Vic fed into it perfectly. He was the underdog who had been attacked but was still standing strong.

His VP, Dean Harkness, was equally enthusiastic, repeating every one of Vic's talking points with a straight face. Their messaging had become a full-on offensive: everything Morales stood for, they attacked. If she advocated for renewable energy, they pushed fossil fuels harder. If she proposed healthcare reform, they blasted it as "socialist" and promised more "freedom of choice." The more absurd the contrast, the better it played with Vic's supporters.

On the other side, Jen Morales was dealing with the fallout. The attack on Vic had dominated the headlines nonstop since the shooting, and the media was relentless. Every press conference she gave seemed to be overshadowed by questions about Vic's "heroic" response to the shooting. Her policies were barely making a dent in the news cycle, and her team was scrambling to regain control.

"People love him now," Tony Vargas, her campaign manager, said during one of their frantic strategy meetings. "He looks like the goddamn Terminator in that photo, standing there with a gun."

Jen sighed, rubbing her temples. "We stick to the plan. We don't engage with the circus. Focus on turnout. Focus on facts. Vic's spinning bullshit and the polls won't hold if we remind people what's real."

But even as she said it, Jen knew the truth. Vic's spin was working.

The staged attack had given him the boost he needed. With a day to go, the race was now tighter than ever, and the constant media coverage of the "manhunt" kept Vic in the spotlight.

The nation was on edge. "We're under attack," Vic said during a rally in Florida, his bandaged hand raised in the air. "But we're fighting back. They tried to take me out, but here I am. And we're going to *win*."

The crowd roared, and the media took the bait once again, amplifying the message across every platform.

Jen, meanwhile, was holding steady, but the pressure was mounting. Her team worked around the clock, hitting swing states with a last-minute blitz of ads, rallies, and interviews. Turnout was key, and they knew that the online voting system—still novel to many—could be their saving grace. The focus now was on reminding people what was at stake, pushing her policies as a direct contrast to Vic's fear-based rhetoric.

The entire nation was waiting, breathless, and anxious for Election Day.

— 45 —

The clock was ticking down, and Jen Morales knew she was running out of time. Vic's attack had shifted the polls, but she wasn't giving up. There was still a path to victory—it just required everything she had left.

Her campaign headquarters was buzzing with activity, people moving in every direction, phones ringing, screens lit up with polling data, social media feeds, and last-minute plans. Her team, Diego, Nathan, Grace, and everyone had been working 24/7 for weeks, but now they were preparing for a final push that could make or break the election.

Jen stood in the war room, listening to Tony Vargas, her campaign manager, run through the latest numbers. The Hispanic vote was crucial. It had always been a key demographic, but now, with Hispanics making up 28% of the U.S. vote in 2036, they were *the* demographic that could tip the balance. Over 51% of American families had some

Hispanic heritage—this wasn't just another voter block; it was the future of the electorate.

"We need to engage them minute by minute until we're done," Jen said, her voice steady but urgent. "We have to go beyond what we're doing now. It's got to be bigger, harder. No one sleeps until Election Day."

Tony nodded, tapping his pen against the table. "We've got something. A channel that could change everything."

Jen raised an eyebrow. "Go on."

Tony leaned in, pulling up a map of the country and overlaying it with voter registration data. "There's a second channel on the major streaming platforms. It's Spanish-speaking, Mexican-American-owned, and massive in Texas, California, and Florida, and even growing in places like Arizona and Nevada. They've agreed to go all in with us for all hours until the end—wall-to-wall coverage, voter mobilization, interviews, rallies, ads, the works."

Jen's heart raced as she processed the information. She had known they needed something drastic, but this could be it. A direct line to one of the most important voter bases in the country, speaking to them in their language, with a network they trusted. It was more than just getting people to vote—it was about creating a wave.

"Hardcore messaging," Jen said, her eyes locked on Tony. "No more middle ground. They need to know what's at stake."

Tony nodded. "Exactly. We're framing it around what Vic will take from them if he wins—healthcare, education, immigration support and reform. All of it. And we push your policies as the alternative."

Tony wasted no time getting the platform on a call. On the other end was Luis Ríos, the general manager of the powerful social media enterprise. The meeting was conducted entirely in Spanish, authentic to the partnership and their shared mission to reach the growing Hispanic population.

Tony Vargas:
"Look, we're hours, not days, out from the election, and we need your full support. You have the largest Hispanic audience in the country, and we know you can move the needle. How can we ensure we reach every home that uses your platform?"

Luis Ríos (General Manager):
"I completely understand, Tony. We have millions of users who trust our content, and many of them have already voted. But we can

do more. We can dedicate our homepage and push notifications to promote Jen's message. We can also schedule live interviews with community leaders, in addition to the ads we're already running."

Tony Vargas:

"That's exactly what we need. We can't afford to lose these people. Jen is with them, and we need to make that clear. Could you also include hourly reminders for early online voting? Many people don't know they can already vote, and we're running out of time."

Luis Ríos:

"Of course, we can do that. In fact, we've seen that direct reminders work best. Something like, 'Your vote is your voice. Vote now to protect your community.' Would you like something like that?"

Tony Vargas:

"Perfect. And make it personal, right? Make them feel like Jen is speaking directly to them, not just another ad."

"That sounds excellent. I want this to be everywhere—they shouldn't be able to open the platform without seeing a message or video from us. And not just for young Hispanics, but for the grandparents and parents too. What else can we do to make sure every kind of Hispanic in the U.S. understands how important this election is?"

Luis Ríos:

"We can do something special in our news section, something exclusive. Maybe an hourly segment of 'Why Vote Now,' featuring respected Hispanic opinion leaders. That builds trust. Plus, we'll make sure our algorithm boosts all content related to Jen Morales so it gets more visibility than anything else."

Tony Vargas (*smiling*):

"That's exactly what we need, Luis. We're going to win this with your help."

As they finalized the Hispanic outreach plan, an unexpected call came through. Jen was intrigued—she'd been approached by one of the biggest Native American marketing and advertising firms in the country. The CEO, a powerhouse in the industry, had built an empire on branding, consulting, and advocacy for Indigenous issues, and she was offering something Jen couldn't refuse.

With the Hispanic and Native American voter outreach in full swing, Jen's campaign kicked into overdrive. The Mexican-American-owned channel broadcasted her message nonstop, rallying the

Hispanic vote relentlessly. Spanish-language ads flooded the airwaves, urging voters to take action and warning them about what would happen if Vic won—stripped healthcare, gutted education programs, and immigration policies that would tear families apart.

The network even aired a series of interviews with Jen herself. She spoke directly to the community in both Spanish and English, laying out her platform clearly and passionately. She wasn't holding back anymore. This was it.

— 46 —

Final Hours to Election Day: The walls of Jen Morales's campaign headquarters were vibrating with energy, tension so thick you could almost taste it. Phones rang nonstop, keyboards clattered as staffers furiously updated spreadsheets, and televisions blared polling updates that worsened with each passing hour. The latest numbers had Jen behind by three points—Vic Ross had pulled ahead, riding the wave of sympathy and his attack.

In the dimly lit corner of her war room, Jen sat hunched over a laptop, her eyes burning from staring at screens for hours. Her social media feeds were open, with constant messages, replies, and live videos. She had been online nearly 24/7 for days, pushing out content, rallying voters, refusing to let Vic's misinformation dominate the narrative. Her hands shook slightly from the coffee and energy drinks she had been downing, her heart racing, fueled by the mix of anxiety and pure stubborn determination.

"I'm not fucking losing, I am not," she muttered under her breath, fingers clattering across the keyboard as she typed out another post, hitting every key with more force than necessary.

Her social media team was gathered around her, discussing strategies. The Mexican-American-owned platform had been a godsend, pushing their voter mobilization campaign to every corner of the Hispanic community. But it still wasn't enough. The margins were tight, and the final hours and turnout would determine everything.

"Jen, we've got the live stream ready," Tony Vargas said, glancing at her with concern. She hadn't slept in days. None of them had. But

Jen? She was driving harder than anyone, refusing to lose and turning herself into a machine.

"Good," Jen said, without looking up. "Put me on. Now. I'll go live until the polls close, and it's what we have to do."

Tony hesitated, then nodded, signaling the tech team to set up the live stream. "You've got this," he said, his voice softer than usual. He knew how much this meant to her. They all did.

Ross's campaign headquarters was a completely different scene. The lights were bright, the energy high, and the atmosphere almost celebratory. Vic had convinced himself that the election was his—his team had assured him that the polls were leaning in his favor, and the staged attack had given him the edge he needed. He felt invincible, untouchable.

Sitting in his office, surrounded by a few close aides, Vic poured himself another glass of Scotch. His hand trembled slightly as he raised the glass to his lips—though it wasn't from nerves. The pills and his breaks from reality because of the positive polling had eased up slightly. It was from the constant stream of Adderall and alcohol that had become his lifeline these last few weeks. He hadn't slept more than a couple of hours in a week.

"We've got this in the fucking bag," Vic slurred, laughing to himself as he took a long drink. "Morales doesn't stand a chance."

His VP, Dean Harkness, sat across from him, his eyes bloodshot from the relentless pace of the campaign. "Yeah, Vic," Dean said, nodding slowly, "but we've still got to make it through tomorrow. The turnout's going to be massive. We need to keep the pressure on."

Vic waved him off, refilling his glass. "Fuck that. We've already won. Tomorrow's just a formality."

Dean exchanged a look with Slater, Vic's new chief of staff, who stood near the door, watching his boss spiral deeper into delusion, yet somewhat calmer than recently. Slater had been holding the campaign together with duct tape and adrenaline, but even he was starting to unravel. He glanced at the empty bottles scattered across Vic's desk and how his pupils were slightly dilated—Vic was barely holding it together, and everyone knew it.

"We're still pushing ads and rallies until the last minute," Slater said, stepping forward, trying to bring some sanity back into the room. "You've got three more appearances lined up. We can't get sloppy now."

Vic smirked, leaning back in his chair. "Whatever you say, Slater.

But trust me—tomorrow, we'll be celebrating. Morales is done."

Jen's headquarters, the tension had reached a fever pitch. They were all running on fumes now. The air in the room was thick with exhaustion and fear. No one knew what the final hours would bring, but one thing was certain—they would fight until the last possible second.

Jen's live stream had been running for eight hours. She had been speaking directly to voters, answering questions, making her case. She spoke with an urgency that was raw, real, and unfiltered.

"Este país está en la cuerda floja," she said, her voice hoarse. "Si no luchamos por lo que es correcto ahora, vamos a perder más de lo que podemos imaginar. No se trata solo de esta elección. Se trata de nuestras familias, de nuestra libertad, de nuestro futuro."

("This country is on the edge. If we don't fight for what's right now, we'll lose more than we can imagine. This isn't just about this election. It's about our families, our freedom, our future.")

Her words were raw and passionate, resonating deeply with the thousands of viewers who tuned in. Tony sat nearby, watching the comments pour in. People were listening. The momentum was building, but Jen knew it wasn't enough, she practiced Spanish. They needed more.

"Get me more interviews," she snapped at one of the aides. "I'll talk to anyone, any platform. Just fucking make it happen, please!"

Things were getting darker. Vic was on his third drink when Slater pulled him aside, out of earshot of the others.

"Vic," Slater said, his voice low, "you need to dial it back. We're hours from the biggest day of your life. You can't be fucked up for it."

Vic's eyes flickered with annoyance, but he smiled, that arrogant, reckless grin that had been plastered on his face for days. "I'm fine, Slater. Don't fucking worry about me."

But Slater was worried. Vic was barely holding it together. The drinking, the pills, the constant stress—it was all crashing down at the worst time. And Slater knew that if Vic didn't pull himself together, tomorrow could become a disaster.

"Just... don't get too comfortable, please, I am begging you," Slater said, his voice strained. "We need you sharp. We need you to win this; we're so close."

Vic downed the rest of his drink in one long gulp, the burn of the Scotch doing little to steady the wild confidence coursing through him. He turned and slapped Slater on the back, its force almost making his campaign manager flinch.

"Relax," Vic said, a crooked grin across his face. "I have good intelligence." He leaned in, his voice dropping to a conspiratorial whisper. "I've already won." He threw his head back and laughed, the sound echoing through the room, careless and full of bravado.

Slater tried to match his smile but couldn't shake the unease gnawing at him. Vic's certainty felt more like desperation wrapped in bravado, and the stakes were too high for empty confidence.

Back in Jen's office, it was nearing 7 am. The live stream was still going, and Jen was running on pure adrenaline. Her body was screaming for rest, her eyes were bloodshot, but she refused to stop. She couldn't stop.

Tony walked into the room, his face pale. "Jen, the latest poll just came in. Vic's ahead by three points. It's not moving."

Jen slammed her fist on the table, her frustration boiling over. "I don't care about the fucking polls, Tony! We still have hours to slug it out until the last second."

Her voice was hard. "I'm not fucking sleeping. Not until this is over." She turned back to the camera, her voice cracking but determined. "We've got hours left. And I refuse to let Vic Ross take this from us."

Her phone buzzed with another notification, and without missing a beat, she answered a question from a voter online, her words slicing through the exhaustion like a blade. "Este es nuestro país," she said. "Y no voy a dejar que lo destruyan." (This is our country, and I won't let them destroy it.)

— 47 —

Election Day, the final hours had finally arrived, and the entire nation felt like it was teetering on the edge of a knife. Months of grueling campaigning had come down to this one day—a day that would decide the country's future, for better or worse.

Jen Morales sat in the war room, surrounded by screens showing the latest polling data, social media trends, turnout reports, answering questions via text, messaging, and live streaming. There was no time left to influence online voting—that had closed 14 days ago. Now, everything hinged on those heading to vote. The numbers had shifted slightly since early voting had ended, but not enough. Jen was behind, and the gap felt like a weight pressing down on her.

"How are we doing in Arizona?" she asked, her voice hoarse.

Tony Vargas glanced at the data. "Tight. We're seeing strong turnout from the Nations, but we need bigger numbers in Phoenix. We're not where we need to be in Maricopa County."

Jen sighed, tapping her fingers on the table. "Push the ads harder, especially the healthcare messaging. If we don't turn out more female urban voters, we're screwed."

Tony nodded, already firing off instructions to the digital team. They were doing everything possible—mobilizing volunteers, hitting social media, and flooding the airwaves with last-minute ads. They had been relentless during early voting, but today was the final push—the last shot to change the trajectory of the election.

"It's all in the turnout," Jen muttered, her eyes glued to the screen. "We can't afford to lose a single voter."

Meanwhile, the mood was drastically different at Vic Ross's campaign headquarters. Vic was celebrating early. He had spent the last hours in the air, meeting with donors and boasting about his inevitable victory. To him, the election was already won.

Sitting in his DC office, Vic raised his glass of Scotch and leaned back, grinning. "We've got this in the bag," he said to his VP, Dean Harkness, who sat across from him, looking worn down.

"Turnout is high in the rural areas," Dean said, scrolling through updates. "But we're still neck and neck in the cities. We need those suburban votes to hold."

Vic shrugged, uninterested. "We're going to win. The online voting numbers favored us; with that done, it's just about getting today's voters out. The numbers are on our side."

Dean nodded, but his eyes flicked nervously to Slater, who was watching Vic closely. The confidence in the room felt overblown— like they were celebrating before the race was even over.

As Vic took another sip, Slater stepped in. "Vic, we need to talk about what happens if this doesn't go our way."

Vic raised an eyebrow and lit another Cuban cigar, "What are you talking about? We're not going to lose."

Back on the plane, as they flew to another donor meeting, Slater laid out the backup plan. "We can start suggesting that early votes were tampered with—especially online voting. Say it was vulnerable to hacking. We can spread rumors about foreign interference, maybe North Korea or Iran. The point is to create doubt."

Vic listened, a slow grin spreading across his face, his eyes gleaming with a mix of arrogance and certainty. "We won't need to do that," he said, waving off the idea with a flick of his hand. "So I don't want to waste time talking about it. No concession will ever be needed, my boy." His voice dripped with confidence, the casual familiarity unsettling.

Slater stared at him, dumbfounded. The easy arrogance, the way Vic dismissed even the idea of preparing for a loss, left him at a loss for words. It felt off—unhinged, almost. Vic acted like the outcome was already written, as if he had some secret assurance that the rest of them weren't privy to. And that attitude, that unsettling sense of invincibility, made Slater very nervous.

The focus was entirely on turnout. Every update that came in from key states was a shot of adrenaline or a punch in the gut.

"We need more in Texas," Tony said, glancing at his phone. "We're not seeing the turnout we expected in Houston."

Jen felt her stomach twist. "We can't lose Texas. Push harder with the ads, the Gram, and the Book. It might be old social, but we take every vote. Hit them with our healthcare message—nonstop."

Her team moved quickly, launching last-minute social media blitzes aimed at undecided voters. Jen was everywhere—appearing in targeted ads, sending video messages, and responding to voters in real time.

"If you haven't voted yet, today is your last chance," Jen said in one of her video messages, her voice raw but determined. "This election will decide the future of healthcare, education, and our freedoms. We need you to vote, right now. Don't wait."

Vic's plane touched down in Florida for another round of drinks with his biggest donors. By this point, he was more than a few glasses deep, his mind foggy from the booze and Adderall.

"We're going to win this," Vic slurred, raising his glass to the gathered crowd. "By tomorrow, Morales will be history."

His donors cheered, but Dean and Slater exchanged uneasy glances. The polling numbers weren't as secure as Vic thought, and the fallout could be disastrous if they didn't win. But Vic didn't care. He was already celebrating, detached from the reality of how close the race had become.

As the minutes ticked down, both campaigns—sans Vic Ross

himself—were operating in crisis mode. Jen's team was running on pure adrenaline, working minute by minute to push voter turnout in every key state they could. The focus was on Texas, Arizona, and Pennsylvania—crucial where early voting had given them a promising start but where Election Day turnout remained critical. Volunteers were making frantic calls, community leaders were rallying voters, and every ounce of energy was being poured into getting people to the polls.

On the other side, Slater was already preparing for the worst. Despite Vic's blustering confidence, Slater knew how tight the margins were. He was working behind the scenes to craft the messaging that would challenge the results if they didn't go their way. The plan was to sow seeds of doubt, question the legitimacy of the vote counts, and, if necessary, throw the entire electoral process into chaos. Money from outside sources had already been secured, ready to be funneled through loopholes that circumvented the new campaign finance rules—another armored car of dark cash to bulldoze through the court system if needed.

While Jen's team fought for every last vote, Slater was armed for a different kind of battle, where winning wasn't about turnout but about twisting the narrative and undermining the system itself. The tension was electric, the stakes sky-high, and both sides braced for a night that promised to be anything but predictable.

As the night ended and the final votes started to be counted, the nation held its breath. Both Jen and Vic's teams were in a full-scale frenzy—texting, calling, and strategizing on the fly. Every state felt like a battle in its own right, every district a potential turning point.

At Jen's headquarters, she had given everything she had, and now all she could do was watch the results come in. "We're going to win this," she whispered to herself, her eyes glued to the screens.

Vic continued drinking, confident he had already won. But Slater and Dean were preparing for the worst, ready to pull the trigger on their backup plan if the numbers didn't fall in their favor.

As the last few polls closed, the entire country awaited the final count. Both sides were poised for victory—or war. Once again, the nation's future hung in the balance, as it does every four years.

*** END OF BOOK ***

12/15/2024

ABOUT THE AUTHOR

Bryan Wempen is an author and entrepreneur living in Santa Fe, New Mexico. Renowned for his candid and insightful storytelling, Bryan explores the intricate depths of human nature, drawing inspiration from his rich tapestry of life experiences and the varied locales he has called home.

His debut novel series, a political suspense saga, is set against a futuristic U.S. presidential campaign, offering a compelling examination of power, ambition, and morality. Bryan's writing reflects his diverse background, seamlessly blending perspectives from farm and city life and domestic and international horizons.

Beyond writing, Bryan treasures time with his wife, exploring hiking trails, and savoring mild cigars alongside the bold flavors of New Mexico's signature green and red chile. Growing up on a cattle farm in a small community, he developed a lifelong fascination with politics and public service through shared stories he heard about farm programs—some of his earliest memories. These experiences continue to shape and inspire his storytelling to this day.

ACKNOWLEDGMENTS

Writing is never a solitary endeavor, and this journey has been shaped by countless influences and the unwavering support of those around me.

To my wife, Michella: Your encouragement, creativity, and resilience inspire me daily. You are my constant support, sounding board, and greatest source of strength. Watching you flourish as an emerging metalwork artist fills me with pride and admiration—I am endlessly grateful for your love and partnership.

To my recovery community and higher power, I owe a debt of gratitude that words cannot fully express. Your wisdom, strength, and compassion have guided me through the hardest times and remind me daily of the beauty of living one day at a time. My sobriety has been a cornerstone of this journey for many years now, allowing me the clarity and courage to pursue my creative passions.

To the many stories, people, and places that have left their mark on me, thank you for providing the foundation upon which my imagination is built. From the small-town values of my upbringing to the broader lessons learned in life's unexpected moments, each experience has informed and enriched my storytelling.

I hope everyone can be kind to themselves and their neighbors during these times of tension, stress, fear, anger, and anxiety. Protect yourself, but strive to face challenges with love, humor, and open communication. Remember to vote—your voice matters, and it makes a difference.

A gentle reminder: while the towns, characters, and events may evoke familiar places or people, they are purely products of my imagination. As they say, life can be considerably stranger than fiction at times, and that truth often finds its way into the pages of a story.